MIDNIGHT'S TREASURY

J. T. CROFT

ELMFIRE PRESS

First published by Elmfire Press 2021

Copyright ©2021 by J. T. Croft

First edition

ISBN 978-1-8381089-5-3

Cover design by Fay Lane:

www.faylane.com

Elmfire Press

Unit 35590,

PO Box 15113,

Birmingham, B2 2NJ

United Kingdom

www.jtcroft.com

Weary with toil, I haste me to my bed,
The dear repose for limbs with travel tired;
But then begins a journey in my head,
To work my mind, when body's work's expired...

— WILLIAM SHAKESPEARE, SONNET 27

PREFACE

You know the story:

Go to bed early after a relaxing bath (scented candles optional), then a bit of light reading before switching off the light and luxuriantly stretching out in readiness for the extended hours of sleep. Then bang – it's midnight, and 'Mr Wide-Awake' pays a visit for an undetermined length of time, like in-laws turning up unannounced with overnight bags.

Those unscheduled hours of waking are often some of my most infuriatingly productive. Ideas coalesce out of the darkness, 'What-ifs' become 'What happens next', and stories emerge partially or fully formed while I toss and turn, powerless to shut off the movie sequences and dialogue that I will barely remember in the morning. Snatches of script make it through to the following day, mere echoes of my midnight meanderings whose memories linger until the moment they are distilled and written, freeing up the insomnia to work its unsolicited magic all over again.

Midnight's Treasury is full of such uninvited guests: gentle ghost stories that focus on the living, strange premonitions, comic retributions and encouragement from the afterlife, difficult choices, and above all, the need to put things right and take control in the face of seemingly insurmountable problems. The stories contained within, with some exceptions, are darker and longer than those in my first collection, *High Spirits*. Whether the global events in 2020 and beyond have affected me at a subconscious level is open to debate. There is no mention of 'you know what' in any of my tales, though I sympathise and concur with a character in one of my favourite stories in this collection, 'The Caveat', when asked:

'What frightens you?'
'Being powerless,' I replied.

I wished I could have hugged the first-person fictional character I created, without regard to social distancing, there in the bible-black dark of one midnight in May. We have all had a fair measure of being powerless over the past year – in our own lives and those around us – and I trust that there may be some solace in the pages that follow.

These stories were cathartic to write, and I hope you find them interesting, entertaining, and thought-provoking. They are a treasury of my midnight ramblings that I was powerless to prevent, but powerful and precious now they are fully conceived and locked away in the words of the page.

I only hope they do not keep you awake past midnight; unless, of course, it is to read 'just one more'.

J. T. Croft
    May 2021

ACKNOWLEDGMENTS

To midnight, and insomniacs everywhere.

With thanks to my Advance Reader Team, *The Muses*:

Audrey Adamson
Siobhan Allen
Richard Brulotte
Tracey Bryant
Matthew Coxall
Lana Kamennof-Sine
Christine Ruiz Noriega-Hollnbuchner

CONTENTS

QUEEN OF HEARTS

C larice Devereux was dead, but that did not affect her ability to bother, befuddle, or berate her young ghost-writer. Even from beyond the grave, the use of the Oxford comma was strictly forbidden while copious adverbs, harking back to the golden age of her romantic fiction career, were actively encouraged.

Dictating from within the free-standing floor-length oval mirror, Clarice composed the same bodice-ripping historical romances to her overworked and underpaid understudy as she had written herself in life.

'*He gripped her tightly, forcing her lustfully against the stable wall. There was no escape for Penelope this time, and she was glad. Feebly waving her hand to protect her virtue, she succumbed to the straw and his—*'

'Stop,' said Kelly, rubbing her tired eyes before the bright screen. 'You used this exact scene in *Champion of the Carolinas*.'

'*Are you sure?*' said Clarice from within the mirror, lounging on an ethereal chaise longue among her many bichon frise dogs and haze from a supernatural cigarette.

'Yes,' said Kelly. 'It was Geraint Malahide going down on Constance—'

'*Going down?*' exclaimed the ghost, rising from her recumbent state and setting the annoying spirit dogs yapping. '*How very coarse of you, my dear. One does not* go down *in any of my historical romances – one gets pursued, overcome with passion, and then dominated by the opposite sex until all resistance is mere prudish memory. Save that other filth for your own work.*'

Kelly rolled her eyes and prepared a smile, turning from the laptop to deliver it to the spoilt, seventy-something southern belle in the mirror.

'Sorry, Clarice, I'll remember that,' she said, watching the self-titled greatest romantic fiction writer of the 1970s settle herself back down on the chaise in her billowing pink chiffon gown.

'*Not even Barbara Cartland would have used such language.*'

'You still used the same scene, though,' said Kelly, returning to her point and the flashing cursor at the end of chapter twenty-seven.

'*Back up a few lines, and have him throw her against the horsebox instead.*'

'You used that in *Pride and Passion at the Kentucky Derby*,' said Kelly, waiting for the inevitable tantrum from the frustrated literary great. Clarice Devereux had all but exhausted her creativity from a career spanning fifty years and one hundred and sixty novels. Not that her dwindling but rabid fanbase minded; any posthumously published paperback from the Queen of Hearts was an extraordinary, though short-lived, event.

'Does he *have* to throw her anywhere?' Kelly continued. 'I mean, couldn't she turn the tables and insist he hands over her inheritance from the foreshadowing in chapter nine to get what she truly wants before joining him sexually as an equal?'

Kelly pushed back her glasses and ground her teeth, ready for the tirade. Even from the afterlife and with no need of oxygen, the intake of breath from Clarice was unmistakable.

'*Who is writing this story?*' demanded the spirit. '*Who is it that provides you with an income to live out your own life here in this unpretty place?*'

'Unpretty place?' said Kelly, defensively. 'I spend most of my waking hours listening to a ghost dictate fiction that belongs in the dark ages, for a pittance.'

'*You are paid the going rate from my publisher for posthumous editions on the understanding you do not breach the confidentiality of our initial agreement. You forget who you are talking to and to who you owe your living.*'

'Yes, but you are always changing things, and it takes twice as long as a normal ghostwriter would take to get the words down,' said Kelly. 'We've been on chapter twenty-seven for over a week, now.'

'*We've been on chapter twenty-seven because you keep interrupting.*'

Clarice came close to the inside of the mirror, peered around the meagre flat interior in stark contrast to the opulent surroundings of the Californian mansion backdrop in the mirror.

Kelly had noted the disparity on their first incredible encounter one morning, two years ago, as she brushed her hair. The room projected from beyond the mirror was opulent, gaudy, and chintzy to the point of distraction. Plush velvet furniture and Italian marble tables completed the dated and heavily decorated interior.

Apparently, one could 'take it with you'.

Paradise, limbo, or wherever Clarice currently resided, unwilling to move on until her reservoir of romance was dry, was a darn sight better than Kelly's current surroundings.

Clarice added further insulting adjectives to describe the

single twenty-something's abode into which she had appeared one evening to continue her declining career from the other side. The offer to write posthumous novels and deliver them to her agent in London had been a lifeline when the local library had closed, forcing the bookish and shy Kelly Somerton, wannabe cosy mystery writer, into an altogether different career path.

'*Furthermore, young lady, you are learning the craft from one of the greatest writers of the genre. Your problem, Kelly, is that you don't understand tropes and what the reader actually wants.*'

Kelly sagged as the dead writer delivered a well-rehearsed diatribe on the benefits of working remotely with a giant of the literary world, albeit in a one-sided relationship. She turned her back and took a swig of diet cola from the bottle. She wiped the back of her hand across her mouth, setting off the spirit behind into a lesson in etiquette. Kelly covertly checked her phone for texts, waiting until Clarice calmed herself down. Finally, the grand dame lit a long cigarette from within the mirror and blew smoke from the next world against the inside of the mirror as a final derisory conclusion to her rant.

'I'm just saying that times have moved on, Clarice,' said Kelly. 'The sales data doesn't lie. Your traditional fans are dying and joining you on the other side. You *are* a great author, but you need fresh context in a world that was changing long before you—'

'*Died?*' said Clarice, raising a heavily pencilled eyebrow from beneath her carefully and perpetually coiffured white hair. '*Yes, I'm dead, but I will not be lectured on romance from someone yet to finish their first novel, let alone someone planning to publish independently.*' The traditionally published ghost shuddered as though the very thought was disgusting. '*If you even mention the word e-book, Kelly, I will scream until everyone hears, not just sensitive little souls like you.*'

4

Kelly reached for the drawer and retrieved her wireless headphones.

'*Don't you dare, young lady!*' said Clarice, stomping her feet and setting off the pampered pooches once more. '*You have a thousand words to do for me before—*'

Kelly clicked on the playlist, and the opening bars of *Madame Butterfly* enveloped her senses, cutting out the sounds of the ghost, the barking of the dogs, and the everyday. She minimised the work in progress and clicked on her draft novel, itching to get a few hundred words down before retiring to bed uninterrupted by 'advice' from the critical Clarice. Transported by the soprano's rise and fall, Kelly stole a quick reflected glance in the screen at Clarice Devereux's soundless and futile attempts to regain her attention and the initiative until peace descended. Kelly cleared her mind to banish all thoughts, apart from the aching beauty of the music, and the spirit vanished, leaving behind nothing in the mirror but a reflection of the simple bedsit and the faintest hint of menthol-infused tobacco.

The following days resulted in multiple rewrites before the epic straw-rolling conclusion of chapter twenty-seven and beyond was reached. Kelly headed into town and posted the hard copy of the revised draft to the Richmond office, ready for their editorial team to rip it apart and remove any minor additions of her own, snuck in to temper the sickly and outdated prose. They knew Clarice's target audience. The tepid, formulaic, two-dimensional characters loosely connected by a semblance of plot would go down a storm among the ageing reader base, locked into the romantic and bygone worlds devised by the Queen of Hearts. One thing the matriarch was undeniably good at was dialogue.

Yet with every book came fewer sales. Younger critics baulked at the submissive natures of Clarice's passive protagonists, who rarely progressed through any meaningful character arc. Devereux's novels were not only deeply at odds with the times, but they were also borderline pastiche. A small but growing LGBT+ movement claimed the unfashionable dead author as one of their own, revelling in the absurd sexual tension and ridiculous resolutions often found in the third act.

It was clear that the brand needed a refresh if future books were to reach a new audience. The telephone call that afternoon from the commissioning editor destroyed any possibility of that.

There would be no more books to write. Devereux's historical romance was as dead as the author herself. The ghostwriter was out of work.

Kelly got off the bus and walked to the edge of town, wondering how she would break the news to Clarice. Would the ghost depart, finally, or sulk as she usually did until Kelly brought her back from despair with kind words and readings from her most popular books? Despite the American's tendency to be acerbic, rude, and ungrateful, Kelly knew the lonely old dame did not have anyone living or dead to turn to.

'*I don't know why I'm still here, Kelly; I only know I have several books still in me before I can move on.*'

Kelly shook her head, trying to rid the novelist from her thoughts and free time, halting outside the independent book shop window. A young man stood on a rickety step ladder, pinning up a display in the main window, utterly absorbed in his work and unaware of her nose pressed against the glass, watching his comical attempts to fix the spring-themed bunting above her. He overreached, tugging at the pennant, and a great section of previously attached display came away, coiling around his arm. Suddenly aware of Kelly frosting up the glass below with the closeness of her breath, he collapsed backwards in alarm into a stacked pile of books.

Kelly raced in, setting the old bell swinging above the door.

'Are you alright?' she said, removing several non-fiction and self-help books from the cardigan on his chest. 'Anything broken?'

The young man squirmed, reached around to his back and extricated a dented copy of *Wisden's Cricketing Almanac*. He held up the split spine in one hand, taking Kelly's offered hand in the other.

'Just the book, thankfully.'

He rose and dusted down his jeans, righting the stepladder before kneeling and colliding with Kelly's head as they both hurried to reclaim the books from the carpet.

'Sorry,' she said. 'For the bump and the tumble. I don't think we've met?'

'I'm Dan,' he said, rubbing his temple. 'Only started yesterday. You a regular, then?'

'Kind of,' said Kelly. 'When I can afford it.' She searched the empty shop for the proprietor. 'Where's Clive? It's unlike him to leave his precious shop for any longer than placing a bet at the bookies in the high street.'

Dan rubbed his back, trying to locate the bruise from his fall. 'He's on jury service till the end of the week, leaving me in charge to manage the place.' He spread his arms wide and glanced around. 'I'm master of all I survey for the time being.'

Kelly looked around at the piles of unpriced books and the mess in the display window.

'It doesn't look as though it is going so well.'

Dan scratched his head and smiled warmly. 'Truth be told, I'm used to writing books rather than selling them. I just needed a bit of extra cash.'

'You're a writer?' said Kelly, following him to the counter.

'Kind of. I write serialised stuff.'

'I'm a writer, too,' said Kelly, putting down the armful of books rescued from the floor. 'A ghostwriter, but I'm ready to move on and go solo.'

Dan pushed aside the untidy items on the counter and leaned over. 'That's a coincidence. What genre?'

Kelly gave the usual response, suddenly embarrassed, as she always was when the subject arose. She suddenly wished she had kept her mouth shut, but the pleasant-looking intellectual in front of her meant a few extra minutes of talking to someone her own age. 'Oh, just bits and bobs, really. Nothing you would have heard of.'

Dan flashed his eyes. 'That's what I always say like it's shameful. Am I right?'

Kelly pushed back her spectacles and looked at her feet, surprised at the honesty and truth in his words. 'Well, kind of. I guess.'

'So go on,' he said, looking at his own feet. 'I'm well-read, so tell me who you are making millions for? I read pretty much everything.'

'Not exactly millions. Alright, you first,' countered Kelly, enjoying the game and needing the time to decide whether to give away her client's confidentiality. Likely enough, the hapless shop boy, charming as he was, wrote for some small, unheard of science-fiction anthology imprint. She decided she would make up a name, which would be the end of the awkward conversation. Talking to young men in the real world was not a strong point, though she never had trouble with dialogue in her own work.

'Don't judge a book by its cover,' he said as though reading her thoughts. 'Isn't that what they say? Clive keeps a fairly broad stock in here; I should know, I come in here regularly as a punter—'

'You come in here a lot? I've never seen you.'

'I'm a bit strapped currently, and he lets me have the damaged stock at a discount.' He pulled out his empty pockets and blushed with the admission. 'I'd rather read and write than eat most days.'

'I agree,' blurted Kelly, desperate to continue the tangent with the potential kindred spirit.

'As I was saying,' said Dan, pointing over to the deep aisles of books. 'Clive keeps a broad church in here, so what do you say? You find your book, and I'll find mine. We'll close our eyes and swap them over to save our blushes, okay?'

Kelly looked at the cheeky smile on the open and honest face. Here was mischief and mystery in one modestly handsome package.

'Go on, then,' she said. 'I know where mine is already because it never gets sold.' Kelly wandered over to the far end of the small romance section and reached up for the copy of her first collaboration with Clarice. Just for a moment, she wiped her hand over the cover of the two main characters, fully clothed but in the act of a passionate, overarching kiss against a backdrop of American Civil War militias. Pride and accomplishment welled up inside with the contact of the novel, and the blood, sweat, and tears put into its transcription.

Passion under Fire by Clarice Devereux.

'Mine doesn't sell well, either,' said Dan, poking his head above the aisle, causing her to startle momentarily. 'Bit old-fashioned and misogynistic, but I have to stick to the script.'

Kelly pulled the book to her knitted sweater to find the young man bashfully doing the same against his bobbled cardigan.

'On three?' he said, shutting his eyes and holding out his empty hand.

'On three,' replied Kelly, adopting the same position.

'One... two... three...' said Dan, placing the heavy paperback clumsily into Kelly's outstretched hand. She flailed around with her book until their hands brushed against each other, and she released the novel to its temporary new owner.

Kelly opened her eyes to see Dan chivalrously holding the book behind his back, awaiting his turn.

She glanced at the dark cover. It was obviously a thriller. An unknown assailant was chasing the running silhouette of a man against a snowy backdrop of mountains and glaciers.

Ice Cold Assassin by Robert Decker.

'You are Decker's ghostwriter?' she said in amazement. 'He was massive in the late seventies, wasn't he? I thought you—'

Dan nodded and looked down at the thriller like a proud parent reminiscing about a newborn child. 'I know what you are going to say,' he said. 'You thought I wrote psychological military sci-fi with dragons.'

'That's a thing?' said Kelly.

Dan broke into a grin and shrugged. 'Probably.'

Kelly flicked through the first few pages. 'Well, I hope Decker's publisher paid you a bundle for it,' she said. 'I get paid by the word, and it's pretty poor for the time invested, all things considered.'

'You are kidding?' he said. 'It barely covered my rent for the six weeks it took to churn it out. You can stop looking for my name, it's not there, but I wrote it.' He hesitated, as though needing to clarify in front of a stranger connected by a passion and profession.

Kelly frowned, unsure of his meaning. 'I thought he died last year?'

'Yeah,' he said, looking across at the zen meditation books lining the shelf. 'His publisher got fed up with me bombarding them with drafts, so I guess I was just lucky to get the opportunity. It's my first and last, sadly.'

'How so?'

Dan shrugged. 'Times change, and his readers moved on to other things; they serialise the brand now in anthologies, which pays less. Can I look at yours now?'

'Not yet,' she said, eager to wrestle control of the fun situation. 'What genre would you say I write in?'

'I can tell you it's probably romance because that's where you're standing,' he said. Kelly stamped her foot, but he held up a hand. 'But I would have guessed that. The genre is massive, though – so many sub-categories.'

He rubbed his cheek and looked Kelly up and down, teasing her with the delay.

'Come on,' she said. 'Make your mind up, Poirot.'

'Paranormal romance?' he offered.

Kelly stuck her fingers into her throat in defiant mockery. 'You are kidding me? You are saying that I look like someone who reads and writes werewolf and vampire love triangles?'

He held up his hand defensively, revealing the book he held. Kelly watched him turn over the novel and whistle.

'Blimey,' he said, flicking through the front pages. 'You're the blooming Queen of Hearts!'

'Not really,' said Kelly, swinging her arms in front of her chunky knit. 'You know how it is.'

He nodded. 'I'm going to write my own stuff one day – maybe publish independently and on my own terms.'

Kelly stepped closer, eager to associate with a kindred spirit. 'Me too. I'm still drafting. Trying to sort out a plot hole in between writing soppy slush for the blue-rinse brigade, but I've got a catchy cover all ready to go.'

'Promise you won't laugh,' he said. 'I'd like to write cosy mysteries with a romantic subplot; my debut is kinda finished, but I struggle with dialogue; I think I'm pretty good at pacing and plot, though.'

'That's incredible,' said Kelly. 'Dialogue has never been a big problem for me. It's scene-setting I find challenging.'

They stood awkwardly staring at each other until a customer arrived, stepped over the fallen books, and headed towards the literary fiction shelf.

'Look, tell you what,' he said. 'Do you know the Independent Authors Guild?'

'Sure,' said Kelly. 'They're the go-to professionals for all things indie publishing. There's a three-day convention running down in the New Forest about making a living as a writer.'

'How would you like to go?'

Kelly stepped back and frowned. 'Don't be daft, it's over a thousand pounds, and besides—'

She fumbled around, desperate to escape from the notion of an overnight stay while equally desperate to go to something life-affirming and potentially life-changing now that her employment with Halcyon Days Publishing had ended.

'Is it the overnight thing?' Dan asked. 'Don't worry; I had the same reaction when I won the tickets on the IAG's podcast. Introvert anxiety always gets in the way, doesn't it?'

'You won two tickets from the Guild?'

He nodded, returning to the counter to serve the lone customer. The bell rang as the door closed behind the departing gentleman, and Dan continued.

'If it's any consolation,' he said, 'I'll be terrified, too, but I'm fed up writing for other people, and I reckon a few days of being socially awkward could end up being something really worthwhile.'

'Why don't you sell the remaining ticket?' said Kelly, still unsettled by the decision. 'You said you could do with the money, and I'd need to bring my work with me – I'm desperate to finish it now.'

'Me too,' he said. 'I've set myself the deadline of the end of the convention; I'll probably have to work all night on it as well as get my other work done.'

Kelly thought about Clarice and how she would have to deal with the awkward conversation closer to the date, not to mention the romantic writer's ignoble ending.

'I'd need to think about it,' she said. 'Plus, I'd need to pay you back somehow.'

Dan held up the romantic novel. 'Sign this copy and buy me your book,' said Dan. 'I'd be willing to give it a go, now I know you wrote it.' He busied himself with items on the counter, shielding himself from a potential disappointment.

'I've never signed a copy of a book before,' said Kelly, twisting around the shop for any mirrors. 'I'm not sure it's strictly legit.'

'Why not? You did all the work, didn't you?'

'Well, I put the words down on the page, if that's what you mean,' said Kelly. 'Tell you what, I'll buy your book, too, if you sign it for me.'

'Done,' he said, smiling. 'I'll put my number down for you. Maybe we can critique each other's work sometime or grab the train together?'

Three days passed, and Kelly's procrastination met its inevitable conclusion.

'*You are going where?*' said Clarice. '*With a boy?*'

'It's a kind of retreat for young writers, that's all,' said Kelly, gritting her teeth and squinting at the screen, trying to avoid the reflection of the spirit pacing back and forth in the mirror behind. 'And don't panic about the guy – he's as nerdy and shy as I am.'

'*And what about me? We need to make a start on the next novel; my readers demand it.*'

'I've thought about that,' said Kelly, ignoring the self-centred delusion from the afterlife and delaying the bad news.

'I can take you with me in my makeup mirror, and we can finish up there. The change will do us both good.'

'*Makeup mirror?*' exclaimed Clarice, her voice rising an octave.

Kelly quickly corrected herself. 'I meant vanity mirror, sorry.'

'*And what do you hope to learn that I can't teach you?*'

'It's more about how to publish digitally, market and distribute as well as meeting up with like-minded—'

'*Spare me,*' said Clarice, collapsing melodramatically onto the chaise like one of her swooning heartbroken characters. '*I have a headache coming on.*'

Kelly rattled her feet against the table leg and bit her fingernails. The ghost had been agitated for days, much more reflective and watchful than usual. Kelly almost missed the overreaction and self-centred stubbornness.

'Clarice,' she said, turning to the mirror. 'What will you do when you no longer need me?'

The ghost twisted from her recumbent position and frowned.

'*Why would I no longer need you? Are you thinking of leaving my employment?*'

The flood gates remained firm, and Kelly elaborated on the lie created to spare the spirit's embarrassment and her own cowardice. A sudden pang of guilt rose, but she ignored it.

'Only that if I publish independently,' she said, avoiding the steely gaze from the woman in the mirror, 'I might not have time to write another book with you.'

To her surprise, Clarice did not explode. The woman buried her fingers in the thick white down of the lapdog and sighed.

'*That's rather a pathetic attempt at deception, Kelly. I thought I had taught you how to write believable lies.*'

Kelly spun around on the chair, knocking over the envelope containing the letter of termination to her contract. 'What do you mean?'

The spirit put down the dog and arranged herself on the floor within the mirror. Clarice pointed to the spilt contents of the envelope.

'*They've cut us off, haven't they?*' she said sadly. '*There is no place in the world for romance anymore.*'

Kelly rushed at the folded letter, meeting the spirit at eye level, inches from the reflective surface. 'How—?'

Clarice placed her hands on her lap and puckered her wrinkled lips. Several dogs joined her, gently nestling and subdued in the velvet of her gown, as though offering condolences to their tearful mistress.

'*You left it lying on the table when you went to get a bowl of cereal last night; you've been reading it ever since. I thought something terrible had happened.*'

Kelly held up a hand against the glass.

'Something terrible has happened, Clarice.'

The ghost held up a hand to meet that of the young woman. '*Why didn't you tell me? I've been waiting to hear what you have concocted.*'

'I can get a job or pursue my writing, but for you... It's all you have left.'

Clarice removed her hand and reached for a silk handkerchief. She dabbed her eyes to avoid damaging the heavy mascara and composed herself.

'*I thought I had a few more books left in me before whatever comes next,*' she said. '*But it appears I have finally died after all.*'

Kelly shook her head. 'Dan says there might be a market in serials; we could explore that option?'

Clarice rolled her eyeballs. '*Can you see me in a* Mills & Boon? *No, it's time for the great Clarice Devereux to put down her pen and retire; I'll need the time to haunt those idiots at the London office in any case.'*

Kelly watched as the grand dame twitched an eyebrow, spilling unchecked tears down her chalk-white face. The attempt at humour landed, and Kelly sniffed back some of her own tears, wiping her nose with the back of her sleeve.

'Don't do that, dear,' said Clarice, impotently offering her a handkerchief from the afterlife. The white silk carried a delicately stitched monogram 'QoH'. *'It's very unladylike.'*

'Queen of Hearts,' said Kelly, pointing to the pretty square.

'Go to this independent convention thing with this boy,' said Clarice, disappearing from the mirror until only her voice remained. *'Go find your author voice and make me proud.'*

Kelly saw the monogram fade and her reflection return. The opulent surroundings vanished, leaving the young out-of-work writer framed within the stark, unpretty reality of the real world.

Dan knocked on the interconnecting door that joined the tired holiday chalets.

'How's your room?' he said. 'Mine has been stuck here from the 1980s and wants to be let out.'

Kelly laughed at the muffled voice from beyond the thin walls and admired the spartan single room with its tilted framed photographs hanging on woodchip walls.

'I've got the suite,' she lied. 'There's a whirlpool bath and minibar on my side.'

Dan chuckled, and Kelly heard the creak from a wooden chair as he sat down, almost certainly the same tired old thing hiding under the solitary table in her room. Dan clunked a plug into the wall, and Kelly listened to his rapid tapping on the laptop keyboard. Something else landed heavily on the table beyond, causing the interior chalet wall to wobble like a cheap *Doctor Who* film set.

'Thanks for the loan of your phone to recharge my own, I'm so stupid to have left the cable behind and yours doesn't fit. Will you need it until tomorrow?' said Kelly.

'Nah,' said Dan. 'I'm good; it'll only be a distraction when I'm supposed to be working. You are doing me a favour.'

'What did you think about today?' she called out, removing her makeup in the mirror she had brought along.

'So much to take in,' he said. 'Got it all down, though. If I could only get some of this dialogue sorted and get a cover done, I reckon I could upload something to Digibooks in hours.'

'What's your book called?' asked Kelly.

'The working title is *Jack of Diamonds* – it's the nickname of my protagonist; he's a jewel thief who solves cosy mysteries alongside a brilliant but dysfunctional female detective side-kick to stay out of jail. The trouble is, she isn't as interesting a character as he is.'

Kelly stared at her reflection and down at her manuscript. 'I know what you mean, Dan. My sleuth is a mystery-solving ghostwriter, but she needs a foil to bounce off against. I invent characters to give her dialogue most of the time.'

Dan grunted in agreement. 'Why is it so hard to come up with something new?'

Kelly folded her dressing gown around her pyjamas and lay on the bed, manuscript and coloured correction pens on her lap.

'We are all good at one thing or another,' she said, biting off the top of a red marker and attacking the first act of her rough draft. 'That's what editors are for, polishing lumps of coal into diamonds.'

They chatted for half an hour before saying goodnight

through the wall. Kelly switched off the water-stained bedside lamp and lay in the darkness. A glimmer of light from beneath the adjoining door faintly illuminated the table's edge and the mirror.

The dark glass showed nothing out of the ordinary. It had been days since Clarice had last appeared, and Kelly struggled to put out the thought that the author might finally be gone for good. She shifted on the lumpy mattress and cleared her mind, hoping and waiting for the well-honed stillness to arrive along with the grand dame. Despite the gentle tapping and scribbling from Dan's room, Kelly achieved complete meditative calm without the spirit's appearance.

Exhausted and in a relaxed state, Kelly succumbed to sleep lulled by the gentle creak of Dan's chair as he shuffled and shifted next door.

After midnight, she was suddenly roused by another voice from beyond the wall, threatening and menacing in its tone and speech.

Someone else was in there, and Dan was in trouble.

'If you don't tell me where the document is, then Salvatori, here, will break every bone in the girl's body.'

'Is that really necessary?' said Dan, remarkably calmly. 'Couldn't there be some other arrangement, just for once?'

Kelly jumped out of bed, sending the loose pages of her manuscript flying around the room. Tying her robe tightly about her, she huddled against the internal door, ear pressed against the flimsy portal, to listen to the muffled voices only a few feet beyond.

'What sort of arrangement, Daniel?' said the voice, lighter and more agitated than threatening on this occasion.

'How about we hand over the plans, knowing they are fake, in exchange for letting the girl go? The timed explosives hidden in the room will go off whether anyone likes it or not.'

Kelly put one hand on the lock, ready to spring to Dan's

aid with the complimentary glass bottle of water firmly in her hand. She peered through the tiny unused keyhole to see Dan seated at the laptop, alone and talking to thin air.

'*Constantine Dangerfield would never allow MI8 documents, faked or otherwise, to get into enemy hands,*' said the voice. '*Besides, we need to get him beat up pretty badly by Salvatori before Dangerfield can wrestle him into the snake pit and kill him with his signature neck lock before launching himself on top of Desiree Gravalax's bikini-clad body before the bomb goes off.*'

Kelly frowned, thrown by the turn of the conversation and the fact that she or Dan may not be in mortal danger. It sounded like dictation, and she laid down the bottle with relief until she saw both Dan's phone and her own lying together, sharing power wirelessly on her bedside table.

'Isn't that a bit far-fetched, Robert?' said Dan. 'Plus, we used an almost identical climactic device in *Cold War Concubine.*'

'*Far-fetched!*' exclaimed the mystery voice, rising an octave. '*Dangerfield is a master of survival, illusion and British stiff upper lip; a mere bomb isn't going to stop him.*'

'Shh,' whispered Dan. 'You'll wake someone up. Keep it down, Robert.'

'*You dare to shush me, the greatest master spy thriller writer of the early eighties, or are you worried your newfound distraction in the next room will find out your odd little secret?*'

'Both, Robert,' said Dan. 'I'm happy to finish this story with you, but then I want to explore other options, and yes, that means working with living writers who I admire, like Kelly.'

'*You need to focus on the words, Daniel. Don't let a woman get in the way of a good story—*'

Kelly launched herself upwards and unlocked the door to the room beyond. Whoever was in there needed a piece of her mind as well as a good tongue-lashing for the noise preventing her from sleeping.

Dan, wearing boxer shorts and a 'Dark Side of The Moon' T-shirt, twisted suddenly, bringing a cheap dresser mirror face down onto the table. He narrowly missed the laptop as he watched the sudden and unexpected arrival of a hot-pink-robed, wild-haired ninja.

Kelly looked around the empty room, searching for the voice. 'Where is he?'

'Wh... where's who?' said Dan, face reddening, as though he'd been caught in the act of something questionable.

'The guy that is putting you and me down,' said Kelly. 'The one dictating dreadful dialogue—'

'*Excuse me?*' said the voice, emanating from the mirror facing the table. '*Who the bloody hell does she think she's talking to? I've sold over a million copies.*'

'Robert,' said Dan, waving at the laptop screen showing nothing open but a word processing cursor and paragraphs of hastily typed notes. 'Time to call it a night; I'll call you in the morning, yes?'

'*Oh, don't be daft,*' said the voice. '*Only you can hear—*'

Kelly raced over and righted the mirror, jumping back in alarm when her intuition proved correct. Within the glass, a white-haired man in his later years sat against a backdrop of military memorabilia and reference books, turtlenecked in blue navy and smoking a pipe.

'I can hear you perfectly fine,' she said, forcing Dan back into his chair as he sought to extricate himself from the awkward situation. 'Mr Decker, I presume?'

Robert Decker limply removed his pipe and stared incredulously back.

'This might take a bit of time to explain,' said Dan.

Kelly put her hands on her hips and addressed both males at the same time.

'Dead author appears to struggling talented wannabe, dead author's books get cancelled because no longer politically correct and ghostwriter looks to move on but can't deal with the situation made more difficult by the arrival of talented dialogue-gifted girl.'

The two men, on either side of death's mirrored doorway, looked open-mouthed at one another.

'Do I have it about right?' said Kelly.

Dan nodded. 'Don't freak out, please. I was going to let Robert know I was going solo after this last serial.'

'I'm not freaking out, but you may be in a few moments,' said Kelly, racing out of sight into her room and returning with the vanity mirror.

'Better be on your best behaviour, gentlemen, there's going to be a lady present.'

Kelly dragged over Dan's bedside table and angled the vanity mirror towards the astonished thriller author and ghostwriter. She closed her eyes and held up a hand to stifle the dissent and confused ramblings coming from the pair of them.

'Shush!' said Kelly, recalling a paragraph of romantic prose committed to memory that always improved the mood of the dead romance writer. A feeling of regret, longing, and urgent need to contact the Queen of Hearts welled up as she began to recite the words:

'"*Jamie tore off his blood-soaked shirt and threw it amongst the flames of the burning Hardcourt Hall. Rebecca backed away, her innocent eyes picking out the ripple of his muscular torso and down to his burgeoning loins—*"'

'What the?' said Dan, peering into Kelly's mirror and seeing a gaudy opulent Hollywood boudoir begin to appear.

Kelly continued, disregarding the interruption and trying to get into a flow state, trying to live and breathe every emotion from the revised text.

"'*There would be no more horse-whipping of women from Jeremiah Hardcourt now that his fortune and body lay broken within the inferno. Jamie had seen to that, and now he would see to Rebecca; his prize, desire and love. Rebecca retreated into the corner of the pavilion, begging for her sensibilities to prevent the union, but relented to the fervent victorious embrace that was now thrust upon her.*'"

'*I may be dead,*' said Robert Decker, knocking out his pipe. '*But that is truly awful.*'

'*I heard that!*' said Clarice Devereux, setting the pack of poodles and bichons yapping in defence. '*And I suppose your smutty sex thrillers are still selling like hotcakes, are they?*'

Kelly opened her eyes to see Dan leaning back against his chair.

'You too?' he said, pointing wide-eyed at the ballgown-bedecked beauty in Kelly's mirror.

She nodded, slumping her shoulders and putting her hands into the pockets of her robe.

'Me too.'

'*I don't write smut, Devereux,*' said Decker. '*I write what men want to read – good hard action with guns, bad guys taking over the world, and a few girls thrown in to spice things up a bit.*'

Dan shook his head. 'It's not what I want to read, or pretty much anyone else given the latest sales figures.'

'*Good grief, Dan,*' exclaimed Decker, pressing his face against the inside of the glass. '*Whose side are you on?*'

'*What's this all about, Kelly?*' said Clarice. '*I thought you were making a go of things without me.*'

Kelly knelt and placed her hand on the mirror, obscuring most of the woman beyond. 'I realised, just now,' she said, 'that we all want the same thing; we all want to write, but each of us has only a single part of the puzzle for these times and these readers.'

'So what are you saying, Kelly?' said Dan. 'That we all team up to create a collaborative piece of work?'

'*I've never collaborated in my life*,' said Decker, folding his arms and puffing on his perched pipe like a merchant ship's captain.

To Kelly's surprise, it was Clarice who took control. '*Well, you are dead now, Robert*,' she said confidently, '*and so is your work if you don't listen to Kelly and the boy. At least my literary career ended with a final flourish – yours is dwindling like a bad investment*.'

'They're both right, Robert,' said Dan. 'Kelly and I could really use each of your talents. Your mystery and plot elements, and Ms Devereux's dialogue and scene-setting.'

'All wrapped up in a cosy modern setting using punchy, flawed characters. What do you say?' said Kelly, removing her hand and turning to the spirit of the thriller writer.

'*I suppose you mean to pursue all of this independently?*' said Decker.

Dan and Kelly nodded. 'We have something almost ready to go,' said Dan.

'We could combine forces, merge novels; maybe do a series?' said Kelly. 'I've got a great idea for book two if we get some interest and sales to make it worthwhile.'

'*Whose name would be on the cover?*' said Clarice. '*You can't acknowledge a dead author without permission from their estate*.'

Dan held up his hand like a schoolboy answering a question. 'Can I make a suggestion?' he said.

Kelly and Dan sat facing each other at the kitchen table in the new shared flat, laptops back to back.

'Have you checked today's reviews?' said Dan. 'Sales seem to be going in the right direction; over three hundred today.'

Kelly pushed back her spectacles. 'Over two hundred reviews, and they seem to be lapping it up. It looks like we have a breakout on our hands; it's the best seller in cosy mystery and crime thrillers.'

'*When you have both finished doing all that silly independent marketing stuff,*' said Decker from the mirror on the wall, '*we need to make a start on book two. What do you say, Clarice? Reckon you have another book in you?*'

The romance author lit a cigarette and nodded. '*Provided there are no bombs, bikinis, or "going down" of any kind.*'

Kelly smiled over at Dan, who looked up, confused.

'I'll tell you later,' she said, watching Dan disappear beneath the table to a partially opened delivery box.

'The hardback proofs came in while you were out doing that podcast interview,' he said, handing over a heavy bound book. 'The playing card on the front with the question mark motif looks great, in my opinion.'

Kelly lifted the heavily bound book and smoothed her hand over the gold lettering.

Queen of Hearts by Robert Devereux

'I don't mind not having my name on the cover. How about you?' he said. 'It feels right somehow.'

'I agree,' she said. 'We are ghostwriters after all, aren't we?'

TREVELYAN'S EYE

T he car rounded the hump of Cornish moorland and I
pulled over into a lonely passing place, eager to soak in
my first glimpse of the sea. The journey from London had
been long in the storms and sleet of early March. Still, here I
was, mere miles away from several weeks of much-needed
downtime and coming home, in a sense, to seek the distant
gravestones and memorials of my once-prominent Cornish
ancestors, while enjoying the remote seclusion away from the
British Museum and the exhibits that consumed my waking
hours.

I lowered the window, and a slam of salt-laden air buffeted
my closed eyes, disturbing the genealogical papers and
crudely drawn family trees in the empty passenger seat.
Memories returned as I turned my face to the weak midday
sun and recalled old summer holidays and halcyon days with
aunts and uncles long gone, sharing warm sand-castled after-
noons in isolated coves, listening to stories of our shared
Cornish heritage, lathered in sun cream while my lips dripped
with an endless supply of iced lollies.

A raucous magpie, high in an old wind-bent hawthorn,

snatched away the daydream with a screech of territorial warning as I closed the window and continued my meandering drive to the rented bothy on the outskirts of isolated Portmellon.

Except for the small inn down by the bobbing boat harbour, the self-catering three-roomed former summer residence of shepherds, smugglers, and the occasional extended family from the now derelict manor house was all that was available. I turned into the stone-walled drive, overgrown with thick pittosporum hedges, and emerged onto a tonsure of lush lawn, tufted and speckled with early violets. Taking a long stretch, I looked around and saw similarly isolated farmsteads further away on the granite tor moorland, white daubed walls reflecting the early afternoon sun. A quarter of a mile away, a headland overlooked the steep descent wherein lay the fishing village, unable to escape or expand beyond the steep ravine it had found itself born into during the late Middle Ages. A modest, squat church tower rose from the upper lanes in solidarity with the granite pillars dotting the nearby fields and cliffs.

I quickly discovered the key beneath an upturned lobster pot, as promised, and nudged open the thick door, disturbing a rook hopping above on the corrugated tile roof. I made my way into the cool darkness of the combined kitchen snug. A close inspection of the sparse but clean room, as well as the functional bathroom and comfortable bedroom, yielded a sense of just enough nineteenth-century adventure and twentieth-century necessities in equal measure. It would be comfortable here for the last week of the closed season, not that the place looked like it would ever be on the tourist radar; this was true Cornwall – tough, wild, enduring, and isolated.

After reading a welcome note pinned to the back of the door and being pleasantly surprised to find fresh milk, eggs, and bread in the antiquated and noisy fridge, I strode out into the broken sunshine determined to begin my ease into accrued annual leave with a hurried walk to the headland and a view of the land thereabouts. Early lambs sprang and darted ahead of my eager and unmarked trespass through the fields and unattended gates until, after some thirty minutes of uphill effort, I reached the pinnacle of the climb and emerged onto the bracken-free ring of springy turf. I looked back at the crows circling the bleach-white bothy peeping from the stunted trees in the distance. The air was sharp and laden with the salt of a prevailing south-westerly swell, crashing against the jagged blocks of fallen granite some forty feet below. It was a lonely place for certain, but one that afforded a great view for miles in either direction, apart from a good view of Portmellon itself now hidden by its rocky enclosure. I sat for a while on a small wind-eroded lump of granite before noticing that four other stones formed a ring of perhaps ten feet across, and I wondered whether to visit the church in the late afternoon light. Though I was eager to search out generations of tomb-stoned Trevelyans, ticking off the decades and centuries on my notes and family tree, the darkening clouds spilling sheets of rainbow-splashed rain threatened a long, wet detour, so I returned to the gate at the lower end of the field, feeling foolish for having a strong sense that if I were to turn back I'd see someone standing in the ring on the headland now high above. My mind fought the ridiculous notion until I could bear it no longer, and I stole a glance back up the path towards the headland while mounting the field gate. For a moment, something darkly cloaked and watchful stood in that lonely place, but it quickly vanished, and I shivered at the touch of the cold iron handle of the gate.

Back at the bothy, I looked closely through the deeply set small windows that illuminated the room as though the house had suffered several hours of cannon fire from an extended siege. The room looked out from all angles, towards the sea, the hedged surroundings of the garden, the weedy gravel of the driveway, and the empty headland. It began to get dark and chilly, so I clicked on the electric radiator, blowing a fuse. The fridge fell silent as I discovered a small torch, which I tapped into brief life before I gave up on the fuse box and its smoking scent of charred wire. A final defiant jolt against my unprotected finger and a flash from an ungrounded electric arc signalled the end of my attempts to light and warm the house by modern means.

I found a disposable cigarette lighter in one drawer and lit several candles, imagining myself as a dramatic character from one of du Maurier's tales while pathetically failing to light the dry kindling in the fireplace. Several burnt fingers later, I coaxed some fiery life into last season's newspapers, and a bright flame began to entertain the walls of the cosy room while I returned to the car for my cases and papers. When I returned, a moment later, the room was thick with smoke.

I rushed over to the fireplace and stamped out towards the small blaze, putting it out. I blinked away acrid tears and headed to open the stiff windows and clear the room. The chimney was blocked, that was certain, but having noticed a set of drain rods stacked in the bathroom closet, I determined to be warm that evening; the clouds were breaking up, and a hard frost seemed likely. I connected the rods and added the threadbare stubble of the disc-shaped broom. Ramming the end up the chimney, I dislodged a fair number of sticks, rook feathers, bird bones, and enough mess to fill the fireplace without needing to resort to other fuel for the rest of the evening. Something croaked and flew away in alarm and resentment as I forced the broom-ended rod one final time into the stone-lined flue, claiming eviction victory over the corvid squatter. As I withdrew the rod, the end caught on a protrusion from within and became stuck. I gripped the closest section of pipe to the opening tightly and pulled sharply, bringing down a cloud of soot, masonry, and something else.

It tumbled onto the smouldering hearth and glanced off the polished crystalline flagstones, clinking as though glass impacting a hard surface. I raised the dying torch to see a dusty leather bundle roll its heavier contents erratically until it came to a stop by my feet. I squatted to examine the object. It was heavy, slightly smaller than a rugby football, but smooth to the touch. Untying the leather thongs that held the chamois leather wrapping, I gasped as a glint of green glass, chipped in one corner from its fall from the hiding place in the chimney, emerged from the dirty covering. It was a bottle, thick and broadly oval in profile, that once may have held a delicate spirit within its thick protective walls. Something lay within, a shape familiar through the bubbled and coarse transparency – a miniature ship.

I examined the chimney to see a clear opening at arm's length on the left side, a square hole illuminated by the fading last light of the setting sun. A void matching the lump of stone in the grate grinned like a toothless gum as I shone the weak beam from the torch against the inside of the flue. There was nothing left within the hole, so I retracted my arm, now covered in soot, carried the ship in a bottle over to the largest of the candles, polished the glass with the leathery rag, and sat down to examine the find.

The ship was exquisitely detailed and sat, listing to starboard, on a painted wooden base diorama. The base was littered with granite pebbles and brittle sea thrift, some of which rolled loosely around the bottom of the ship as I turned the wooden craft, static for so long in its dark, confined harbour. I saw, backlit by the candlelight, the silhouette of an ancient three-masted sailing ship; its stained calico sails were torn and tattered against its severed rigging. Parts of the boat were missing. A plank here, a whole section in other parts, until I realised I was looking upon a wrecked ship or a ship breaking apart. A glint of brass grabbed my attention, and I rubbed at the glass to read the tiny nameplate fixed to the base of the scene.

'*The Surprise*,' I whispered, breaking into a smile. I twisted the bottle to examine the stopper; the initials '*TT*' were melted into the blood-red wax that covered the cork stopper. The lack of any meaningful phone signal prevented me from searching for any hint of the ship's heritage or contacting the bothy's owner, a Miss Roscoe, to inform her of my discovery as well as the sorry state of the bothy's electrics.

A distant door slammed shut, and I rose to the window to see the lit windows of a remote farmhouse in contrast to my meagre candlelight. The light of a waxing moon broke free of its cloudy embrace, and a faint flickering light appeared on the headland, now all but indiscernible. It bobbed and weaved as though being raised and lowered, going out periodically, as if in some silent communication before reappearing once more to continue its dance against a moonlit sky. I watched for several moments before a larger bank of cloud covered the moon, and at that moment, the light on the headland ceased.

I returned to light the fire, which rose through the open chimney and warmed the room in a short time. I opened a bottle of wine and drank from a chipped teacup while reading my papers, occasionally glancing over at the bottle on the deep windowsill. Its sparkling glass-like sunbeams reflected against the irregular whitewash of the other side of the room. The fire spat, and the flames rose higher for a moment, scattering the fractured light and silhouette of the wrecked ship across the far wall. A strong smell of the sea, bitter and acrid, enveloped the room, and I rose to close the windows before settling down sleepily in the lush seventies corduroy of the single high-backed chair.

Intoxicated by sea air, wine, and a crackling fire was, perhaps, enough to explain how I fell into a doze for several hours before the overpowering stench of the sea and all that was rotten woke me suddenly with a gag.

I twisted to see the windows closed in the dark room, lit only by the embers of the dying fire. Moonlight poured in like a sieve through the many portholes, illuminating the puddles of spent candle wax and the bottle on the granite ledge. I instinctively pinched my nose, but my mouth was already open in amazement as I glanced across at the whitewashed wall.

Projected via the moonlight, the ship in the bottle tossed and listed on the makeshift screen as though replaying the final moments of its precarious existence in a thunderous gale centuries before. There was no sound, and I rubbed my eyes, watching as the ship struck a jagged outcrop of barnacled rock, briefly uncovered by the heavy seas. The waves returned to lift and toss the vessel mercilessly as its rigging and aft mast snapped under the intense forces of nature. Small figures of men fell from high points on the rigging into the sea as I turned to look directly at the ship in the bottle on the opposing window ledge.

The ship was stationary, locked into its endless list on the diorama within its glassy prison, unlike its cinematic counterpart on the whitewashed wall. I returned to the moving image, heedless of the foul smell of the sea, and placed my hand on the scene. A lone rowing boat, crewed by several men in tricorn hats, moved away from the ship in desperation as *The Surprise* began to break up. I followed the boat and flinched as it crossed the back of my hand and into the shadow cast by my silhouette.

I rushed for my phone, switched it on and watched as the small startup message appeared.

'Come on, come on!' I whispered at the device, eager to record the moving images. I turned back to the wall to see *The Surprise* split in several places; one final and monstrously high wave broke over the boat and turned it in to an unrecoverable position before the image faded to be replaced by another.

A solitary figure of a hooded man stood on an image of the headland, braced against the elements. The grass was devoid of stones, and I could see from his frame and demeanour that he was a tall and broad set man. He lowered a lantern, shielding its light against his cloak and signalling to others on the beach below. Men with torches and lanterns raced across the sands towards the half-drowned sailors, lucky enough to reach the shore. Exhausted and tossed onto the beach through the final breaking waves of the coast, they realised, as did I, that it might have been preferable to have drowned and gone down with the ship. The villagers were not coming to save them.

They were coming to kill them, cudgels raised.

I watched in horror as they brought down the crude weapons sharply against the skulls of the sailors crawling out of the surf, arms feebly raised to ward off the repeated and heavy blows from the wreckers. After a mercifully short time, the resistance failed, and the backwash of the sea reclaimed dark pools of blood. I watched as the figure of the wrecker in charge mounted a horse and rode down out of sight before emerging later to regroup with his murderous cohorts on the beach. The rowing boat, crewed by five men, headed for safety at the far end of the cove, but they were seen, and the wreckers moved to intercept. The boat beached, and the men sprang from the flooded craft, exhausted but alive. It was then that I recognised the red jerkin coats of soldiers, whitesashed and buckled. Their officer, brass insignia around his neck glittering against the broken moonlit clouds, issued the order to load and raise muskets to no avail.

Their powder was wet, and their time was up.

The wreckers swarmed the exhausted attempts by the redcoats to fend off the vicious slaughter until the leader dismounted his horse and raised his pistol to the face of the officer who clutched a small chest in the crook of his arm. The flintlock fired its charge at point-blank range, and I caught sight of the explosive tearing off skin from the side of the poor man's face before he sank to his knees and fell forwards, still clutching his strongbox.

I was momentarily blinded by the screen on my phone as my finger shook, trying to locate the video capture app. The image on the wall faded, and I glanced out of the window as the moon began to dim behind a veil of high cirrus. I got a final and single fleeting glance of the beach and the wreckers pulling ashore a great bounty of flotsam, barrels, and drowned men. 'No, not yet. Show me more,' I cried, running to the window to look out upon the hazy sky now too weak to project the image through the ship's bottle. The intense smell of the sea returned sharply, and I opened the window instinctively to be met by a frigid, frosty cold. The lawn outside glittered with rime, but there was something else out there too.

Figures of men.

I could not determine their number immediately, but someone was out there, just at the boundary of the shadows cast by the white-frosted hedge. They stood motionless, except for occasional shifting. I heard the jangle of metal and buckles shiver against tarnished brass buttons, reflecting in the brief interlude of a moonlit sky. When the clouds returned, the figures faded almost to beyond sight before brightening again, though still shadowed when the moon blazed forth its silvery light. I turned over the brightness of my phone and checked the lock on the door while my eyes became accustomed to the dark. I crept into the bedroom and peered around the moth-eaten curtain to gain a different perspective.

The moonlight briefly brightened, and I saw that there were indeed five of them.

Five redcoat soldiers, their uniforms horribly tattered and moulded with time. The white sashes across their chests still holding powder charges covered with blood, barnacles, and bile. Their down-turned faces still lay hidden, deeply shadowed by their battered tricorn hats. One stood slightly forwards and swayed gently, as though struggling to remain upright in a chest-high current of water, and raised his head. I shot back into cover, my mind reeling with the sight of his partly missing face, bloated, pale, and very dead.

I remained crouched and panting until the lactic acid in my legs forced me to rise, but I toppled over, banging my head against the iron bedstead, and fell into a swoon on the flattened towelled rug beneath the window.

It was the crow that raised me, blinking and bruised into a confused and cold morning. A splitting headache mixed with the sound of gulls circling the headland meant I was at least painfully alive, and I raised my hand to my head to check for any signs of a cut. I smoothed over a lump on the side of my temple, but my hand came back clear of any blood. Staggering to the mirror in the bathroom revealed little more than a duck-egg-sized bruise, hidden by sleep ruffled brown hair, so I freshened my face with water before changing into a clean set of clothes. The sun peeped through the curtains, and I drew them back to see a thick frost covering the lawn. My eyes drifted towards the edge of the dense shrubbery, and

I was relieved to discover no footprints or signs of any trespass.

Had I imagined the whole affair? I had heard of people suffering blows to the head and losing a sense of time and was unsure of whether I had been party to the strange projection of the ship on the wall, and the possible spectral encounter, or whether I had hit my head and the rest had come afterwards in some semi-conscious stupor, my mind later rearranging the event to make some sense to my logical and materialistic outlook on life.

After a cold breakfast of mixed fruit and cereal, I headed out of the door with my pack containing my precious family history file, banana sandwiches, and a flask of hot tea. I glanced at the ship in the bottle, casting its green shadow obliquely across the ledge in the rising sun, and resolved to take it, with its leather wrapping, to the village to locate the owner of the bothy, a Miss Roscoe, and to discover any further history once I had visited the church.

The wind had dropped, and it was a chilly but altogether pleasant experience once my eyes adjusted to the bright sunshine and reflections bouncing off the glimmering sea. I strode down the driveway path to meet the lane with my paracetamol-placated headache and the sound of a few hardy sheep bleating their steamy breath like small woollen steam engines.

Passing the early morning postman, I made it to the church in less than half an hour, and I creaked open the sea-rusted metal gate to the modest but well-kept graveyard, searching for those stones with a Trevelyan in the surname. I found several in one area and got out my camera and notebook, enjoying the solitude and the outlook over the sea. Many of the stones were intricately carved and dated from the early Georgian period. There were even older relations in a far corner whose stones listed like the ships they would have depended on in life. I made several rubbings of the names with a lump of black crayon, mildly disappointed that the churchyard was missing one of the more allegedly interesting and wealthy Trevelyans, once a resident of the nearby derelict manor house and former squire of Portmellon.

Rounding the church on the east side revealed a new internment with flowers freshly placed, recently marked by a headstone belonging to a Cadan Michael Roscoe. The man had died before Christmas, and I wondered if it was a close relative of the holiday cottage owner.

A great white gull heralded my closer inspection of the church's interior, which was typically plain and functional, with several squat diamond-leaded windows. They were mostly clear, with coloured panels casting hues like a harlequin's costume across the wall memorials on the opposite side of the nave. I studied many of the stucco wall urns and carved pieces, many relevant to the maritime wars of the last three centuries, but a larger, older, and plainer memorial bearing the name of Trevelyan caught my lasting attention.

It was a family memorial from the late seventeenth century declaring the virtues of Reginald and Isadora, who appeared to be great benefactors of the village and the church, and whose graves lay outside on the southern side of the graveyard. The name Thomas Trevelyan stood out as one of their children – the only Trevelyan whose burial I had yet to discover, although my research had uncovered that he'd inherited a sizeable fortune from the tin mines further along the coast. A brief inscription lay within a panelled wooden framework.

May God protect and nurture this place
My line for ever more.

I sat for a while in the peaceful place, surrounded by distant family I had never known, and tried to imagine their presence in the very plain wooden pews long ago while shutting out the sound of squabbling gulls squawking outside the thickly set granite walls. With a warming cup of tea nestled within my chilly fingers, I flicked through my notebook for the address of the holiday bothy owner and made a mental note of the location on a map I had fortunately sketched.

A look at my watch indicated eleven o'clock, and I left the pleasant cool for a brisk walk down to the centre of the village with its tight meandering streets. I located the correct small paint-peeling door at the start of a row of charming fishermen's cottages raised and retained upon a terrace of cut granite blocks from the houses below. Several knocks yielded no response, and I left a note beneath the door and headed for the harbour.

The sandy stretch of beach lay sunbathing at low tide. Boat lines, limp on their iron rings cemented into the sea-weeded granite, stretched out to the little outboard motor-boats lying impotent until the earth and moon turned, bringing back the rise of the sea once more. I glanced down the coast to the end of the cove, and the shallow waves spilling over a submerged plateau of rock only a quarter of a mile distant, the same outcrop that seemed, to my cloudy recollection of the previous night, to be the very same that had claimed the great ship. I lowered my pack and withdrew the heavy bundle before unwrapping the bottle and holding it up to the wrecking rocks against the distant horizon. The ship in my outstretched hand positioned perfectly in scale against the scene beyond, almost as if the maker had once stood close by with intimate knowledge of the wreck. Putting the bottle under my arm, I collected my pack and headed for the only visible open doorway in the village, that of the Mermaid Inn.

I entered the empty dim bar, the smell of bracing sea air replaced for the time being by centuries of spicy spilt ale, and pulled on a small bell rope to summon the landlord.

'Morning,' said a wiry man, getting up from behind the bar with some surprise. 'Didn't expect to see anyone today, what with the market on at Penzance and all.'

I sat on a stool and placed the loosely wrapped bottle on the counter. 'That explains things. Apart from the postman, you are the first person I've seen all day. Could you make me a coffee?'

The landlord snorted. 'It'll have to be instant; we don't do any of that fancy stuff around here; no call for it.' At that moment, the leather rag slipped from the top of the bottle, unfolding to display the bottled ship. The man behind the bar froze from spooning the cheap coffee into a white mug.

'Mother of God!' he said. 'I'll ask you kindly to put that thing away. Frighten away all my customers that will.'

I looked around at the empty room while he approached the ship gingerly, as though the bottle was radioactive.

'Save us,' he whispered upon reading the name on the brass plate. 'Bad luck to bring a bottle like that into an inn, especially a wrecked ship such as this. Best put it away if you please; we are superstitious about things like that.'

His pained look seemed genuine, and I complied. I quickly wrapped the bottle and returned it to my pack; the cloud of anxiety evaporated from his stubbled face.

'Sorry, I'm just visiting the area. My ancestors came from Portmellon,' I said, trying to kick-start the conversation on a friendlier note.

He passed me the mug and a bowl of faded, tea-stained sugar packets.

'Are you the Trevelyan staying up at Drover's Light?' he said, fixing his eyes on my pack once more. 'Ally mentioned someone was coming to look around the area for a few days. Begging your pardon, we hoped—' he corrected himself suddenly and turned his back to examine the optics of the whiskies that lined the bar wall '—thought that the line had died out.'

'I'm the last as far as I can tell,' I said, wondering if the peculiar behaviour was down to me being an outsider. 'Likely to be the last, too, as I'm not married, and my work at the museum doesn't allow a great deal of free time.'

I watched his reflection in the grimy glass as he looked up and spoke. 'Where did you get the bottle?'

'The electrics failed in the cottage, and it was cold so I thought to use the fireplace. There was a blocked chimney when I arrived, which I cleared, but a loose piece of masonry dislodged, and the bottle came with it.'

'The last Trevelyan and the return of *The Surprise* on the same day?' he muttered. 'Very strange indeed.' He turned and waved away my attempts to pay for the hot drink. 'On the house, and welcome home, if you like.'

I swallowed a pair of painkillers and sipped at the coffee. 'Can you tell me more about the family and *The Surprise?*' I said.

'Ally Roscoe is the one for history around here. She'll be the one to talk to about that and the electrics – she inherited Drover's Light as well as the trinket shop.' He pointed over his shoulder. 'It's halfway down the lane behind the inn.'

I was grateful for the information and rose, offering my thanks. He nodded silently and watched me cross-armed until I closed the door behind me. The sign of the smirking mermaid above swung back and forth as I peered back to see the landlord still staring at my departure, leaving me in no doubt that my presence had unsettled the man and his quiet coastal existence.

Behind the inn, the side lane narrowed and disappeared around a tight right bend to join the main street leading out of the village. Past several low, wide stone cottages appeared the aged and flaking sign of 'Roscoe's Curios'. A cobwebbed, wide bay window stretched past a narrow open doorway displaying dusty maritime items of questionable age and provenance, sitting jarringly next to neon-coloured buckets, kites, and other modern holiday paraphernalia.

I poked my head into the doorway opening to see boxes of unsold stock stacked within the modest space. A glass cabinet counter housed several delicate items of shell and scrimshaw, and I glanced my head on the ceiling-hung harbour lights and sailboats for sale as I entered the shop.

'Hello?' I called out towards a radio broadcasting from a small backroom.

'Be right with you!' came the reply of someone amid hurried industry. Within a short time, a woman in her mid-thirties, fair-haired and wind-tanned by a lifetime next to the sea, appeared, wiping her hands down her navy blue sailing club top.

'Didn't expect tourists today,' she said with a strong Cornish lilt. 'Sorry about the mess, Father wasn't one for tidiness, and now he's gone and left me with all this I thought I'd have a sort through. Seen anything you like?'

I was surprised and humbled at the openness of her welcome and the mention of her loss to a stranger. Her sea-glass-green eyes and smile-creased lips showed no hint of sadness, just a hopeful and optimistic sense of an early spring day when anything was possible with a future of independence lying ahead.

'I'm sorry,' I said, taking off my pack. 'I was up at the church this morning looking for old headstones from my own family – was it your father's grave I saw overlooking the sea?'

'It was,' she said, nodding and coming to stand behind the counter. 'You must be Jack Trevelyan, staying at the cottage. I hope everything is comfortable for you?'

'Yes, apart from the electrics,' I replied. 'I'm afraid the fuse board might need some professional attention.' I raised my fringe to display the red mark on my forehead. 'Stupid, here, banged his head last night when the lights went out.'

Miss Roscoe raced around the counter and pressed her face close to mine with a genuine look of concern.

'I'm so sorry. That wiring needs looking at, and I've been so busy with Dad and the shop and all that I've not got round to it. I could run you down to the infirmary in Penzance if you like?' She wandered off to the back room and returned with witch hazel ointment and a packet of cotton wool.

'I'm fine,' I lied, not wanting to cause a fuss and glad of the opportunity to feel brave in the company of a young woman likely having gone through recent personal hell. 'Would it be possible to send someone to look at things? I had to unblock the chimney last night, too, because it was getting cold.'

'You are a real treasure, Mr Trevelyan,' she said, passing me the ointment. 'I'll get on to someone I know in Marazion, and he'll sort it for you. If not, you are welcome to stop over in the flat above; I moved back to the farm. Come to mention it – I wondered why there was candlelight coming from the old place last night; I thought you were having an atmospheric night alone with a copy of *Jamaica Inn*.'

I dabbed my bruise with a soaked cotton pad and shook my head. 'Don't worry, it won't affect your Tripadvisor score,' I said, breaking into a smile. 'I'm glad to be away from the museum for a week under any circumstances.'

'You look too young to be a fusty old professor,' she said.

'I'm not a professor; I'm in acquisitions.'

'Don't look too closely around the shop then, most of it is just tat from local house sales and boot fairs, but there are one or two pieces of nineteenth-century wreck salvage in the window if you are interested.'

I reached down into my pack and withdrew the heavily

wrapped bundle. 'Actually, I'm hoping you might be able to tell me more about this?'

Her eyes widened as the wrapping fell away to reveal the ship in the bottle. I passed it over, and she lifted and turned it before whistling with astonishment.

'Few of these were ever made by him and every one a ship that he had cause to wreck. I suppose it was some kind of trophy, that he got a kick out of reminding himself. This would have been the last one he made, thankfully. It's a family heirloom and no mistake, though one I wouldn't want to hold on to.'

'Why do you say that, and who made the bottles you are speaking of?' I asked.

She tapped at the initials on the wax stopper. 'Why, Thomas Trevelyan, of course. He made one for every ship he had wrecked. It's worth a pretty penny, though.' She examined the chipped section of glass. 'Shame about this bit of damage; looks recent?'

'Actually,' I said, 'it doesn't belong to me; it belongs to you, technically. It was hidden in the chimney at the cottage. I accidentally caught it with one of the drain rods as I unblocked the rook's nest.'

She placed it down sharply on the glass counter and whispered to herself. 'A long-lost Trevelyan turns up and *The Surprise* on the same morning...'

'That's just what the landlord at the Mermaid said – can you tell me more about the ship? I had what you might call a funny experience last night.'

'Before or after you banged your head, Jack?' interrupted Ally.

'I'm not sure, but I thought I saw something when the moon was out. I'd drunk half a bottle of wine, and it was a long drive.'

I watched as she studied my face, seeking some additional

information like a key waiting to unlock a chest of centuries-old secrets.

'What kind of something?' she asked in a quiet voice, glancing over to the window into the empty lane as though fearing to be overheard.

I held back for fear of sounding stupid and sensational.

'Just someone out on the headland shining a torch about.'

She returned to my face and looked up at my forehead, which I hurriedly covered with a lock of my brown hair.

'Too much sea air,' she said finally, leaving an awkward silence.

'I couldn't find Thomas Trevelyan in the churchyard,' I said. 'He was mentioned in the memorial inside the church but didn't have a—'

'He's not buried in Portmellon,' said Ally. 'He and his gang were betrayed and taken to Bodmin and hanged for wrecking. His wife and son didn't want him commemorated in the village after what he'd done. Later, the manor house fell into ruin, and the family moved away. We remember that some of them went to America, which was probably for the best.'

'Yes,' I said. 'According to my records, the line died out but not before a sole heir returned in 1869 to live in London; that's whom I ultimately descended from. The last, as far as I know.'

'The last Trevelyan finds the last bottle he ever made,' said Ally. 'What are the odds?'

'Pure coincidence,' I said, 'but I'd like to know more about it.'

Ally peered into the glass and twisted her mouth as though recalling some distant memory.

'Grandfather always used to talk about this one, the last ship that finally did him in,' she said, pointing to the bottle. 'It's a three-masted barque longue from what's left of her, quite advanced for the time. Not earlier than 1710, but I know for a fact she was wrecked over on Soar Rock by Trevelyan and his gang. We sometimes get divers come looking for treasure, but we don't say that there's nothing left 'cause they drink a lot in the Mermaid, and they charter a few boats, which makes things easier during the off season.'

'Why did Thomas Trevelyan turn to wrecking? I thought his money was in tin,' I said.

'Even tin runs out eventually,' she said. 'He was a powerful man, old One-Eye.'

'One-Eye?' I said. 'You make it sound like he was a pirate.'

Ally stared, transfixed by the boat.

'Worse than any of that lot,' she said. 'But he got his comeuppance in the end, though he lived long enough in hiding to make this before he went mad and handed himself over to the authorities.'

'You said there was treasure on the ship. Is that what he was after?' I said, watching as she exhaled, as though unburdening a long-held memory.

'He was after brandy and port, but on board was something else, heavily guarded, that he knew nothing about. A great jewel, by all accounts, sent from Cadiz as a gift for Queen Anne to seal an alliance. When the ship got blown off course on its way to Plymouth, it caught sight of the light and made the mistake of thinking it was Penzance.'

'He lured the ship onto the rocks?' I said.

Ally nodded. 'We all know the story hereabouts, long history of the same families in Portmellon, told to us by those that came before. Poor men drowned or worse when they got to shore, all for smugglers' liquor and to avoid the revenue men.' She held me long in her gaze, gauging my honest, middle-aged face.

'But there was something they hadn't bargained for.'

I lowered my voice instinctively, sensing some deep and painful collective secret rarely broached with strangers.

'Five redcoat soldiers in a rowing boat carrying something of great value?' I said.

Her eyes widened, and she raised her hand to her mouth.

'How the hell would you know that?' she said between her hands.

'It was part of what I thought I saw or imagined last night, in the cottage. The bottle seemed to show things that happened by the light of the moon.'

I realised I had overstretched my willingness to share the bizarre and frightening events of the previous night. Ally dropped her hands and the tension in the air cleared.

'That idiot Jethro told you in the pub, didn't he?' she said. 'It's not funny, and I don't like being made a fool of. It's my family history, too, whether anyone else believes it.'

I shook my head and held up my hands, uncertain how to resolve the sudden collapse, attempting to deny any attempt at mockery as she grabbed her coat and keys, bustling me out of the shop. 'I'm off to Penzance, Mr Trevelyan, to sort out the electrics, and I'll be happy to come to some sort of settlement on the cost of the cottage for the inconvenience.'

She passed me my pack and locked the door behind us before I had the chance to offer apologies for any offence, desperately and pathetically attempting to ease any notion that the landlord had put me up to any tomfoolery.

'A lot of men died, Jack,' she whispered. 'The sea is tough enough without men such as Squire Trevelyan or Madern Roscoe piling on more misery, and I don't need reminding of it, not now.'

She turned and strode off, putting on her brown suede jacket and flicking out her flowing hair on her way to a rusted old Fiat at the lane's bend.

I turned to the shop window to see the bottle lying on its wrapping on the counter, the muffled sound of the radio obscured by the crying of the gulls that circled above, mocking my feeble attempts at recovery from a situation in which I had been a naive player.

I wandered over the roller-coaster coastal path for several miles before stopping at a secluded bay to eat my sandwiches and a dry Cornish pasty picked up from my stop at a service station the previous day. I sketched several interesting rock formations and a distant container ship traversing the horizon before returning via a straighter route back to the cottage.

The rook in the chimney pot took flight from its new attempts at nest building as I entered the snug to find the electrics still off. I dropped my pack and took a lukewarm shower, thankfully fuelled by the gas tank hidden by a mat of brambles and overgrown tamarisk.

I lit the fire early and restocked the basket from a metal bunker in a small outhouse before toasting thick slabs of bread struck through with the cleaned end of the iron poker. I warmed soup on the gas ring and sat down to watch the setting sun sinking into the sea and the first stars twinkling into life in the dark blue beyond.

I set out the remains of the candle stubs, realising it would be an early night; at least my headache seemed to have subsided, and I did not have any ship in a bottle to worry about.

The sound of an approaching car on the gravel drive broke my reverie of the nautical twilight from the snug window. It was followed by a loud knock on the door.

I peered out of the front window to see the rusted Fiat, and I admit to being a little nervous about opening the door, following my previous attempt to protest my innocence. Ally stood in the doorway, overloaded with shopping bags and a mouth gripping onto her purse.

'Sorry about earlier,' she mumbled. 'I brought you some things.'

I breathed a sigh of relief and grabbed several bags of food, candles, new paraffin lamps, and bottles of wine. Ally crossed the threshold carrying the leather-wrapped bundle of the ship, and my heart sank a little despite the promise of her company.

She put down the bottle on the windowsill and moved her purse to her pocket, instinctively trying the light switch to no avail in the gathering fire-lit darkness.

'That bugger Pete said he'd sort it this afternoon,' she said, hands on hips. 'I'm going to kill him.'

My disappointment was mollified by the several bottles of wine and the tapas urgently removed from the bags before I had a chance to react. Ally wandered over to the kitchen, oblivious to the fact that it was technically my cottage for the week and rifled through the cutlery draw.

'Peace offering,' she said, uncorking a bottle of red with a wooden handled corkscrew. 'Get the paraffin lamps out of the boxes while I get some glasses and plates; I'm starving.'

'Will you be alright to drive after this?' I asked as she poured a large glass and one for herself.

Ally pointed out of the front window. 'That's the old farmhouse,' she said, pointing to a dimly lit cottage about half a mile away, nestled in the rusty bracken of the upper slopes of the hillside. 'If I can't drive, I'll walk home and leave the car. If you want the company, that is? I've got something important to show you.'

I flustered my way through some sort of acceptance before she handed me a glass of supermarket Merlot.

'I spoke with Jethro, the landlord,' she said. 'I know you

didn't hear it from him, so either you are telling the truth, or something else happened last night.'

I motioned for her to sit. 'It was probably just my imagination,' I said. 'Coincidence, if you like, but I got the feeling I had seen or dreamed the things you spoke about after my tumble. I'm sorry if I upset you this morning—'

'It's fine,' she said, breathing out and throwing herself back into the armchair. 'That damn ship is still taking lives, even after all these years.'

She must have seen the puzzled look on my face as she continued. 'Dad used to run the divers over to the wreck, but last October, he had a heart attack, and it was an hour before the divers surfaced to discover it was too late.'

I realised the sudden trigger of grief I had unwittingly released, both with my presence and that of the ship.

'I'm so sorry; I would never have—'

She shrugged her shoulders and batted a palm in my direction. Her hair comically flopped over her face, and she reset her locks and composure. 'No need to say any more, not your fault.'

'Thank you for the supplies and the lamps,' I said, looking at the items still with their price tags attached. 'You mentioned you had something important to show me?'

She slammed down her glass and launched out of the chair towards the windowsill, removing the ship from its wrapping. To my astonishment, she brought over the leather rag and stretched it out on the floor.

Ally pointed to the centre of the dirty wrapping.

'There is writing here,' she said. 'I only discovered it by accident when I hung the thing up out of the way.'

I followed her finger to the spidery letters, written in a hurried hand:

A wrecker's moon lights a way to the midst of God
The five guard it still

TT

'The time for secrets is over, Jack,' she said. 'Blow to the head or no, what did you see last night?'

I recounted the evening up to the moment that the moonlight faded through the bottle as best I could remember, and Ally listened, admitting that she too had seen the headland light.

'It's only happened twice in my lifetime; once when I was a girl, and they teased me mercilessly for the rest of the school term. The second was last night, which made me touchy this morning. Both times the wrecker's moon was out.'

'Wrecker's moon?' I said.

'It's what old Cornish folk call the full moon in March. It's a time when gales and strong seas can cause the first ships of the season to come to grief.'

'Like *The Surprise*?'

'Exactly,' said Ally. 'It's full tonight and will be rising soon over Pendennis Tor if you want to put your ghost story to the test.'

'What about the writing?' I said, pointing at the leather on the floor. 'It all sounds a bit Enid Blyton to me. What is it describing?'

'Trevelyan's Eye,' said Ally, pouring herself another glass of wine. 'The soldiers onboard *The Surprise* were tasked with delivering a great jewel to Queen Anne before they were waylaid and murdered down on the beach. They each swore an oath to defend the jewel, living or dead, until it was in the hands or proper place of its rightful owner. Trevelyan wore it in place of a glass eye for security and for reminding folk of his reputation. He couldn't sell the jewel once word got out because none of the dealers would touch it. It's what the divers that come here every year are after.'

'You seem to know a lot about this, Ally,' I said, stamping

out a fiery ember smoking on the rug. 'What is it you aren't telling me?'

Ally drained her glass and placed her hands before her, staring down at the floor like a child about to confess the location of a stolen biscuit.

'Madern Roscoe was my ancestor and deputy to old One-Eye,' she said, glancing up at my puzzled face. 'We both have bad blood in the family, Jack. Madern was the first to be caught and turned Queen's justice; he betrayed his fellow-men, which is a crime worse than smuggling around these parts.' She twitched an eyebrow. 'Seems I owe you an apology for sins of the father and all that.'

'Ancient history,' I said, motioning for her to continue.

She breathed out a sigh of relief and squatted down next to the fire to warm her hands, staring into the heart of the flames. 'They couldn't catch Trevelyan, no matter how hard they tried. Almost a year had passed, which I guess explains how he could make the ship in the bottle, but word got out about the state of his mental health.'

'You mentioned he went mad and turned himself in,' I said, kneeling beside her to catch her softly whispered words.

She nodded. 'Trevelyan told of being pursued by some-thing that haunted him. Even when he left the jewel in a safe house, which drove him mad to be parted from it, he complained about being watched. He turned himself in to the parson after the following moon in March 1711 but not before hiding it somewhere in the village or round abouts.'

Ally's fire-lit eyes turned to gaze into my own. 'These words he left on the leather tell us where it is if only we can decipher them.'

I looked out of the window to see the darkness descend. Starlight poured through the windows, and a glimmer of moonshine appeared above the silhouetted massif of the granite moorland.

'I think you should go before the moon rises,' I said, gently squeezing her arm as we both rose. 'The five that still guard it, the redcoats—'

'What about them?' she said, placing her hand against my own.

'They were here last night, outside at the far end of the lawn. It's what caused me to bolt into cover. I fell over and banged my head as I tried to get up.'

I watched as her confusion spread to abject horror.

'They were here, Ally. I couldn't see them, apart from a glance at the officer, but they are dreadful. You need to go now.'

She wandered over to the window and clenched her fists tightly before turning, framed against the front window and the first rim of the rising moon.

'I'll not have it said that a Trevelyan was braver than a Roscoe; I have my pride, you know, and besides—' she pointed towards the headland with a shaking finger '—it's too late, it's already started.'

I raced to the window, grabbing her around her shoulders, and peered through the darkness to see the lantern candle-light bobbing erratically on the distant headland.

'Do you think it's—' she whispered, as though fearing that the frosty air would somehow relay her words across the open fields to that lonely place.

'Yes,' I said. 'Bolt the door and get those paraffin lamps lit.'

We spent a furtive and frightened half an hour securing the cottage as best we could while we took turns at the windows. We ate a little but avoided any further alcohol, short of a shot of 'on offer' brandy that Ally had rushed to the car to fetch before I barricaded the door with brooms and the two wooden kitchen diner chairs.

'What do we do now?' she said, throwing a split lump of oak onto the fire.

'We wait and hope that the night is not eventful,' I said. 'If it's of any consolation, the five did not harm me or attempt to break in; they seem to be impotent. They didn't kill Thomas Trevelyan after all, did they?'

'You think they are trying to fulfil their mission?' she said. 'You know, getting the jewel back to the rightful owner?'

I smiled nervously. 'Which one of us is going to tell them that Queen Anne has been dead for over three hundred years?'

'I vote you do that,' said Ally, returning a grin. 'We still don't know where the damn jewel is. What do you suppose *"in the midst of God"* means?'

I looked down at the notes I had made, rearranging letters, looking for anagrams or codes that might reveal some hint of their meaning.

'It's not here, in this cottage,' I said. 'Sounds like the church would be—'

I was cut off mid-sentence as the moon cleared the hillside and shone like a searchlight through the cottage windows. The horrific stench of rot and sea-salted brine smothered the clean air within the snug, and Ally raised her hand to her mouth to prevent herself from being sick.

'It's started,' I said, turning to the whitewashed wall to see the silhouette of the ship in the bottle begin to change into a moving projection. 'Dim the lamps; we need to see what happens after Trevelyan takes the strongbox.'

Ally moved over to the wall, casting a shadow with her hand as *The Surprise* was lured onto the rocks in a repeat performance of destruction and death.

'It's... It's not possible...' she muttered.

We watched in silence, heedless of the foul air. The wrecker's moon, free from any cloud, was at its fullest, shining an unbroken and unsullied light through the green bottle. The image was clear but rippled as though the moonlight wafted through the irregular glass and onwards against a thin, wind-blown veil.

Back on the wall, the soldiers made it to the shore, and Trevelyan rode up, pistol in hand.

'It's the five, isn't it?' murmured Ally, wide-eyed and stricken by the unfolding scene. The officer looked up into the barrel of the flintlock, and I threw myself into the path of the light to prevent her from seeing the man's face torn from his skull.

'Cornish or no, you didn't need to see that,' I said. 'No matter how tough you are.'

She nodded in gratitude as I moved away to see Trevelyan grab the strongbox and ride out as the gang retrieved the beached plunder and dispatched the sailors making it to shore.

'Madern must be there somewhere,' she said. 'I'm so ashamed.'

'Different times,' I said, placing a comforting hand on her shoulder.

The image faded, and we both spun round to hear glass grating on stone as the ship bottle was twisted by unseen hands until the wax stopper bearing the initials of Thomas Trevelyan faced the incoming beam of light. Ally grasped me.

'One-Eye's here!' she whispered.

'Yes,' I said, trying to control my shaking and heart thumping in my chest. The image on the wall changed, lit except for a circular eclipsed shadow formed by the stopper. 'But I think he is here to show us something, not to harm us.'

Her fingers relaxed as a new scene played out upon the wall. Trevelyan rode as though pursued by some great urgency through the fields from the headland, horse close to collapse. Something pursued behind on foot, ever-present and equidistant each time he turned to look over his cloaked shoulder. No matter how fast the wrecker rode or ran, they were always behind him.

The figures of five men in tattered red uniforms.

Trevelyan threw himself from his moving horse as he approached the village, which was remarkably familiar and intact considering the intervening centuries. Clutching a small bag, he jumped over the dry-stone wall to the church-yard silhouetted against the moonlit sky.

'He's going in,' said Ally, turning frantically between the scene of the wall and the unseen visitor in the room. 'You were right; it's somewhere inside the church.'

The image faded, and we turned to see the ship in the bottle twist back to its sideways profile. I glanced out of the side window to the lawn to see the faint line of the hedge. Nothing stood there, but an overwhelming sense of expectation struck me along with a renewed stench of the sea.

'They are coming,' I said. 'They are still after him; we don't have long.'

At that moment, a curious scratching sound coming from the glass bottle on the windowsill caused us both to stop and draw closer to each other. Something was being scratched into the glass by the unseen hand of Thomas Trevelyan, the wrecker master general.

I saw the imperfections projected in the glass against the whitewashed wall. It was handwriting, the same spidery script from the leather wrapping.

Hurry.

'We have to get out, to the church, now while they're still formless!' I said, unblocking the door against Ally's frantic attempts to prevent me, always looking out on the gathering shadows at the edge of the side lawn.

'You are one crazy emmet, you know that?' said Ally,

searching for her purse and car keys. I looked up, unsure what she was planning.

'We don't have horses, and I'm sure you aren't suggesting we walk to the church? It's over a mile away.'

She pressed the button on the car fob, and the old vehicle squawked, unlocking its doors.

'Age before beauty?' I said, one hand on the latch of the door, ready to sprint over to the car and check that nothing was waiting to waylay either of us.

She looked up at me wide-eyed, but very much still in control. 'Both together,' she said. 'I'm driving, so you'll have to run around the front to the passenger side.'

I nodded and counted to three, throwing open the door to the bitter freshness of the frosty night. Ally launched out of the protection of the cottage, and I followed, twisting to see something take form in the shadows to the side of the house.

She threw open the door, and to her credit, she leaned over and opened the side door before slamming her door shut. The engine spluttered into life, and we reversed as I clung to the door, closing it as we sped out like a rally car down the drive.

'Lights!' I cried as we careered into part of the shrubbery.

'Sorry!' she cried, switching on the headlamps and leaning forwards into the tightly gripped steering wheel.

I looked back and saw nothing in pursuit and turned around, pulling my seatbelt into position to stop the alarm from sounding.

'You can relax,' I said. 'And leaning forward won't make the car go any faster.'

We sped down the lane, and I was glad she knew where the twists and turns were. I feared the short journey would come to a sudden and suicidal end as we raced through one blind bend after another. I saw the church approach as I clung to the armrest to prevent myself from being tossed around by the frantic but expert handling of the driver. We pulled up in a short lay-by, got out, and ran for the church door. My prayers were answered as it swung open, and we tumbled inside to the moonlit solitude of the nave.

'Where should we start?' said Ally, catching her breath and leaning on the closest pew.

'No idea,' I said. 'But it has to be somewhere accessible; Thomas's parents remodelled the church, and it's barely been touched in three hundred years.'

'You think it's in a vault or something?'

I shook my head. 'There isn't one, and I think it's likely to be somewhere where God is present in figure or words.'

Ally strode to the altar and felt around the walls of the small alcove. I glanced over at the dark memorials on the wall, trying for the second time that day to make sense of them or locate anything to do with Thomas Trevelyan.

'Nothing over here,' said Ally, walking back towards me. 'I've been in here hundreds of times. I would know if there was anything suspicious or hidden.'

'*A wrecker's moon lights a way,*' I said, glancing down the nave at the moonlit puddles of light casting their beams against the far walls. 'It has to be something lit by the moon at this time of year.'

I strode along to every patch of moonlight until I reached the panelled memorial of the Trevelyans'.

May God protect and nurture this place
My line for ever more

The light cast from the opposite window illuminated the first half of the first line; a red light cast by a stained-glass diamond glowed against the word 'God'.

'*In the midst of God,*' I whispered, raising my finger to trace over the letters. The central 'o' was recessed more deeply than the other letters. I ran my finger over the same letter in the adjoining words to confirm my suspicion.

'Enid Blyton,' I said, smiling as I returned to the second word. 'In the midst of God, or the middle if you are living in the twenty-first century.'

I pressed my finger in between the central 'o' of 'God', and a sharp click echoed through the empty stillness as a hinged panel on the upper left swung open to reveal a small hollow space.

Ally gripped my arm in excitement. 'All these days I spent listening to boring sermons and it was here under my very nose. Well done, Professor.'

'I told you I'm not a professor,' I said. 'I'm in acquisitions.'

She smirked and pointed to the hidden cubby hole. 'Then go acquire something, Mr Trevelyan.'

I breathed in and reached into the hole. For a moment, I thought it was empty until I hit the back wall and spun a hidden trapdoor to discover a side compartment. I recoiled, suddenly scratching my wrist on touching something clammy and skin-like.

'What is it?' Ally said. 'Booby trap or spiders?'

I shook my head, recalling the feel of the leather wrapping. I stretched into the dark space once more and prodded the soft, leathery skin of a small bag. My finger hooked onto a leather thong, and I dragged the bag through the opening and into Ally's outstretched hand.

'There's something else in there,' I said, returning to slide two gold coins from the same space.

'Doubloons?' said Ally, unable to contain her excitement. 'They won't laugh at me now we've solved it!'

I turned over the precious metal. 'Queen Anne golden sovereigns,' I said. 'Still valuable, though.'

Ally held up the bag. 'It belongs to you, technically.'

I untied the straps. 'It belongs to neither of us.'

Pinching my fingers, I groped in the bag and felt the cold touch of something smooth and broadly spherical. I withdrew the marble-shaped stone from its hiding place of three centuries and dropped it into the palm of my expectant treasure-hunting colleague.

'It's beautiful,' gasped Ally, holding the giant ruby up in the moonlight. I clicked shut the panelled door, and the central recess of the letter 'o' returned to its previous position.

'Trevelyan's Eye,' I said. 'Seems to be about the right size for the glass eye of a wrecker general.'

The ruby was smooth, slightly irregular, and virtually flawless; large enough to rival the great Black Prince's stone that adorned the front of the imperial state crown.

It was priceless.

'What do we do with it?' said Ally, wrinkling her nose suddenly at the rising of the sea-stench within the confines of the church.

She shook and hurriedly handed the stone back to me. I placed the jewel back into its bag and pulled tightly on the drawstrings. 'We give it back,' I said, watching her nod in agreement.

The rotting air grew thicker with the stinking residue of the sea, and we rushed to the door, realising we were trapped. Outside, among the stones, stood the five redcoat soldiers, come to reclaim their charge.

I slammed the door shut and opened the small portcullis hatch, watching as the shapes shimmered and vanished with each appearance and disappearance of the wrecker's moon.

'They are out there, aren't they?' said Ally, squirming past my face to catch a glimpse. To her credit, she did not recoil. 'It's like they are reflecting the light of the moon; they keep appearing and disappearing.' She twisted and panted suddenly, throwing up a hand to her mouth.

'I saw the officer's face,' she mumbled. 'You weren't kidding.'

I returned to the portcullis, acclimatising myself to the faces of the dead. Bloated and rotten, they stared back. Barely shifting in the moonlight, the officer raised a hand as though signalling a parley.

'I think he wants to talk, not eat us,' I said, trying to inject a moment of terrified gallows humour.

'Why don't you just chuck it out of the door and see what happens?' said Ally.

I nodded and parted the door to swing my arm far enough to launch the bag into the air towards the ghostly figures. The bag plopped onto the rime between several stones, only eight feet away from the redcoats. The officer advanced and bent down. His ghostly hand swiped through the leathery pouch, unable to interact with it. He stood and raised his blasted face to the sky, showing me every terrible detail of his ravaged, pale face. A rasp of exhaled frustration came from the hollow skull, and he stepped back to join his men, raising his hand once more.

'It's no good,' I said. 'The soldiers can't fulfil their mission.' I laid my hand on the door latch, lifted the handle and opened the door. Just as I was about to leave, Ally's hand pressed into my own.

'They can't eat us both if they can't pick up a bloody bag, can they?'

Her weak smile filled me with courage, and we left the sanctuary of the church and stood on the tomb-stoned grass not less than twenty feet away. The officer lowered his hand and withdrew a musket.

'It's not a parley; it's a trap,' said Ally, twisting me back into the open doorway.

'Wait!' I said, watching as the musket was pointed downwards, drawing out something in the frosted grass.

The officer shuffled with the musket until he had completed the formation of two letters, traced upside down for our benefit. He pointed towards the bag wherein lay the precious ruby.

A R

'What is that supposed to mean?' said Ally.

'It's not a what,' I said, understanding suddenly. 'It's a who. Anne Regina, Queen Anne.'

The redcoats shuffled with the mention of the name, setting off the metallic clink of buttons against buckles.

I addressed the officer directly. 'The ruby must go to Queen Anne. Is this what you want me to do?'

The officer nodded and shouldered his musket.

'Now might not be the time to mention that she's as dead as they are,' whispered Ally.

'Queen Anne lived at Kensington Palace, if I recall,' I said, wracking my brains for any information on the grand dame of the English monarchy, 'but the jewel house in the Tower of London would be where it would have ended up—'

The redcoats shifted once more, exhaling through dry and dusty lips, skin pulled tight over their decaying skulls. The officer nodded once more.

'Perhaps one queen is as good as another on this occasion,' I said, turning to look into Ally's trusting eyes.

I released her hand and took several steps forwards to reclaim the jewel bag. Holding it aloft, I turned to the ghosts of the men.

'You have my word as the last descendant of the man who robbed you of your charge and your lives that I will deliver this stone into the hands of the jewel master of the Tower. Is that enough for you to find peace and leave this place?'

The soldiers turned and huddled as though in silent,

shambling communication. The officer turned and raised a rotten hand in salute, stepping back to join his retreating men within the shadows of an overhanging yew tree. A stiff breeze blew all foul air from the place, and a bank of cloud obscured the moon. The soldiers faded, and all became still.

'I think it's time to go,' I said. 'Your place or mine?'

'Definitely mine,' said Ally, giving the yew tree a wide berth on her way to the car. 'No more candles and moonlight; I want good old-fashioned electric light and Dad's expensive cognac. You're welcome to the spare room, if you can sleep much tonight.'

'I don't understand why you want the donation to be anonymous, Jack,' said the tall, spectacled man, placing the leather bag in the car's boot. 'It's the British historical and monetary find of the century.'

'Trust me, Bill,' I replied, turning to Ally in the farm-house's doorway. 'We have our reasons. I'm just glad an old museum alumnus trusted my urgent request on a Sunday and made the journey from London to pick it up personally.'

The keeper of the Jewel House of the Tower of London slammed shut the boot of the car. 'I don't know if I can keep this under wraps for long,' he said. 'Secrets get out somehow.'

He got into his car, and I waved him off on the six-hour drive back to the vaults beneath Tower Bridge.

'Will that be enough?' said Ally, crossing her arms in front of her chest.

'I've known Bill for a long time; he'll keep it safe in the place it should be. I think we've done what we promised, and besides,' I shrugged my shoulders and leaned in for a closer inspection of Ally's sea-glass eyes, 'if anyone steals it, they've got a nasty surprise awaiting them.'

The sun warmed the headland ring as we began to pack away the picnic rug and Tupperware boxes.

'The ring of stones,' I asked, pointing at the granite blocks. 'Neolithic?'

Ally folded the rug and shook her head. 'Madern raised a monument for each of the soldiers when he learned about Trevelyan's ghosts. I guess he hoped by marking memorials for them they'd leave both of them alone.' She halted and held me long in her gaze.

'Do you think they'll leave us alone now?'

'I'm sure of it,' I said, 'but just to be sure, I've brought this—'

I lifted out the ship in the bottle.

'What are you going to do with that?' said Ally.

I spun the smooth glass into my hands. 'I tried to hide it in the secret compartment in the church, but it's too wide, so I was going to bury it here, but the soil is too thin.'

'Looks like you are stuck with it, and me, at least until the electrics are fixed on Wednesday,' she said with a flirtatious wink.

'I've done all the family research anyone could want for a lifetime,' I said, throwing her an empty flask with my free hand. 'I've not started on my holiday yet.'

'Are you angling for a free week or something, Mr Acquisitions?' she said, catching the tartan cylinder one-handed and placing it in the hamper.

'Is it available next week?' I asked hopefully.

'It's free until the beginning of May if you want to stay that long.' She smiled mischievously.

'It'll only cost you a single Queen Anne sovereign.'

I opened my mouth in mock shock and amazement. 'For that spartan bothy?'

'And my charming company,' she said hopefully. 'I could use a hand in the shop if you get bored.'

'Throw in a bottle of that brandy we had the night before last, and I'm in.'

Ally spat into her hand and extended it in true country fashion. 'Deal,' she said.

I instinctively threw forwards my right hand containing the glass bottle to grab at the offered palm, sending the ship sailing into the air and over the cliff edge before I could do anything about it. We rushed over and crept close to the ledge to see the bottle bounce several times before smashing onto a plateau of granite outcrop below.

'That was stupid of me,' I said, slamming my fist into the turf by my side.

'Wait,' said Ally. 'The ship – it's afloat for the final time.'

The miniature model of *The Surprise* lifted, caught by a spilling wave which dragged it into the sea, its bobbing form barely visible against the sea foam and spray colliding with the lower cliffs.

We lay there for a blessed time, our arms folded around each other, watching the small ship reach open water before it disappeared out of view. The last ship to be wrecked and the first to escape and complete its journey out from the confines of Portmellon and onto the sundering sea.

THIN AIR

K aye's lungs and legs burned with the exertion from the Austrian mountain climb. At twenty kilometres in, the steep obstacle in her ultra-marathon training run was always brutal. Head down, she strode on, ignoring all rational pleading from her brain to stop, pause, gulp in the precious air, and to give up. Defending champions didn't quit, but they hurt just like everyone else.

She tapped the sweat-soaked smartwatch on her wrist and focused along the stony forest track that disappeared into the misty Tyrol plateau. The rise from the valley floor was ending, and the relief that it would bring to body and mind lay blissfully ahead.

'Pace – *Six point two kilometres. Time – One hour, forty-six minutes, twelve seconds.*'

'Not bad for a thirty-something,' she mumbled to herself, a light-headed response to the thinning air. She knew the signs as a seasoned athlete and had the foreknowledge that her head would clear once her breathing was under control again at the high altitude.

'I've got this. It's going to be a personal best if the rain hasn't turned the cutting through the trees into a bog.'

The parallel lines of crushed white limestone led on and levelled out as the tortured climb to the zenith of the mountain pass came to an agonising end. Kaye splashed through the milky-white rivulets, knowing there would be no stopping, not until she completed the half-marathon distance. Her coach, Hans, would be waiting for her on the other side of the pass, grunting his satisfaction at his long-distance protégé. She would have words with him for deliberately putting that cheesy and annoyingly catchy tune on the radio before the drop-off point in the valley this morning. This time it was the Macarena, and the repetition in her head had driven her mad for the past two hours.

It had also done its intended job of distracting the body from the painful build-up of lactic acid, and her mind from wandering without focus. The high-altitude training was going well, and there were a few more extended training runs before the key event at sea level at the end of the month. She would fly around the course; her body coursing with greater red blood cells from the reduced oxygen training environment. She would come home with the gold medal once again.

It would get easier from here, and she could recover now that the remaining distance was over level ground before the descent to the valley floor. There would be no glorious views over Innsbruck today, though; the steep slope of the mountain and the view across to the opposite range was now obscured by cloud and mist. All but the nearest trees, goats, and abandoned shepherd huts became shrouded from view.

The testing point of giving up and going home had passed; she had beaten the inner demons this time. The sweat and clinging damp streaked through her tied-back hair and teased its way into her mouth. She spat out the weak brine, promising to reward herself with a few sips of the electrolyte-rich sports drink from her hand-held running bottle. There might even be a carbohydrate fruit gel to fuel her depleted reserves if the imposter in her head stopped bleating on about slowing down or pausing for a breather.

She whispered to herself, in a mild delirium, of the hot shower in an hour, bananas and flapjacks, and the slap on the back from her Twitter followers for going out into such dank and miserable weather. The lightheadedness was normal at this stage, and she noted it by greeting the lonely, washed sun with a wave as it rose above the peak. It was good to have something as company this far out into the wild; barely a soul walked, drove, or rode the high track. The ground levelled out, and she glanced up at the gap in the dark resinous pine forest, leading her on to food, shelter, and warmth.

A massive glacial boulder marked the end of the steepest section. Kaye had passed it many times and was no less empathic for the weather-worn wooden cross leaning at its base. There were many accidents in the mountains and not every mountaineer who went up into thin air came back.

She glanced up to spit sideways and noticed someone was ahead – an indistinct man-sized form that lay briefly out of focus through the dense mountain cloud. The unease of being so isolated and alone replaced the urgency to quit, and she forced herself to determine any potential notion of danger this far out from home.

The figure remained elusive and out of clear sight, as though running away, maintaining its distance from her – another runner, perhaps? There were fleeting glances of cadence in the way the person was moving. The muddy section of the route lay near a bend in the trees, and the distant figure picked their way through the ruts that typified the boggy section ahead.

The sound of an approaching and heavily revved engine had been growing ever since the monolithic moraine boulder signalling the end of the climb. Wondering how close the vehicle was, Kaye looked back into the disappearing track. The low cloud made it difficult to determine the direction, but one thing was clear – it was travelling at high speed. Kaye raised her arms and shouted in warning to the distant figure at the blind bend ahead, unsure if they were aware of the danger. The person halted and looked around, confused by the signal. Kaye cupped her hands and bellowed a last shout, leaping over to the forest edge in readiness to avoid the vehicle – it was certain the driver would not see them until it was too late.

The figure ahead turned and sprinted on, not heeding the warning, and ran into the path of the light of the emerging vehicle. It appeared suddenly, but indistinctly, slipping and sliding at breakneck speed, with only a single headlight for warning. The figure ahead disappeared, and the headlight veered uncontrollably to the left and off the road. Kaye heard the tumbling and rolling of the vehicle as it gained momentum down the sheer slope, splintering trees and breaking apart until it came to a distant terminal shudder far below.

Kaye sprinted to the bend to determine the fate of the other runner and the point at which the vehicle left the road. She peered over the cliff edge; there was almost no chance anyone would have survived such a fall. She approached the bend, calling out to no reply. The figure had been in the centre of the road, and Kaye checked the steep wooded slope on the left for any sign of a casualty, knowing there was little chance they could have escaped the vehicle that lay now at the bottom of the ravine.

She scanned along the muddied track, searching for signs of footfalls, tyre marks, and the crashing void where the car could have left the road. There was no sign of recent travel by any, save the passage of a herd of goats some days prior. It made little sense, and she retraced her steps to double-check. The cloud lifted briefly, and the track sparkled in tributaries of white. In either direction, there was not a soul on the disused road.

'*Time – two hours,*' signalled the app on the phone.

'Oh, shut up,' said Kaye, adrenaline coursing through her body. 'I don't understand. It was right around here.'

She called out until the chill from the sweat made her shiver. She swallowed a strawberry gel for comfort and gulped some bottled water to settle her nerves before plodding on through the virgin mud.

Fifteen minutes later, she collapsed onto the bonnet of Hans' pick-up, having made up time for searching the bend. Hans leaned against the car door, stopwatch in hand, and gave a disapproving shake of his head.

'Where the bloody hell have you been?' he asked.

Kaye bent over, retching from the exertion and the shock of the earlier encounter.

'I... I'll... tell you later. Accident... back about two kilometres – car came out of thin air... went over the cliff. Might have hit another runner, but there are no signs in the... mud. I don't understand.'

'What are you talking about?' he said, coming over to lift her, allowing her lungs to process the low oxygen levels fully. 'Thin air is right; you hit that hill too hard; I keep telling you.'

Kaye grimaced, shook her head, and limply pointed to the watch to show the contrary.

'There's been no one through all morning, runner or car,' said Hans, taking the sweaty device off her arm and checking the stats, unconvinced. 'No one uses this track anymore, and I'd have heard a car rolling down the mountain from here.' He wiped the smartwatch on his fleece jacket and pointed towards the opposite mountainside.

'You can't see it today, but there's a quarry over there, and that's six kilometres away. I can hear that fine, even over your whining,' said Hans sarcastically. 'You could have come up with a better excuse for the crappy time.'

Kaye gave him a withering glance, trying to stabilise her breath.

Hans opened the passenger door. 'Get in before you get hypothermia,' he said. 'Let's get you down and into that nice ice bath.'

'Well, spit it out,' said Hans, concerned about Kaye's unusually contemplative mood. She sat in front of him, cross-legged.

She put down the pair of partially cleaned trainers and shrugged up at the best long-distance trainer in the business, sprawled on the sofa.

'I know what I saw,' she said. 'I just can't explain why there were no tracks.'

'We've been over this,' said Hans. 'Sound carries in these valleys – it could have come from twenty miles away. It was lack of oxygen, Kaye. I got overtaken on the Andean plateau by Napoleon once, just before I lost consciousness – I always hated being beaten by the French.'

Kaye rolled her eyes and returned to picking out the dried mud from the soles of her shoes.

'You said you saw the car swerve, but there was nothing on the track to explain why?'

She put down the trainers and knelt, picking up and placing cleaning items to show the incident like a general mapping out a battle. Hans watched as she arranged several waterproof wax sticks.

'The runner was ahead of me, about two hundred yards at the edge of visibility,' she said, picking up a shoe to symbolise the car. 'They disappeared before the car with its sole head-light came round the bend, swerved to avoid something that wasn't there, and tumbled down the ravine.'

'You're sure it was a runner?'

'Had to be,' said Kaye. 'A good one to keep ahead of me. They must have come up the hill about a few minutes before me, though I saw no one in front till the forest cutting.'

His pensive face peered down; head cocked amusingly on one side, as it always did when he was deep in thought.

'It was a trick of the light – you know, a sun dog or some-thing. You said there was no sound of impact and that there was no sign of tracks when you got to the spot you last saw the figure?'

'No, just the sound of the car going over the edge. It wasn't a trick, because the sun was in front of me. I spent a few minutes calling and checking the slope, but I didn't tell you about—'

Hans leaned forwards. 'About what?'

'You are going to think I'm crazy, but the runner looked like they knew or recognised me, but they just ran on regard-less, as though they knew the accident was going to happen.'

'Maybe it was a competitor – I wouldn't put it past the Italians to train on the same mountain as us?' said Hans.

Kaye ignored the change of subject.

'Will you ask Maria when she comes in to tidy up, Hans, just to put my mind at rest? She knows this area and the people.'

'Of course,' said Hans, putting his hand on her shoulder. 'Rest day tomorrow, which is just as well, because the forecast is for more rain. I've got some lovely weights lined up for you in the morning; that will take your mind off things.'

'What about if it was a ghost or something?'

Kaye had been desperate to bring up the idea, despite her reservations about the supernatural and the absurdity of bringing the topic up in front of her closest confidant. To her relief, Hans joined her on the carpeted floor and pressed her hand.

'I believe you saw something up there that spooked you,' he said. 'Whatever it was won't be any clearer the more you tie yourself in knots about it. You did what any normal human being would have done and shouted out; the runner would have heard and seen the car way before you did.'

She squeezed his hand and nodded.

It was 3 am before weariness, and the circular reasoning in her head, allowed sleep to claim her. The image of the figure in the centre of the track had been so close to being fully discernible before the single headlight of the hidden vehicle had scattered the form to the clouds.

Maria arrived at mid-morning to prepare breakfast. The elderly housekeeper looked after the chalet complex and the walkers during the off season. The promise of snow brought the skiers and her four-month sabbatical until the summer returned to the lush green valley and she once again cooked and cleaned for the gentler tourist.

Kaye stabbed her foot against Hans' shin, causing him to cough on a piece of marmalade-laden toast. He had avoided any hint of broaching the subject until then.

He leaned down and rubbed at his leg, frowning at Kaye innocently eating her porridge.

'Maria, was there any news about an accident or missing person this morning when you did your rounds?' he said.

The housekeeper turned round and collected several empty plates from the kitchen table.

'Why ever would you ask that?' she said.

'No reason. It's just I was up on the south pass yesterday

and thought I heard something, that's all,' said Kaye, inter-rupting before Hans could reply.

'No one was up there except you yesterday. I wish you wouldn't go up there in such cloud; it's not a place I would go at the best of times.'

'How so?' said Kaye.

'Long time ago, before you were born,' said Maria, sitting down to impart the tale. 'There was a girl at my school who used to tend the goats up there, often saying there was some-thing strange up there and telling tales of things she saw in the cloud.'

'Did she tell you what she saw?'

'Nonsense, mostly, and no one believed her till it happened; a coincidence of course, but she maintained the story right until she died, about twenty years ago.'

Hans put down his toast and tapped at his watch, signalling that it was time for work.

Kaye nodded back, but asked another question.

'What happened exactly?'

'She had been telling tales of a quarry lorry coming off the road. Her father had been up there to put the child's mind at rest, but saw nothing. Whatever she thought she saw only revealed itself when she was high up and alone. She had an overactive imagination, and the thin air was likely enough to explain it, but when the accident finally happened, just as she described, they stopped thinking like that. It was a quar-ryman that died and left behind a young family too. There's a cross, or used to be, near the spot.'

'I've seen it,' said Kaye. 'It's leaning up against a large boulder near the top.'

'Sounds about right,' said Maria. 'I'm glad it's still there, but few go up there now. The quarry closed the route after the accident and made the new road go around it.'

'Are there any other runners in the village at the moment?' said Hans.

Maria shook her head. 'No, you told me to keep a special lookout, and I've done what you asked, Mr Schaffer. There are an elderly British couple and a party of schoolchildren, but no athletes or anyone like Miss Kaye here.'

'Thank you, Maria,' said Kaye, watching as the house-keeper bustled back to the sink with the crockery.

Hans jerked his head towards the spare room and the weights set up inside.

'I don't want you filling your head with coincidence and ghost stories, Kaye,' he said. 'You've got to focus on Salzburg, okay?'

She waited as Hans set up the equipment, watching the rain outside the steamy window obscuring all but the lowest slope of the mountains. Maria's battered 4x4 and Hans' gleaming pick-up stood outside, like metallic sheep clustered together to endure the mountain weather. She picked out the distant limestone scar and the start of the track, bright against the brooding sky.

'I know,' she replied. 'My mind's at ease knowing there wasn't anything bad that happened yesterday – at least, nothing I could do anything about.'

———

The cloying, thick alpine fogs continued under the still air conditions of the high-pressure system. Kaye, run-starved, ventured out into the pre-dawn gloom to scratch the itch that could only be sated by elevated heart-rate and the pounding of the ground beneath her. Thoughts of the incident in the cutting had receded after Maria had reported that nothing out of the ordinary had happened in the intervening days. Kaye's fear of discovering some news of a missing person in the papers did not materialise, and she warmed up, ready to repeat the run.

Hans dropped her off at the starting point, radio blaring out 'Gangnam Style'. He smiled as she gave him a friendly and curt middle finger for the choice of music that would cycle endlessly in her head for the next two hours.

The going was rough, and Kaye danced across the flooded fields to avoid the boggier parts. She reached the base of the hill climb, glad to see the firm ground beneath her sodden trainers. The ground rose, and her heart-rate pounded to its peak for the twenty-two-kilometre run. The path was soggy, and the floodwater from the mountainside was carving its way through the track, turning it into a bubbling stream of chalky tributaries. She steeled herself and ran on, onto the marginally drier centre ground between the ruts, wrestling with the imposter within who wanted warmth, the dry, and a chocolate brownie instead of this torment. Determined to push on, she increased her speed, desperate to stretch herself and get this section over with as soon as possible.

The climb was as unforgiving as ever, more so considering the amount of surface water she needed to negotiate. The cloud was down, and she all but forgot about the previous incident until she glanced back to see the indistinct figure behind her through the mist.

She forced herself to ignore the urge to look back, but gave in as she mounted the rise and approached the boulder and the cross. The figure seemed to keep pace, though there was no sound of footfall or splashing over the pounding of her own heart and the gasping of her breath. The figure raised a hand as though waving at something intangible and continued their exertion up the track. Kaye sped off, nervous once more about the prospect of meeting someone so far from help. The going would be slower ahead, and the runner would gain on her. If he or she proved worrisome, then she had plenty left in the tank for a full two-kilometre sprint towards the towering German, dozing in the cab of the warm and dry pick-up.

She heard the approach of the heavily labouring engine, the same as it had sounded before. Its direction of travel was again unclear, hidden from any sense, but with a broad signal that it was getting closer.

Kaye passed by the boulder and halted to see the figure gesticulating wildly at her. That was enough to spook her, and she raced on ahead in the centre of the rain-washed track. The softened ruts and the recognisable footfalls of her strides were clear from two days prior. Kaye picked her way around the larger puddles, noting the haphazard impressions of her frantic search for the runner. There were no other recent marks around the blind bend, and she knew no other person had been out to the spot. Considering the current poor weather, it was unsurprising.

Kaye looked back once more to see the figure emerge onto the rise behind her and become recognisable. It was a woman, or so it seemed, leaping from the track and onto the verge, urging her to get off the track.

Kaye slowed, unable to make out whether it was a cry for help; it sounded more like a warning. Through the thickening cloud, the approach of a single headlight confirmed the heavily worked vehicle was approaching towards her from the tree-lined cutting. The light was closer this time, brighter and more intense. Ahead, the figure of a female runner materialised, vaulted over something unseen, and ran into the path of the approaching light. Kaye glimpsed a hint of the vehicle before it veered to the left, one hundred yards away and off the track, tumbling over and over until it echoed with a final shuddering boom. She removed her shaking hands from her mouth and leapt to the spot she knew lay ahead.

The steep edge showed no signs of any impact, and she

saw nothing on the ground or through the mud. A lonely goat bleated ahead as the visibility briefly lifted. Turning to call for the runner behind, she caught a glimpse before the mirage disappeared. There was something familiar in the appearance, almost a reflection of herself against the thick cloud. One thing was certain – the runner had the same blue clothing as she had worn two days before.

'I don't want you coming up here again,' said Hans, moodily gripping the wheel as he negotiated the uneven road back to the chalet. 'We'll try another route that doesn't turn you into an emotional wreck.'

Kaye put down the recovery oxygen canister and held on to the armrest as the pick-up ploughed through a pothole.

'I'm not bullshitting you, Hans. The damn thing went off the road as it did before.'

He wiped the fogging windscreen and threw the cloth into the rear of the cab. 'I didn't hear a thing, and I'm still going to kick your ass when we get back for overdoing it on the climb.' He pulled out the smartwatch and dangled it in front of Kaye's flushed face as exhibit A.

Kaye swigged some water and broke the silence. 'It wasn't a quarry truck, if you want to know.'

'I don't,' said Hans, 'but how would you know that?'

'I was closer to it this time because I was faster on the climb. I could make out it's a large car with a single headlight. It's got damage to the passenger wing, the same side as the light is out. The runner ahead of me would have clearly seen it.'

'You mean the steeplechaser vaulting over invisible objects?' said Hans. 'Maybe they know the runner behind you, too? You know, the one that steals your running clothes when you are out and follows you for a run.'

Kaye unwrapped an energy bar and munched noisily to annoy her mentor. Hans did not allow any food in the truck; it was his pride and joy. To her surprise, he let her get on with it.

'You can clean those crumbs up when we get back,' he said, glancing over to see Kaye sticking her tongue out in defiance.

Kaye swallowed the grainy snack and wiped her hands down her leggings. 'What was the time?' she asked.

Hans snorted. 'Good enough, for a crazy lady that won't do as she's told. That hill will be the making of you, or the death of you, if you don't listen up. Tell me about this runner in front – you're sure it was a woman?'

'Absolutely. She was in that chequered red, white and blue, like the Commonwealth Games kit I have. I felt as though I should know her or she should know me – like the one I saw further behind me.'

'You said there were no tracks apart from your own from the other day?'

'I know it sounds crazy, but after what Maria said yesterday, I'm thinking it's not the past I'm seeing...'

A loud clunk interrupted Kaye as the pick-up dropped into a flooded pothole and emerged rattling and buckled.

Hans slammed his hands on the steering wheel and swore in several languages.

'What is it?' asked Kaye, rubbing at her shoulder, bruised from the sudden lurch to the right.

'The bloody axel rod has snapped by the steering, not to mention the brake line.' Hans pumped the pedal, and the pick-up veered to the right, showing that only one side was braking. 'If we get back in one piece, then we aren't going anywhere for a few days, by the looks of things.'

The following day, Hans was preoccupied with getting the pick-up fixed. The journey through the pothole had slashed the tyre, and the passenger underside was a mess of bent and buckled metal.

It rained, and Kaye headed on to the monotony of the running machine for a gentle 10 km to stretch her calves. After forty minutes Maria came in with the washing and opened up the wardrobe, hanging up the blue running clothing worn earlier in the week and the black outfit she had worn the day before. Swinging on the hanger beside them was the red, white, and blue of the England uniform from the successful summer of the previous year. It was her lucky kit, and she kept it, superstitiously, for international events and trials she felt she needed that extra bit of confidence to win. It was a fast suit, to be sure, and even the smell and feel of it next to her skin made her feel like a champion.

She paused the machine and took a swig of water from the holder.

'Maria, can I ask you a question about the girl you spoke of the other day?'

The housekeeper puckered her cheeks. 'Mr Schaffer's asked me not to bother you with silly old tales,' she said. 'I think it's best if the past stays where it belongs, and you look forward to that race of yours.'

'Just a single question, you might not know the answer...'

'What is it?' whispered Maria, cautiously watching Hans outside in animated discussion with a local mechanic.

'How many times did the girl say she saw the lorry before...' Kaye sought for the words, but Maria gracefully answered.

'She saw it twice and never got the chance to see it again, thankfully. She stayed at home on that Saturday. I remember because she wasn't allowed out to play when we called in the morning.'

Kaye grabbed a towel and gripped it tightly, carefully wording her next question.

'How long between the last time that she saw the accident and it happening?'

Maria stared out of the window, looking further away towards the mountain, recalling the sad day forty years before.

'It was the very next day, in the afternoon. We saw the dust and smoke from far away near the playing field, and then we heard the boom echoing around the valley. We knew something was wrong straight away.'

Kaye joined her at the window and put her arm around the kindly housekeeper.

'If you knew what you know now, about your friend's conviction, I mean,' said Kaye, 'would you have gone up there and tried to stop it from happening?'

Maria turned to look into the bright young eyes, wide with questions.

'With all my heart,' she whispered. 'With all my heart.'

———

'Don't overdo it in the pool while I'm out,' said Hans, putting on his jacket. 'One mile maximum, okay?'

'Okay,' said Kaye, ushering him out of the leisure centre towards the small hire car. 'Go. You'll miss the registration, and I'll have to watch from the sidelines next week.'

'I'll be back in two hours. We can get to work on tactics once I know who's running.'

Kaye nodded, swung her arms around him, and pecked him on the cheek.

'What the hell's that for?' he asked, unused to a display of affection despite their close working relationship.

'Just because I feel I owe you, and I never told you that.'

Hans was temporarily speechless.

'I'd – better go... will be late,' he said, still puzzling over the affectionate gesture.

He turned, and Kaye watched him through the glass doors of the complex, still struggling to comprehend the exchange.

'I just thought you should know,' she whispered. 'Just in case.'

Kaye changed into her red, white, and blue chequered outfit, rolling aside the swimsuit and locking it away in readiness for what she knew she must do. Get up into that thin air, run faster, and stop the inevitable from happening. She would get an almighty bollocking when Hans found out, and it could jeopardise the training programme they had both worked so hard to achieve. She thought of the runner ahead in the cloud, so similar in appearance and wearing her race kit, and knew that destiny would ultimately decide if she was strong and quick enough to reach beyond her physical limits and stop the car going over the edge of the ravine.

She caught the empty bus back to the chalet but did not get off, instead choosing to carry on to the lay-by that signalled the usual starting point for her training run. She had her bottle and gels arranged on her belt, like a bandolier, but something was missing.

'Sing me a song,' she asked the driver.

'Eh? What kind of song?' he asked. 'Not much of an audience for me today.'

'Something catchy, you know, memorable,' said Kaye.

'The English tourists always ask for "Edelweiss"?' he replied. 'Will that do?'

Kaye groaned at the prospect of the famous tune inhabiting her most sacred space for the trial ahead.

'Perfect!' she said as the driver crooned out the first verse. Several miles later, she was off and into the damp air, looking up at the distant mountain and the old quarry track climbing into the cloud.

Kaye gave up trying to avoid the watery sections of the valley floor; the entire area seemed saturated. The sound of newly created waterfalls accompanied the brisk and chilly wind that funnelled against the mountainsides, condensing at a low level into impenetrable cloud.

'*Pace – Five point two kilometres. Time – One hour, sixteen minutes, twelve seconds.*'

'Ahead, but only slightly,' she murmured. The lactic acid and exertion were already taking their toll, and she still had the climb to traverse. She knew it would have to be faster than she had ever run.

Would there be any need for the final two kilometres after the blind bend if she was unsuccessful?

'Need... maybe... two hundred yards to be sure,' she said to herself. Kaye swigged the remaining water from her bottle and cast her belt and pouches aside, trying to reduce the load.

As she approached the mountain base, she knew it was going to hurt.

'*Edelweiss, Edelweiss...*' she murmured despite the lactic build-up in her legs. '*Every morning you greet me...*' The initial zig-zag was through, and she leapt like a mountain goat, searching for the most direct route up to the straight and steepest section.

'*Small and white, clean and bright...*'

A goat appeared suddenly from the cloud in front and panicked with the appearance of the runner in red, white, and blue. Kaye snapped back to reality and the pain of the exertion, trying to shut out the imposter in her head screaming for her to stop.

'*Pace – Four point nine kilometres. Time – One hour, thirty-eight minutes, nine seconds.*'

Kaye knew she was ahead from the effort, but the mental torture and fatigue were affecting any reasoning or calculations. She screamed out loud and slapped the sides of her thighs to force an adrenaline response.

'Not yet... not faster... yet. Wait for the...'

Out of the cloud and marginally early loomed the form of the boulder. The cross emerged alongside, recumbent in its memorial to the quarryman. Kaye hummed the last line of the tune that had occupied her:

'*You look happy to meet me...*'

The monolith appeared, clear and dripping in the saturated air.

So did the sound.

The sound of the approaching vehicle.

'What do you mean she's not here?' said Hans, picking up his jacket in readiness for a return to the heavy rain of the chalet porch. 'She should be back by now.'

'I called the pool, Mr Schaffer, and they said she left over two hours ago,' said Maria, wringing her hands. 'I should have listened to you and not given in to her questions.'

Hans spun sharply. 'What did you tell her?'

'She asked about the girl and the accident. I told her I wasn't supposed...'

'Maria, what did she ask you?' said Hans determinedly, as he glanced out through the curtain of rain to the far mountain.

'She wanted to know how soon after the girl's prediction did the accident happen. I told her it was the next day.'

Hans didn't finish listening before running through to the

spare room and throwing open the wardrobe. The Commonwealth Games kit was missing.

'Shit!' said Hans, grabbing his keys and flying out the door. He got to the pick-up before he realised the wheel was missing. He looked over at the small city car and then over at Maria's battered jeep.

'I need your 4x4,' he said to the housekeeper at the door. 'She's gone up that cursed mountain. This car won't make it up the track on the other side – I need to hurry!'

Maria disappeared in and returned, throwing the keys out to him. 'Be careful, Mr Schaffer, the steering is not good, and the brakes are very soft.'

Hans caught the keys, one-handed, and wrenched open the battered door of the housekeeper's antiquated mode of transport. The starter motor slipped and ground its way through several more geared teeth before finally forcing the engine into rattling and rasping life. Hans floored the clutch and crunched the first gear he found. He released the pedal, and the jeep lurched away in a cloud of gravel.

'Come on, you piece of crap!' he shouted, trying to get the vehicle above fifty miles per hour.

The engine screamed in response to the handling, like a runner begging for release from the exertion of the track. A single, ineffective window wiper flip-flopped pathetically against the torrent of rain hitting the screen. Hans took his eyes off the road momentarily, searching for the headlight switch. He switched it on, but the sudden squeal of scraping metal across the passenger wing jolted him back to the road, and he straightened back into the lane, assessing the glancing blow from the road edge barrier. Something metallic tinkled down the road behind him, but there was no time to stop and figure out what had come off.

He had to get to Kaye, and he knew where she would be.

He glanced at his watch, trying to calculate distance over time.

She would be on the climb right about now. Hans reached the entrance to the far quarry road and took the turn at high speed. He felt the jeep rise off the passenger-side wheels as he completed the turn. The jeep jolted back onto its chassis and Hans bobbed violently inside, urging the struggling motor onwards, into the cloud and towards the cutting.

Kaye stared back down the track, making out the black-outfitted form of herself from two days prior. She'd been right. With no time to take in the mirage's reality or not, she turned and raced on, knowing she was ahead in terms of distance.

Was it going to be enough time?

There was a shout from much further down the track, and she recognised the call, finally. She was reliving the events of the past two runs, and if no other image of herself appeared in the seconds that remained, then the accident would come to pass; the vehicle approaching would be real.

A creaking groan like that of a whale broke her reverie as a large tree, with its root plate washed away from the torrential downpours, tilted and swung over into the track ahead, showering the old road and opposing trees with splinters and flying branches. Kaye shielded her eyes and sprinted towards the obstacle, with the rain lashing down, steaming on her face and lower arms from the furnace inside her.

'Faster, Kaye, faster!'

The single headlight appeared, bright and close. It would not see the tree until it was too late.

But it might see her.

She gambled her remaining strength and launched herself

over the metre-high trunk of the fallen fir tree. She felt her stride falter, her legs unable to continue with precious little oxygen.

The car emerged from the fog as she threw herself into its path, arms outstretched in warning and surety of her destruction. There was a split-second recognition of the battered jeep and its driver before she instinctively raised her arms to protect herself. The car slammed on its brakes, veering and weaving. It would not be enough. The car was travelling too fast and would see the tree too late and go over the edge.

Kaye flung herself to the ravine side of the track, forcing the driver to swerve towards the bank on the opposite side. It deluged her with mud as it passed, inches from a collision, and she slipped, rolled, and turned to see the jeep slide against the bankside, slowing it down. The driver saw the tree in the path and swerved for a final time, throwing the passenger wing of the jeep into the trunk. The jeep lifted on its driver-side wheels from the impact, teetered at a steep angle, and came down with a springing lurch.

Kaye gagged with the sudden demand for air and the suddenness of her collapse. She writhed in the mud, trying to sit up, desperate to see if the car was still there and if the driver was alive. It was too much, and too soon, but just before she passed out, she had a wonderful feeling of euphoria; the car had not careened off the road and into the ravine. Kaye had the feeling of being lifted, of being weightless or being carried.

As she lost consciousness, she smiled from the trick of the thin air.

She almost thought she heard Hans telling her she was going to be alright.

'You'll rub the silver off that medal, you know,' said Hans. 'It's not solid like the old days.'

Kaye smiled and slipped the trophy that had been around her neck into its presentation case. It snapped shut, and she looked out of the pick-up window.

'I suppose I should be grateful even to have come second, after...'

Hans turned on the radio, evasively trying to shut down the conversation. Kaye leaned over and switched it off.

'Alright, alright,' he said. 'It was a quick time, and it was a miracle you were race fit at all after...'

'After?'

Hans glanced over and cocked his head. The bruise on his forehead was receding into a sickly yellow, and the cut to his lip was healing well. He always looked comical when unsure of what to say.

Kaye laughed and was even more surprised when he spoke again. His eyes welled up as he returned his concentration to the road back to the chalet.

'I owe you, Kaye,' he said. 'I just thought you should know that.'

Kaye beamed and took out two flapjacks from the bag between her legs.

'Want one?' she inquired, handing him the snack.

'Sure, why not?' he said, ripping open the plastic and showering the dashboard with toasted oats.

'Crikey, you've reconsidered,' said Kaye, tucking into her bar. 'I didn't think you allowed food in your pick-up.'

Hans munched the flapjack, spilling crumbs onto the seat.

'It's not mine anymore,' he said. 'I'm giving it to Maria for what you did to her jeep. A hire car is waiting for us back at the chalet.'

'What I did?' said Kaye, recognising the start of the game

beginning to play out between friends. 'You were the one who...'

At that moment, Hans clicked on the radio and turned up the volume.

Over the sound of 'Mambo No.5', he barely heard the chatter of her reply and the inevitable assassination of his good and honourable character.

NEIGHBOURHOOD WATCH

'Evening, Tom,' said the ghost, leaning on her gravestone. 'You're looking dapper this evening.'

'You say that every night, Mel,' said Tom, smiling. 'But I thank you all the same.'

'They don't bury them like they used to,' she said, admiring the waistcoat and three-piece suit of the apparition. 'You had real class back in the sixties. Every bloke buried these days turns up as a ghost wearing the same £99 throw-away suit.'

'Times are hard,' said Tom. 'It's such a pity we only have the choice of what we were buried with or died in, to last us. I've got a choice of this or my boiler suit.'

'Electrocution?' asked Mel. 'I never thought to ask how you died.'

'Nah,' said Tom. 'I fell off a ladder in the days before anyone had ever heard of health and safety. What about you?'

'Rare form of cancer,' she said. 'I died in my cat-print pyjamas, so I'm kind of stuck wearing this other ensemble.'

Tom rubbed his chin and puckered his lips.

'Nice, though,' he said. 'Whoever dressed you had good

taste; as far as eternity goes – it'll never date.' He turned to scan the large municipal graveyard. Around the myriad of broken and upright stones, long grass and spent wildflowers shed their seed into the shared earth. The ashy fluff of fire-weed drifted across the tombs to the hedgerows and housing estate beyond.

'It always looks so peaceful in early autumn,' he said, looking across at the avenue of beech trees. 'I'm surprised not more people are about on a warm night like this.'

'There haven't been more than a dozen living folk all day,' said Mel, pointing to a far headstone. 'That woman over there has been here a while though.'

'That's Onesie's wife,' said Tom. 'Come to give his ears a bashing and read the local digest. We should be thankful neither of us was married, I suppose?'

Mel folded her arms and half-shrugged. 'Never had the chance, but maybe you're right. Why do you call him Onesie? I thought his name was Clive.'

'It's his nickname because there's a few Clives about the place. He's mad on cricket and used to follow Worcestershire all over the country wearing a one-piece rabbit costume.'

Mel smirked. 'You're kidding?'

'No, I'm not,' said Tom. 'He used to be part of a band. You know the ones that make a racket, get the fans singing, and all worked up? Well, they used to wear all sorts of silly costumes to stand out, and one sweltering day, he put his trumpet to his lips to start another rendition of "Jerusalem" when he had a heart attack and died. There was a bit of a to-do because he had been prescribed medicine by someone later found guilty of tampering; they are still sorting out the mess.'

'Poor fellow,' said Mel. 'I suppose he's glad he can wear what he was buried in?'

Tom shook his head.

'His wife knew he spent all his free time at the cricket-ground, and his mates thought it was a good idea, so she buried him in the outfit.'

Mel's eyes widened in horror. 'You mean he's stuck wearing a rabbit suit for eternity?'

Tom nodded. 'Along with that blasted trumpet of his. You've heard it when his team are playing?'

'The theme to *The Great Escape*? I thought it was someone from the estate; I didn't realise it was a ghost playing. How terrible! We've met, but I thought he'd died as a children's entertainer or something and was having a laugh with me; I was new to the cemetery at the time.'

Tom raised a hand in greeting to the ghost materialising by the side of the old woman.

'Well, he's coming over. Just don't dwell on what he's wearing, he can get quite self-conscious, especially around Easter time.'

A large ghost wearing a ragged white rabbit costume approached. His pink fluffy belly bulged and stretched the plush around the dead man's stomach. Apart from the space for his head and his bare hands, the giant rabbit outfit was complete and ridiculous.

'Evening all,' said the rabbit-costumed ghost, putting his hands on his hips and sticking out his tongue at a passer-by. The man wheezed and puffed with his walking frame as he meandered his way to his long-dead wife's grave.

'Be seeing you soon, Alfred. I always remember you pinching my girlfriend at the dance, and we are going to have a few words when you pass over and turn up here.'

'He can't hear you,' said Tom.

'I know,' said Clive. 'But it makes me feel better.'

'I see your missus is here?' said Tom, admiring the home-grown marigolds from a distance. 'Your grave's looking splendid.'

'Don't remind me,' said Onesie. 'I've had to listen to all the gossip about the Women's Institute. If she really loved me, she'd read the cricket scores.' He got out a spectral pipe, pretending to smoke it from decades of habit.

'I've come over here to give my bloody ears a rest.'

'What has she had to say for the past hour, Clive?' said Tom.

'Prattle, mostly,' he said. 'What I really want to know is the match scores from the rest of the county, not "who is seeing who", or "who's been into hospital" for whatever reason.'

'Well, we might get that on the sports radio tomorrow when the grounds apprentice turns up and pretends to do some work,' said Mel optimistically.

Clive folded down a large rabbit's ear, deep in thought.

'Well, he'll have plenty to do,' he said. 'The state of plots 100 to 130 is an absolute disgrace, not to mention what some moron has graffitied on the wall memorial. It's getting worse.'

'What have they written this time?' asked Tom. 'It's only been two weeks since they wiped the last smut from the marble.'

Clive blushed, and Mel saw the colour rise in his cheeks.

Unusual, she thought, smiling to herself. *Ghosts don't hold colour, as a rule.*

Clive looked at the ground and kicked at a stone on the path; the booted rabbit's foot passed straight through.

'Well, I had to ask young Billy over on plot 167 what it meant,' he said. 'I've been dead a long time and don't know all these modern swear words. When he told me, I wish I hadn't asked!

'I won't repeat it, Tom, it's filthy talk, and there's a dead lady present.'

'Is it the same hooded guy with the red trainers?' asked Mel, nodding her appreciation at the courteous behaviour.

'The one we saw in the high street tagging the telephone box
–*Nemesis* or something?'

'That's the scumbag,' said Clive. 'Signs his scrawl "Nemo".
I followed him one night up Wordsworth Close to that row
of dodgy houses; it's number seven.'

'It's about time someone did something about it,'
said Mel.

'What are you proposing?' said Clive, raising his fluffy
arms in front of him. 'That we rattle our chains and shout
boo? I got his bull terrier barking, but that's about all I
could do.'

'I don't know,' she said, furrowing her brow. 'There's an
awful lot of antisocial behaviour lately, and the police don't
have the time or resources to deal with it. What we need is
someone from the other side who could pass on information.'

Tom folded his arms. 'We could see Betty?'

'Betty Somerton?' exclaimed Clive, shaking his head.
'She's as nutty as a frog!'

Mel shrugged her shoulders as Tom explained.

'She's a medium,' he said. 'The whole family's got the sixth
sense; Romany blood and all. We could see if she'll listen to us
and get the police to take action?'

'I'm in,' said Mel. 'I've never been to a seance before, and
it beats waiting around for the place to go to the dogs.'

Tom looked over at the giant rabbit.

'Oh no,' said Clive. 'You won't get in without an appoint-
ment, plus I've got better things to do—'

'You're not knocking about with the Victorians again?'
said Tom.

'Well, someone's got to do it,' said Clive, sharply. 'No one
comes to visit them, and they like a bit of news; anyway,
they're the only ones with a cricket set in the entire
cemetery.'

'Then lend me your trumpet,' said Tom.

'Whatever for?' said Clive.

'In case she won't see us,' said Tom with a wink. 'I've got an idea.'

'Can she really speak with the dead?' asked Mel, passing through the doors of the bus to join Tom at the closest stop to Betty Somerton's house.

'Apparently,' said Tom, watching as a woman with a pram passed through them on the pavement. 'She's like the local telephone exchange if you want to get in touch with someone, providing that person is open to receiving, of course.'

'You mean she can hear us and pass on messages? I thought that was all nonsense when I was living.'

'I've never tried it myself, and there's a long waiting list, but I know the guy on the door.' He pointed towards a semidetached house with the figure of a large ghostly bouncer wearing a smart tuxedo standing sentinel in front of the petunia-lined path to the house.

The ghostly doorman shuffled as they approached, and got out a small notepad, upon which appeared a list of names.

'Evening, Mr Carson,' said Tom.

The bouncer furrowed his brow, as though trying to place the man.

'Is that young Tom Haines?' he asked. 'Haven't seen you since the late sixties. How have you been keeping?'

'Very well, thank you, Mr Carson,' said Tom, before introducing the female ghost to his side. 'I was just explaining to my new friend here how you used to referee the football matches when I was a lad; you were tough, but always fair.'

The doorman smiled and puffed out his chest. 'I miss those days,' he said. 'What brings you around here? I hope you're not coming to see Betty; she's fully booked this evening.'

Tom puckered his lips and raised himself on tiptoes to whisper in the giant's ear.

'Isn't there anything you can do, Jack? My friend here, she's in a bit of a state – recently crossed over; you know how it is?'

Mr Carson looked down at the smartly dressed young woman, doing her best to look meek and upset about being dead.

'Boyfriend, no doubt?' said the doorman.

Tom nodded. 'Needs to say goodbye and all that.'

The bouncer swung open the gate behind him and tapped a finger to his nose.

'Thank you, Mr Carson,' said Mel, leaning up to peck him on the cheek. 'We'll be as quick as we can.'

Tom led her through the front door, literally, and into the snug.

An old woman, wrapped from her shoulders in a silk-tasselled scarf, sat at a small circular table with two living guests. She leaned over a crystal ball in the dim light, crowded upon by many ghosts waiting to speak.

The ghost of a small dog sat barking upon the table.

'Is that you, Mr Pickles?' said Betty, staring into the crystal ball. 'Your mummy and daddy are here to say hello.'

The dog barked again.

'I hear him,' said Betty, closing her eyes as though to hear the animal more clearly.

The old couple opposite clasped hands, remembering the spoilt animal loved for over a decade until its demise at the hands of an out-of-date pack of sausages.

'He's quite well, and having a lovely time running around the green fields above, digging holes and biting deceased postmen,' said Betty, embellishing the seance with several rocks in her chair, and moans from her heavily painted lips.

'She's very good, isn't she—' said Mel, before being accosted by a nearby ghost.

'Shh!' said the stranger. 'And wait your turn. We've been here an hour already.'

Betty's brow furrowed as she heard the ghosts' chatter.

'Mr Pickles wants to return to his basket now,' said Betty, one eye on the clock. She knew a packed house of spirits was ready to come through and impart their words to loved ones. She would have a busy time transcribing them later. Betty also knew that *Celebrity Snakes and Ladders* was on in half an hour and she wanted to get the kettle on and the pack of custard creams to hand in readiness.

The dog jumped from the table and vanished, but not before cocking a leg against a nearby ghost.

'He's gone now. Back to the ether, Mr and Mrs Wilkins. See you next Thursday, same time?'

The couple rose and clasped each other tightly. Childless and bereft of animal company, they nodded and handed over a ten-pound note. They showed themselves out, comforted by their weekly reach out to the pet they had adored above all things, including each other.

'Right,' said Betty. 'Who's next?'

Tom strode forwards into the path of a ghost at the front end of a sinuous queue.

'I'm sorry, friend,' he said. 'This is an emergency.'

The ghost screwed up his face. 'So is mine. I need to tell my daughter her husband's been cheating.'

'Settle down, settle down!' said Betty. 'No queue jumping—'

Tom put the trumpet to his lips and blew a few awkward and untried notes. The medium put her hands to her ears.

'Alright, alright!' she said. 'You'll wake the dead—'

A round of laughter and some slight applause filled the room as Tom lowered the musical instrument.

'You may not remember me, Betty,' said Tom. 'It's Tom Haines; I used to read the meters when your mum was alive.'

'Didn't you get electrocuted?' said the medium, gazing into the crystal ball.

Tom rolled his eyeballs into his non-existent head.

'Something like that. We need your help.'

'We?'

Mel strode forwards and peered through the other side of the crystal ball. The medium jolted back as though stung.

'Got yourself a fancy woman, have you?' said Betty.

'I'm not his girlfriend, Betty,' said Mel. 'We need you to go to the police station or call the local community support hotline. Tell them that the graffiti around the town is being caused by a man in his early twenties, hooded, red trainers, and lives at 7, Wordsworth Close, Shambleton. Tags his spray paint with "Nemo" and a smiling face.'

The ghosts murmured and interjected with messages of their own.

'I've seen that scrawled across the bus shelter on Mayfield road,' said one.

'He's signed his name to a load of thingies,' said another.

'Thingies?' asked Tom.

The ghost pointed to his groin. 'Thingies,' he repeated.

'That's disgusting,' said Betty. 'But why should I get involved? They'll not believe me.'

'If you don't call them this minute,' said Mel, 'Tom will start practising his trumpet here every Thursday night, right?'

'Right,' said Tom. 'Come on, Betty, just a quick call; your mum would be proud, and I'll tell her when I see her next – she's over at Highfield cemetery, isn't she?'

Betty struggled to her feet and dialled the phone number, putting the speaker on hands-free.

'*Hello, Hambleton Police Station. How can I help you?*'

'Hello,' said Betty. 'It's about all the graffiti around the town – I'd like to give you some information, in confidence, of course.'

'*Can I take your name and address, please?*'

'It's Betty Somerton. 9 Helston Avenue.'

The voice on the end of the line was joined by another, whispering about the inbound caller's notoriety.

'The person you are after is a man in his early twenties, wears a hood and red running shoes. Lives at 7 Wordsworth Close in Shambleton,' said Betty. 'That's what my source says.'

'*And can you give me the name of your source, please, Betty, and a contact address?*'

'It's Tom Haines, but he's been dead for sixty years.'

'*I'm sorry, Mrs Somerton,*' said the voice tersely, '*but you mustn't waste police time.*'

'But it's true,' said Betty. 'Tom says he'll blow his blasted trumpet every Thursday during my meetings if I don't tell you about Nemo.'

'*I will pass the information on to our community support team. If they need anything further, they will be in touch. Goodnight, Mrs Somerton.*'

The phone clicked dead, and Betty replaced the handset.

'Told you,' said Betty, slumping back into her chair.

'What do we do now?' said Tom, glancing around the room.

The ghosts shrugged.

'What about possession?' said Mel. 'Is it possible to possess someone like in the films, Betty?'

The medium sighed. 'I can see where this is leading. Yes, it's possible, but you'll never be able to channel the connection for long enough for you to possess the moron and hand yourself in to the police station.'

'But you could show me how to do it?' said Mel expectantly.

'It's just like putting on a pair of tight gloves or one of them fancy wetsuits, or so I've been told,' said Betty. 'If you are going to try then hurry because my telly programme's on in ten minutes.'

'What do I do?' said Mel.

'Follow my movements or sit inside me, then imagine yourself wearing me like a set of clothes. Body first, mind later.'

Mel moved to sit within the space occupied by the medium. Betty flinched as the feeling took hold, as though someone was sliding into the space between her every sinew.

'It is like wearing a pair of clothes,' said Mel, sliding into the medium's hands and waving at Tom who stood nearby. 'It's really weird, and it takes some effort, but I can get control.'

'Not for long,' said Betty, tensing and grimacing at the uncomfortable sensation. 'Now try to imagine what I'm seeing and copy it in your thoughts; you'll be able to complete the possession that way. No poking around in my head, though, and only for a moment or two, alright?'

'Agreed,' said Mel, staring out at the crystal ball. Momentary snatches of the old woman's life came to mind as Mel took control.

Standing up, she looked around the room, conscious of touch, taste, smell, and hearing from a living world long since departed.

'I can't see any of you,' she said through the old woman's mouth. 'But I've got it. I've got hold of her, Tom.'

Mel shuffled around the room and opened the front door.

'Mr Carson,' she shouted to the unseen doorman at the gate. 'Thank you for being there and sorting out the numbers. I've never told you so, but I think you're doing a terrific job.'

Mel slammed the door shut and froze.

'How do I get out?' she said to the not-quite-empty room.

The answer came sharp and painful from her right ear as Tom blew a mighty screeching note on the trumpet. The shock severed the connection to Betty's mind, and Mel withdrew from the medium's body, leaving the old woman panting and shaken.

'If that's all,' said Betty, on her way to the sherry decanter and the television remote, 'I'll be calling that a night.'

The ghosts in the room groaned as they filed out of the room.

'Thank you,' said Mel, grabbing Tom by the ghostly arm and heading for the door. 'You've given us a chance to sort this out for ourselves.'

Betty nodded, sipping on the sweet liquor. 'I never want to hear from you or that trumpet again, Tom Haines, do you understand?'

A week passed, and the graffiti was removed, readying the white marble canvas once more.

The residents of Shambleton Cemetery watched and waited for signs of the hooded young man with the red trainers. Damage, litter, and graffiti from neighbouring graveyards kick-started a sense of ghostly civic pride, encouraged by Tom and Mel's efforts, as they investigated the claims. A small gang of miscreants had formed around the central character, known by his tag as Nemo.

'Take out the linchpin,' said Tom, 'and the rest will tumble.'

'We need to find him first,' said Mel, on vigil near the war memorial. 'I can't remember anymore what I did before patrolling the graveyard.'

'Isn't that the job description for being a ghost?' said Tom, smiling as he scanned the rows of dark graves for signs of movement. 'It's created a network that we never had before, and that's a good thing; you should be proud.'

The rabbit-costumed form of Clive appeared, animated and excited from his sentry post at the graveyard entrance.

'He's here, at the gates. He's doing the chapel wall as I speak!' said Clive, pointing back at the entrance. 'He's as local as he gets. Whatever you've got planned, now's your chance.'

The three of them hustled along the beech avenue, reaching the gates to see the miscreant, hooded and beginning his scrawling art on the blue engineering brick of the exterior chapel wall.

'And what are you going to do?' said Tom. 'When you possess Picasso here?'

Mel scanned down the road. 'Wordsworth Close – how far is it from the council leader's house on Carmichael Avenue, over there?'

Clive scratched at his rabbit ears. 'Dunno, maybe a quarter of a mile? Ten minutes' walk?'

'I'll only have half of that if I'm lucky,' said Mel, slipping into the young man's body. 'I'll only be able to hear you, so stay close and follow me!'

Nemo stopped and looked at his hand, suspiciously. The marking of his territory halted as he felt a loss of control in his extremities. His hand would not react to the spray can. Mel completed the possession and slipped into the mind of the breacher of the peace.

'I'm in,' said Mel in the deep voice of the youth. 'Over to the councillor's house, quick.'

'We are right behind you,' said Tom. 'You'll be able to run faster if you pull those jeans up; they are almost round your knees.'

Mel turned, lowering the hood to reveal a bleached-blond crop of shaven hair.

'They're supposed to be like this,' she said. 'It's fashion, not sports gear.'

'Can you imagine dying or being buried in that?' Clive said as he puffed, struggling to keep up.

Tom raised an eyebrow at the giant rabbit alongside him.

Mel turned into an avenue of smart houses with expensive cars parked off-road. She stopped and took out the spray can, covering a silver Mercedes at number twenty-two in her best imitation of the youth's tag.

'Not bad!' said Tom. 'You've got talent! Now what?'

Mel painted the lower part of the tarmac drive with the address of the young man. The paint was running out, and so was her time in control. She lifted her feet and spray-painted the soles of the red trainers with the remains of the fluorescent yellow, adding a dollop on top of the man's head to the amusement of her fellow conspirators.

'I'm nearly out of time,' said Mel. 'Time to go!' She chanted and screamed her way through the only football song she could remember, waking the residents and setting off dogs and light switches across the neighbourhood.

She raced towards the end of the avenue, leaving a trail of yellowed footprints in her wake. The others followed towards the youth's home.

'The paint's coming off,' cried Tom as they collapsed into Wordsworth Close.

'Which one's seven?' shouted Mel, feeling her grip on the situation falter. She shook the spray can vigorously for one last coating of a single foot.

'The one with the wheel-less car on bricks,' said Clive.

Mel ran towards the house as her possession of the trouble-maker ended. She retreated from the rest of his body and fell backwards onto the weedy path. Nemo halted, confused why he should suddenly find himself back at his house, when moments before he had been enjoying a night out at the chapel wall.

He tossed the empty can into next door's hedge and scratched his head, coating his hand with the yellow paint as he lifted the door handle and went in.

'That was bloody well done,' said Clive, clapping his hands and wiggling his tufted backside in glee.

'I only hope it was enough,' said Mel, placing her hands on her hips.

In the distance, the sound of a police siren pierced the stillness of the September night. Bright blue flashes heralded a patrol car.

'I think so,' said Tom. 'It's who you know in this world; good thinking about the councillor.'

'It's about who you know in the next world too,' said Mel, smiling to her companions as the police car came to a screeching halt at the end of the broken path.

'They got him, then?' said Tom, leaning on his gravestone.

'According to my missus,' said Clive. 'It's all over the papers, as well as some other good news.'

'Oh?' said Mel.

'They're digging me up next Thursday.'

'What!' said Tom. 'An exhumation?'

Clive turned and punched his fists in the air. 'Oh, yes. They are doing post-mortems across the district for those people suspected of being given the wrong medication; Jim from plot 144 is getting done too. The missus is upset, but she'll get a nice pay-out if they find anything, which I'm certain they will.'

'Why are you so happy about it?' said Mel.

'Don't you see?' said Clive, bending down his fluffy rabbit ears. 'They'll cut all this rotten costume away to get at me. Likely put me back in the box with something smarter, more conventional. In a few weeks, I'll be nearly as dapper as you are!'

'Congratulations,' said Tom, turning to see the old medium shuffle up the path, searching the gravestones. 'Looks like we have a visitor?'

Betty Somerton wandered over to the gravestone and stood, head bowed for a moment.

'I'm off,' whispered Clive, turning to leave. 'You can deal with the old nutcase yourselves.'

'You there, Tom Haines?' she said.

'Yes, Betty. Mel's here too. Sorry about the other—'

'Oh, don't worry about that,' she said. 'I heard they caught the beggar, and I figured you and the young lady had something to do with it. They sent around a community officer wanting to know if I had any other bits of information that might prove useful.'

'Looks like the councillor has set the cat among the pigeons,' said Mel.

Betty laughed. 'You could say that. They want to know if I'll be part of a neighbourhood watch along with a few *colleagues* of mine. It seems they have become a bit more open-minded suddenly. As long as I don't go into too much detail about how I'm getting the information, they seem receptive to making enquiries.'

'That's great news, Betty. I'm sure we'd be happy to let you know anything we come across. You could assign each one of your *colleagues* to a particular graveyard.'

'Just what I was thinking,' said Betty. 'Keep your eyes open for a woman with a large brown dog – been seen fouling the park and verges and never picks it up.'

'Will do,' said Tom. 'Can I ask for a favour? Do you know Clive Tunstall's wife, Mary?'

'Play bingo with her every Saturday – aren't they digging the old beggar up for something?'

'That's the one,' said Tom. 'Can you ask her not to rebury him with that trumpet?'

THE CAVEAT

'What's the present for?' I asked.

'Don't you know?' said my aged employer, handing over the beautifully ribbon-wrapped box with a shaking bony hand. 'It's been a year since you gave up your sanity to care for a grumpy senior like me. It's an anniversary gift from the last of the Carmichaels; one lonely old soul to another.'

I sat on the mayfly-buzzing lawn overlooking the Cotswold country house, basking in the contentment of falling on my feet with this charming, eccentric, and lovable rogue, sick as a parrot and every bit as colourful. I caught my reflected smile in the metallic blue of the wrapping and glanced over at Carmichael, perched on the edge of his wheelchair and wrinkled like the crackled vinyl armrests upon which his hands were placed.

I resisted the urge to rip open the paper and carefully opened one end to slide out an antique black leather jewellery box.

'You forgot my birthday last month,' I said, worried that

the old fool had bought something expensive and unnecessary.

'Did I?' said Carmichael. 'The only positive thing about senility is that you get to blame all sorts of useful mistakes upon it.'

I turned to see the usual mischievous look on his creased face as I opened the box. Inside, on a small pad of midnight velvet, lay a delicate filigree silver brooch, with intricate forms of wildflowers interwoven around its central pea-sized garnet. The main stone was held by a thin axle, allowing it to spin freely with minimal friction. I breathed gently upon the jewel, and it disappeared into a coloured blur, coming to rest like a spent toy gyroscope ten seconds later.

'My mother used to amuse me with it as a child until I stopped crying.'

'It's beautiful,' I said, 'but I can't—'

'Yes, you can,' he said, waving his hands in the air to ward off any further dispute. 'You've worked like a trooper these past twelve months. Don't think I haven't noticed what you get up to when you are supposed to be taking time off.'

'What do you mean?'

'The clocks in the study,' he said. 'You cleaned them the other day without asking – you lied about going to the pictures.'

I blushed, but replied with my customary parry to keep the old man entertained. 'So did you,' I said. 'You told me you were sleeping.'

'Touché,' he said. 'A pair of liars thrown together through mischance or happy coincidence; I haven't decided which one yet.'

I fingered the smooth semi-precious stone and confessed that it was my first piece of serious jewellery at twenty-eight years.

'It belonged to my mother,' he said. 'I'd like you to have it.

No point in giving it to you when I'm gone; where's the pleasure in that?'

I nodded and gave him a smile of affectionate gratitude as I snapped shut and pocketed the box with its wrapping.

His sparkling eyes betrayed his eighty-six years of mischief and fair-hearted hedonism.

'Are you just going to grin like a silly young woman all afternoon, or are you planning something wicked behind my back?' said Carmichael. 'I beat you fair and square at Scrabble last night.'

'You changed the rules so you could win,' I said, recalling with a slight blush the words that belonged more in the Urban Dictionary rather than the Oxford English edition.

'House rules,' he said, beckoning me to push him further along the drive towards the scent of rhododendrons flowering in the woodland garden. 'And I have looked after this place since my father died in 1942, so I get to change them whenever I like; he planted those azaleas over there, you know.'

'Yes, you told me, and no, you will not get me to push you all the way around the perimeter so you can avoid your medicine before lunch.'

Carmichael screwed his face into a mock spasm of disgust and winked. 'Just to the view over the churchyard, and I'll promise to be good for the rest of the afternoon.'

'That'll be a first,' I said, checking the pipeline of the drip attached to his arm and chair. 'Agreed.'

His skeletal hand rose in a sudden act of affection, and I grasped it, coming to stoop in front of the old man.

'I'm very fond of you, my dear,' he said with genuine warmth. 'I don't know what I'd do without you; paradise can be so lonely.'

I gently squeezed the brittle hand and nodded. 'The feeling's mutual, Jeremy,' I whispered, lest the four-hundred-year-old country house overheard and disapproved of the informality. I was once a desperate young woman needing a job, and he an old sickly gentleman in need of live-in support; a man of breeding and seemingly infinite wealth, with a lifetime of retirement in which to have spent it.

'Just to the churchyard, then,' I said.

The wheels of his chair crackled over the thin gravel pathway, and I recalled walking the path for the very first time in May of the preceding year. I was anxious and barely listened to the tall, austere solicitor explain my duties as valet, personal carer, chauffeur, and foil for all of Carmichael's eccentricities and whims. My worry was short-lived when I understood that an answer to a single question had secured my employment.

'*What frightens you?*'

'Being powerless,' I replied, without understanding the question and attempting to sound prosaic and intelligent.

Two others had been employed but I had lasted the longest of them, and apart from an afternoon or day off here and there, I was happy to look after the old rogue in the most beautiful house and estate imaginable. He took some getting used to, but Jeremy Carmichael, enigma and recluse, was free and generous with all manner of pleasantries and remuneration if one did the work and never complained about the never-ending nature of it. Business was business, even in paradise, and I never forgot it or took advantage of my terminally ill charge, a gentleman in all senses of the word.

'What are you thinking?' he said, as though aware of my meditative recollection of the past twelve months.

We skirted the edge of the yew avenue.

'I was thinking about this time last year when Mr Southwaite walked me around the estate at breakneck speed trying to get the measure of me before I met you in the drawing room.'

Carmichael laughed and rubbed his bony, arthritic knuckles. 'Well, you'll be able to relive the pleasure of his company tomorrow when he visits along with that dull priest. Southwaite is breaking in a new apprentice by all accounts, and it won't be long before our dear Father Jessop needs a new understudy. I'll be damned if he outlives me, and I do so enjoy the look on their faces when they see her for the first time; I remember mine—'

Carmichael ceased abruptly.

'The house?' I said, unsure of his meaning, but he ignored me and turned to the gravestones listing in the Cotswold clay of the churchyard. He continued as though speaking to someone distantly remembered.

'That's the trouble with time, all your closest allies and necessary evils grow old with you and need replacing.' He twisted and returned to the moment with a grin of his false, porcelain teeth. 'Present company excepted, of course.'

A breath of southerly wind funnelled through the entrance to the walled garden as we traversed our way past the bumblebee-buzzing yellows of tree peonies and early Canary Bird roses.

'Have you known each other long?' I said, avoiding the hosepipe laid out sinuously by the garden help.

'A long time. He was exactly the same back then, no personality, and just out of short trousers when he joined his father's firm,' said Carmichael, suddenly pensive as we passed through the walled gate and out over the half-acre of wild meadow that brushed against the dry-stone wall of the churchyard.

He raised a hand as we approached the corner of the garden's extent, signalling a stop. 'Still,' he whispered to himself and staring across at the patch of wildflowers, partly shaded by the puberty of a grand oak's newly emergent leaves, 'well-suited to the job at hand – I wonder what his new apprentice will make of it by this time tomorrow.'

'Make of what?' I asked, trying to gain any hint of why this particular area always put the usually jovial man into a melancholic and contemplative mood. I wondered if it was the church's closeness, given his age, and the proximity with the gravestones of his family whose long tenure of the estate had existed since the seventeenth century.

Carmichael's gaze did not venture over to the church. His eyes remained fixed upon the gentle ripple of the oak shadow upon the lush grass dotted with snake's-head fritillary and forget-me-not.

'Have the gardener cut the area of grass in readiness for tomorrow morning,' said Carmichael, signalling a joyless end to the morning trip. A cloud passed across the sun, plunging the corner into a brooding shade.

'Wilkins knows the spot, but not the reason why.'

The afternoon rain subsided, and the sun once again came out to highlight and brighten the dust motes dancing in the comfortable lounge as well as Carmichael's mood.

'Is anything the matter?' I said, surprised, as he took his tray of pills to task without complaint or customary jests of mock defiance. 'You were like this the first day I met you, do you remember? I thought you were going to be the ogre everyone warned me about.'

He stifled a guarded snort. 'Is that what they call me?'

'You are avoiding the question,' I pressed. 'Is it the solicitor's annual visit and the priest who accompanies him? It seems like an unlikely partnership – I didn't know you were religious.'

'I'm not,' said Carmichael, 'though my worldview on that subject is rather fluid at this time of year,' he said, pointing to the decanter of port on the mahogany Chippendale commode. 'You and Wilkins will take the day off tomorrow while I deal with important matters.'

I did not offer my usual resistance to the alcohol despite the concoction of drugs absorbing into his thin blood as we spoke; God knows he took it behind my back on occasions, and it had not yet killed him. I passed a small glass of the sweet tawny spirit into his unusually fitful hands and helped him raise the glass to his lips.

'I insist,' he said with a note of finality and uncharacteristic brevity, passing me the empty glass and swivelling around to face the sunbeams in the bay window overlooking the distant church tower. 'Now leave me to my thoughts until tomorrow's communion is over; I feel strong enough to put myself to bed this evening – you can check on me first thing tomorrow.'

I got up and collected the empty tray and the china cups with their tea leaves stuck to the sides of the delicate and expensive porcelain.

'Fran,' he said, not turning as I opened the door to leave.

'Yes?'

'You remember what question I asked you when we first met?' he said.

'You asked me what I was afraid of, and I replied, *being powerless.*'

He nodded. 'I'm sorry if you feel frightened right now, and I want you to know that I understand completely; it's what has frightened me for the last seventy-eight years since I first understood that living here in paradise comes with a caveat.'

'I don't understand,' I said, watching as he held up a hand in defiance towards the church tower where a petrol-powered grass strimmer whined, cutting down the long grass.

'You will,' he said, barely in a whisper. 'If things go very well... or very badly.'

Carmichael appeared uncharacteristically late the following morning, as though shortening the day ahead would somehow limit the anxiety of his meeting scheduled for noon. My curiosity was tempered with professionalism as I completed several tedious and overdue chores, usually impossible once my employer awoke and became the centre of my attention for the rest of the day. I checked in periodically to see the old man slumber and wheeze through fitful sleep until he rose and entered the lounge fully dressed in a morning suit that once had been tailor-made for his tall and impressive frame but now hung loosely across his slumped shoulders. He leaned on his crystal-topped ebony cane like a Victorian fop and attempted a twirl before grabbing hold of the nearby chair back to steady himself.

I rushed over, but he recovered.

'How do I look for an octogenarian?' he said.

'Dangerous,' I said. 'I could drop you into the village later if you want to parade in front of the baby boomers that sit outside the tearooms?'

He considered the jest for a moment and turned to look out of the window with the sound of an approaching old Jaguar motorcar coming down the drive in a cloud of yellow dust.

'I'd rather do that for all the money in the world right now,' he said, resigning himself to a slump into his wheelchair. 'Can you show them into the study and then make yourself scarce?'

'What about your morphine drip?' I said. 'You know the patches don't agree with you.'

He shook his head. 'Neither today. I need my head clear until they've gone.' He caught my disapproving look. 'I promise not to overexert myself, alright?'

He pointed to the door as the car outside the main entrance came to a stop. I got to the door as Carmichael wheeled himself laboriously into the panelled room opposite. I appeared just in time to stop the tall and immaculately presented solicitor from pulling on the chain to the bell.

'Miss Simmons,' said Mr Southwaite. 'A pleasure to see you again. I trust you and the old scoundrel are well?'

'Both very well, thank you,' I replied as two others, a man in his late twenties with boyish hair in a dark suit that he wore with unfamiliarity, and a silver-haired catholic priest, carrying a Gladstone bag, emerged from behind the entrance pillar.

'May I introduce my recently chartered colleague, Mr Mackenzie Soames.'

The young man broke into a charming smile that utterly dissolved his otherwise pensive face. I couldn't help but smile back until he lost eye contact to prevent further colour from blushing into his high and pale cheekbones. 'He is undergoing client familiarisation, and it is hoped that he may take some of the more irregular call-outs as time progresses.'

I turned to the priest.

'And this is Father Jessop, who I think you may recall from this time last year,' he continued, nodding over his left shoulder.

The renewed smile on my face vanished when the priest's emotionless face rejected any gesture of geniality.

'Won't you all come in, and I'll get some tea?' I said, opening the heavy oak door widely. 'Mr Carmichael will see you in the study.'

The three men graciously entered, and the young man, obviously the junior partner in the proceedings, wiped his feet generously on the entrance mat. He stole a second glance in my direction, making me self-conscious of my woeful attempt at putting up my hair.

'Keep up, Mackenzie!' came his master's voice from within the study.

He flashed another smile of hesitant embarrassment, which I returned quickly; sadly, the last time that he smiled for the rest of the day.

I brought in tea and biscuits on the unused and rickety 1970s hostess trolley, feeling rather too young to pull off the intended partnership successfully. The air was thick with tension and devoid of small talk once the newly qualified Mackenzie Soames introduced himself. Southwaite and the priest silently laid out several documents in front of Carmichael for him to sign. The young man tapped his fingers in uncontrolled anxiety on the side of his leg, as though waiting for a trial or interview to begin. I wondered if Carmichael's reputation had escaped the confines of the pleasant valley and reached his ears in the Cirencester office twenty miles away.

'No need to worry,' I whispered, hoping not to offend his male pride as I handed him a cup of Earl Grey. 'He's really rather sweet.'

Mackenzie exhaled with the reassurance before returning to his taut and tense state as Father Jessop opened his leather bag.

The priest laid out several items on the desk, followed by a folded and stained cloth; it was worn and stitched in places to hold the coarse calico together.

'That will be all, Frances,' said Carmichael, using my full name and catching the confused look on my face. It was as good a sign as any that my curiosity would have to wait, and formality now ruled our working relationship for the present.

I hold myself blameless for any snatches of conversation I may have heard because of the construction of the house. Sound carried readily throughout the lower rooms, making things easier when locating the geriatric wanderer at a moment's notice. Mackenzie was here to develop a relationship with Carmichael following the imminent retirement of Mr Southwaite. However, it sounded from the snippets of conversation that he was due to prove himself in some capacity to progress at the firm. He spoke little, and in short, startled bursts, mostly signalling his intentions and agreements. I felt sympathy for him but a certain feeling of comradeship too as we were both operating in a world that had long since departed to the pages of history. Once grand households and landed gentry now retreated to quiet corners of the countryside with their attendants, growing cold like dying embers of a fire, blown out by modernity and social change.

Polishing the picture frames on the staircase, unnecessarily, I overheard a heated exchange on death duties and inheritance; Carmichael, I knew, had no living relatives and had not married. Voices rose and fell until an impasse on the activities of a trust, set up to deal with the post-mortem management of Delford Grange and its assets, was reached, and Carmichael got his stubborn way on the matter of succession.

'If you don't choose soon, old boy,' said Southwaite with blunt sincerity, 'we'll be forced to assign a new guardian; we've done it in the past. You know we do that for the good of everyone.'

Carmichael's voice rose to match.

'Not for the good of the one whose responsibility it is to live alongside the damn thing,' he shouted.

The solicitor's voice quietened, and I strained to hear the soft reply.

'She'll need to know soon, old friend, if you insist on pursuing the matter, and so will we. You aren't a well man.'

There was a long pause, and Carmichael continued in softer speech. 'I want to give her a few more months of innocence before offering the choice. Can you remember the days before we knew, old friend? Look at your understudy, South-waite; he's like a rabbit caught in the headlights. When did you tell him, on the way over in the car? It's not so easy now, is it, when you risk frightening away all the good ones?'

'Mackenzie has been aware of the unusual situation here at Delford for some time,' interjected the smooth voice of the priest. 'I have prepared him as best I can for what to expect for his first time.'

'Then let's put him to the test,' said Carmichael, 'and get this year's damn communion over and done with.'

I heard the clattering of papers and teacups as the men prepared to leave the room. I abandoned my sudden polishing of the staircase bannister and tiptoed upstairs to my second-floor room.

Mackenzie and Father Jessop emerged outside onto the path beneath my bedroom window overlooking the sun-splashed walled garden and distant churchyard. Southwaite appeared shortly, pushing a sober-looking Carmichael in the wheelchair that was usually my prerogative. I felt a little aggrieved – jealous and possessive of the old soul as he gestic-ulated to the corner of the wild meadow recently trimmed into an irregular crop circle. They crossed the lawn and reap-peared following a short disappearance among the avenue of ancient yews, Mackenzie lagging like a mourner walking at half pace. The priest turned and collected the young man, placing a hand on his shoulder and hurrying him along to meet the others making their way into the mown section of meadow.

Billowing clouds covered the sun and plunged the corner into shade, but the distinct reflection of a silver cross flashed in the priest's hand as it was withdrawn from the Gladstone bag. Father Jessop raised it, and I made out a few words from his lips as he laid it down into the centre of the ring. He with-drew and unfolded the stained cloth upon the ground, as though in readiness for a picnic. Even from this distance, I could see Mackenzie Soames shaking with fear as he stepped back, averting his eyes from the ugly material. Several times the young solicitor looked round as if to weigh up the possibility of escape. A barked command from Southwaite, audible through the glass even at six hundred metres' distance, snapped him back into a forwards concentration.

Carmichael sat motionless, bored, as though one sitting through a ritual for the umpteenth time, with one exception; his eyes fixed on the young solicitor and I recalled the old fool's words from the previous day.

I do so enjoy the look on their faces when they see her for the first time; I remember mine...

Jessop stretched the cloth tightly and pulled it back and forth until he halted with a quick step back. He regained his composure and beckoned the others closer. I lost sight in the shade as the men clung onto each other around the cloth, and I reached for the binoculars on the windowsill that I usually reserved for distant views of buzzards circling on thermals across the vale.

I watched Carmichael, now magnified, standing and supported by Southwaite and the priest on either side. Mackenzie inched forwards as though approaching the rim of a deep pit, completing the ring, and looked down upon the cloth.

Nothing happened for several seconds until a sharp stab from the priest's hand focused all eyes to an upper corner of the cloth laid upon the fragrant turf. They watched with heads bowed, as though searching for something I could not see from the angle of the upper floor. Whatever it was, Mackenzie saw it for the first time.

He screeched and covered his mouth before turning towards the house with a look of such profound terror I had to put down the binoculars momentarily to compose myself. I watched as he twisted, trying to break free from the grip of Southwaite and the priest. I raised the lenses to see the merciful release of both restraints, and Mackenzie unceremoniously raced over to the church wall and leaned over in a fit of spasmodic vomiting. Southwaite shrugged his shoulders and joined the man, patting him on the back in sympathy and compassion. Carmichael stepped back into his chair, ashen-faced but otherwise unmoved as the clouds parted and the sun shone once more upon the house. I was too late to lower the binoculars as the sun glinted off the lens, and I saw my employer glance up at the window. I twisted around out of view, knowing I was almost certainly too late, heart pumping with the strange ritual, the rush of covertly watching proceedings, and finally the notion I had been caught.

When the men arrived back to the hall, I was nonchalantly unabsorbed in a jigsaw, hurriedly laid out onto my sitting room table. I heard the clink of several crystal glasses as some fortifying spirit was shared, along with some muted appreciation for the young solicitor's courage if not for the fortitude of his stomach. They removed to the drawing room, and I stole quietly down the stairs with the honest intent of retrieving my phone.

That was until I saw the open door of the study, and I risked a glance inside.

The room was in some disorder, as only a group of men can hastily accomplish. The cloth was the focus of my attention, speckled with blades of damp grass as it lay draped across the back of Carmichael's wheelchair.

I hurried over and lifted the stained material about the size of a single bed sheet. It was in a disgusting and unwashed state and appeared to have considerable age to it. In one corner, in fine writing, were the names of several clerics, prefaced by their rank, with dates ranging back as far as 1624. I raised it to my nose instinctively, smelling the unmistakable odour of rotting earth and mould despite it being bone dry. A great tear, as though something had once erupted through its centre, showed a repair with coarse sailor's stitching, completing the macabre priest's totem.

Apart from the watermarks – stains of what may have originally been bodily fluids –the handwritten names and dates, and the spots of historic mould, there was nothing visible that would have caused a grown man to suffer a sudden collapse into an unbridled panic. The cloth slipped from my grasp, and I bent over to retrieve it, conscious that the men could return at any moment.

And then I saw it.

It was as though I gazed upon a fluoroscope, a moving x-ray revealing items through the cloth and into the floorboards beneath. I moved the fabric, and the image shifted, revealing the nails and joists of the study floor. I snatched at the cloth and patted the rug beneath in disbelief, before returning the sheet to its revelation of things buried beneath the floor – screws, old coins, and the sudden appearance of a mouse, appearing as startled as I was. Whatever the cloth was or did, it seemed to work both ways, revealing things below to those above and vice versa. I shelved my confusion and disbelief as I heard movement in the hallway outside and hurried to throw the cloth back over the chair before someone entered the room.

Back to the door, I attempted to sweep up something from the rug to cover my stupidity and clenched my teeth before the person behind me revealed themselves.

'Miss Simmons?' said a soft voice. 'Excuse me; I'm just retrieving some items for discussion next door. Have you lost something?'

I twisted round to see Mackenzie cross the room to the central table.

'My contact lens.' I bit my lip at the ridiculous fable.

He came over to stoop nearby and helped in the vain search for an item that did not exist. He ran his smooth ring-less right hand across the Persian rug, over the hidden metal treasures and rodents lurking beneath, and I felt a pang of guilt.

'I wouldn't want you to waste any time on my account,' I said. 'I probably lost it on the stairs, now that I come to think of it.'

It may have been the panic I was in or just my innate ability to blurt out things without thinking, but I realised too late that I had opened my mouth to speak before my brain had time to engage and filter.

'How are you feeling now, Mr Soames?'

The young man got up and frowned, unsure of my meaning.

'I mean about earlier,' I said, digging myself deeper into a hole. 'You looked a little unwell.' I had intended, of course, to mean the moment I had passed him a cup of tea.

He brushed back his hair and misunderstood in the worst way possible.

'It's just Mackenzie,' he said. 'Only Mr Southwaite calls me Soames – it's all dreadfully formal. Forgive me; I wasn't aware you knew about Delford's caveat yet. How was your first time? I confess my own left me rather shaken.'

My blank look gave it away, and he retreated a step, turning to the cloth with a look of unease.

'You don't know, do you?' he said, covering his mouth instinctively to prevent any further revelations. 'You won't say I told you anything, will you, Miss Simmons? I only just passed the test this afternoon and wouldn't want to jeopardise all I had accomplished so far.'

'It's Frances,' I said, offering my hand in a gesture of confidence. 'And no, I won't as long as you don't mention to Carmichael that I was in here searching for invisible objects.'

He stood puzzled for a few moments as I puckered my lips and scanned the floor like a naughty child.

'I don't wear glasses or contact lenses.'

I glanced up, hoping to see the warm smile returned to his lips. He twitched his nose mischievously.

'Agreed,' he said. 'I expect and hope we may be able to share or keep more secrets in the coming years – Mr Carmichael's health withstanding, of course.'

'You got the gig, then?'

He shrugged. 'I guess so. They are discussing it now. It looks like we might see each other again at some stage?'

'Oh, I hope so,' I blurted out like a love-struck teenager. 'What I mean is, we don't have many guests and—'

Southwaite's booming voice rescued me from further embarrassment and summoned Mackenzie back to the drawing room.

'Until this time next year, Frances,' he said, turning away with an armful of documents.

'Until then, if not sooner,' I said as he disappeared into the hall.

I crept back upstairs to process my discovery of the cloth's strange qualities, but it made no sense. The sound of the men leaving jolted me from the jigsaw, and I peeked out of the window. Each one shook Carmichael's hand, and I caught a quick wink from Mackenzie as he stole a glance in my direction. Both solicitors and Father Jessop, carrying the Gladstone bag – presumably containing the cloth – got into the vintage car and drove away in a drizzle. My employer wheeled himself within the entrance and threw the door shut with an echoing shudder. I froze, holding my breath, hearing nothing from downstairs for several moments.

'You can come out now, Frances. Time we had a little talk.'

We sat by the hastily arranged fire in the parlour. Carmichael tended the smokeless coal in the grate with an iron poker as I fitted his cannula and pain-relieving drip. I made some pretence of scolding him for going outside in the drizzle and for missing his medication, in a vain attempt to spark some guilty gentle-hearted banter or precursor to the ticking-off I was overdue.

He stared into the flames, silently musing until I finished and sat down opposite in a high-backed moth-eaten armchair.

To my surprise, he opened my disciplinary with a smile. He put down the poker and held out an unsteady hand.

'What do you think of Mr Soames?' he said, squeezing my returned hand.

'Mackenzie?' I said, puzzled.

'Mackenzie, already, is it?' he said, tutting with a raised eyebrow. 'Sounds like you had a busy and eventful afternoon.'

I ignored the last comment and the heat of the blush rising in my cheeks. 'He seems to be of good character; did he meet your expectations?'

Carmichael nodded. 'As have you, but I ask that you refrain from questions about today. There is nothing to worry about, apart from my mood swings and nonsense, which is, as you well know, part of the job description.' He squeezed and released my hand.

'He will be overseeing Delford's affairs and what comes next.' He held out a palm to stifle any reply. 'I will not live forever, Fran; you know that. What will you do after I'm gone?'

I folded my arms in front of my chest and picked at my bobbled cardigan. My fingers brushed against the cold silver of the brooch, hastily pinned as a protective amulet against potential family wrath. 'Apart from going into permanent mourning like Victoria, I haven't thought about it, and I don't want you to think about it either.' It was my turn to hold out a palm to restrict his counterargument.

'You have been so very kind to an inexperienced young woman in need at the time I met you. I've learned a great deal about judging books and their covers and that I rarely follow the rules to the letter, but then, I've only got my teacher to blame.' I leaned forwards and gave him my best look of remorse for my indiscretion on something beyond my comprehension, which was obviously a personal family matter. 'I'm sorry for today – I felt powerless and confused.'

The old face relaxed into gentleness, and he sat back, eyes still fixed upon my own.

'As did I,' he said. 'You'll miss me when I'm gone, I know, but I want your solemn promise on two things when the time comes.'

I gently nodded, and he continued.

'First, you will not spend all the years you have ahead alone, as I have done. Go find yourself a gentleman and share the same fun and enjoyment that we have spent together.'

'That's easier said than done,' I remarked. 'Private service has a way of monopolising time, if you'll beg my pardon.'

'Then stick with someone with whom you might share that particular world, someone that might operate within the same circles and who might benefit from your *joie de vivre*.'

'Like who?'

'I think you know, Frances. I'm not that blind yet; I can almost smell the chemistry that might develop with a certain young solicitor.'

'He's good-looking for sure, but unlikely to be interested in someone like me,' I said, fishing for compliments.

Carmichael's mischievous eyes sparkled and reflected the flickering flames as he evaded my attempts to deflect any notion of romantic conversation.

'That's what you think,' he said. 'But I'm not thinking of your happiness; I'm thinking of his.'

'Charming!' I said, glad that the mischief was back in place of the solemnity that had clouded most of the day.

He winked. 'I'd hate for that young man to grow up and turn into another Southwaite; it's a travesty but inevitable without someone like you intervening.'

I glowed with the thoughts of companionship other than that with my employer, as satisfying as that was.

'I'll consider the promise on its merits, if that will suffice?' I said. 'And what is the second you spoke of?'

Carmichael returned to the fire and stuttered in his attempt to find the right words.

'Promise me you'll forgive me for a choice you will have to make and for my lack of courage in not being able to deliver it in person.'

I frowned. 'You are obtuse today. You aren't taking those red pills again, are you?'

He remained transfixed by the flames. 'Just promise you'll forgive a selfish old coward who didn't want to lose you whilst I lived.'

I sat back, speechless.

He turned with a look of such profound sadness that I thought my heart would burst. His eyes landed upon the brooch that I unconsciously fingered.

'Just promise me. I'll make sure you'll be safe when I'm gone, whatever you decide –this I swear to you.'

Summer burned bright and joyful, but Carmichael was failing. We took to spending fewer hours outdoors, despite the fine weather, and there were several weeks where he spent time in hospital during the early autumn. I took to wandering the empty house and gardens, trying to fill my time with chores and little things to take my mind from the inevitable farewell that would break my heart.

The grass in the lower meadow dried and bent over with the gales of early winter, and I stopped my visits to the churchyard for fear of bringing a contagion of melancholia back to Carmichael. The area disturbed me more than ever but held a fascination, like a child putting fingers to a burning match, knowing that it would burn. I felt the need to have my irrational anxiety tested beneath the leafless oak, desensitising myself to an unknown fear. Thoughts returned to the cloth and its bizarre revelations in the study.

I knew that whatever had caused Mackenzie to have such a violent reaction lay beneath my feet. How far down and what it was, he would not say, even during our stolen intimate moments.

'One day, there will be no more secrets between us,' he would say. 'By my actions, you know me to be true-hearted and I will betray no confidences you may have.'

Mackenzie was frequently away, travelling across the country. He would call me occasionally, and I could tell that whatever he was up to in some distant county involved the fellowship of Father Jessop or some other priest. Whatever was beneath my feet was also in other locations. On those occasions, I could hear the quake in his voice from the moment he began speaking, desperate to reach out to someone just to calm his thoughts. It didn't matter what we talked about; he just needed to hear my reassuring voice.

I cursed the ground beneath, and whatever lay there for keeping him from me and our future.

I felt guilty for considering my options while the old man was still alive. I threw many agency registration letters into the parlour fire, criticising my self-interests when all my efforts should be focused on the challenging months ahead.

There was always something in my head, a small voice, quiet but attention-grabbing when it appeared.

Still time, not yet...

Christmas was a merry time, and the old man perked up with the season and several powerful injections of medicinal rocket fuel. In a separate room, Mackenzie stayed over on the pretence of checking the accounts and helping Wilkins with some of the glasshouse repairs.

January and February blew bleakly, and I picked late-emerging daffodils to adorn the vases in the lounge, now the location of Carmichael's bedroom. His decline continued into the spring until the approach of May, when the doctor recommended additional medical support in the form of two night-workers, much to my protestations.

'You have to sleep, too,' said Mackenzie on a rare visit. 'I have a power of attorney in this matter, and it's that, or he is moved to a palliative care home.'

In between periods of extended sleep and rest, Carmichael remained remarkably lucid and entertaining. If there was one difference, it was in his reflectiveness of someone about to hand over a great burden with the long days of guardianship behind him. Even when he thought I wasn't aware, he watched me as though fearing some sudden disappearance or breaking of spirit on my part.

The second week of May arrived, and I was surprised and fearful to see him dressed in the baggy morning suit during the handover from the night-care.

'It's that time again, isn't it?' I said. 'You are going down to that dreadful place one last time, aren't you?'

He nodded. 'And you are going to make yourself scarce when Mackenzie and Jessop arrive.'

'I don't think so,' I said. 'Not this time.'

'I've asked Mackenzie to lock you in the wine cellar if you don't do as I ask; he has my authority and speaks for me.'

I put my hands on my hips and opened my mouth to object.

'You know he'll do it. I know he's kept back something you are desperate to understand, and yet you still love the ridiculous-haired hero.'

'And has he ever discussed any of my secrets with you, perchance?' I said, trying to regain some control of the argument.

'Not a dickybird, and God knows I've tried. I even offered him the bottles of '52 when I'm gone, and he didn't even give it a thought. You've got a good one there, Fran.'

He raised a weak hand to his mouth to blow a quivering kiss.

I caught it casually in an instinctive interplay that had been going on since last year.

'I'd challenge him to a duel or something if I were sixty years younger,' he said. 'Now do what we both ask of you, one last time, please. It's very important.'

Mackenzie and Father Jessop duly arrived, and I admitted them to the study in a repeat of the preceding year. I grabbed my confidant by the right arm and pecked him on the cheek.

'For luck,' I said.

'Thanks,' he replied. 'This might be the last time for Carmichael, so we need to honour his wishes.'

'He's already told me you planned to lock me in the wine cellar if I didn't play ball.'

His eyes widened, and a much-missed smile broke his handsome face. 'Did he now? I said no such thing, but now you come to mention it – there are some bottles of '52 down there you could sample. God knows we could use a bottle when we get back from out there.' He glanced over at the church tower through the lobby window and sighed. 'Best get it over with; maybe we can catch up for a moment later before I have to take Jessop back to the seminary?'

I released him and watched as he strode confidently into the study. I never thought I would find the demeanour of a solicitor in any way attractive, but just then, I wanted to rush over and tell him how proud I was of him for whatever he had been challenged by and overcome.

It didn't take long for voices to be raised once more. I made no pretence of any cleaning because most of the borderline shouting appeared to concern me.

'You should tell her, Mr Carmichael,' came the strong voice of my partner. 'It's not right she learns it from me or someone else after you've gone.'

'You will do as I ask unless you wish me to find another solicitor in the short time I have left?'

I overheard the priest trying to calm the situation down. 'Gentlemen, please. Might I suggest we continue our discussion outside and in private?'

'You'll not silence me in my own house, Jessop,' replied Carmichael. 'This isn't that monastery you and the others hide in.'

'Then end the need for silence or secrecy,' shouted Mackenzie, 'and grow a pair of balls, you old fool. Tell her!'

I stepped back into the nook of the lobby and covered my mouth. I wasn't sure whether to be terrified of Mackenzie's outburst and its repercussions or proud of his confidence in dealing with the old curmudgeon; I certainly did not 'have the balls'.

The silence was deafening, and I heard the pounding of my heart in my head until the soft voice of a calm Carmichael spoke once more.

'Open the door.'

I twisted out of the shadow to see the double doors swing open as though in invitation. I hesitated in the silence, wondering if there was some cue to follow or whether the young solicitor was being invited to leave. I grasped the brooch on my shoulder and opted for the former.

'Tell me what?' I said, entering the study where the three men were already turned in anticipation of my arrival.

Mackenzie relaxed his clenched hands and looked over for guidance from his employer. Carmichael nodded and buried his face in his hands.

'Tell her,' he murmured.

Mackenzie straightened his suit and cleared his throat. 'I, Mackenzie Soames, acting as solicitor and power of attorney for Mr Jeremiah Cosgrove Carmichael Esquire of Delford Grange, do discharge the intentions of my client concerning the disposal, inheritance, and guardianship of said property and its environs to Miss Frances Simmons, current employee and resident of said property in perpetuity to include an annual allowance not exceeding eight hundred and thirty-five thousand pounds per annum, to be reviewed bi-annually.'

'What?' I said. 'Don't be absurd—'

'Furthermore,' continued Mackenzie, performing his due diligence, 'the benefactor, Miss Simmons, agrees not to sell, develop, or partition any of the land, fields, or buildings during their tenure and guardianship of the property and its caveat.'

'Caveat?' I said.

Mackenzie looked across at the priest in a moment of hesitation. Carmichael nodded through his hands, still avoiding my gaze.

It was Father Jessop who spoke first.

'Mr Carmichael is discharging his inheritance to you, my dear, on the grounds that you keep safe the property, especially that which is buried in the southeast meadow adjoining the church wall.'

'In addition,' said Mackenzie, 'annually during the second week of May, you are required to present yourself along with your legal representative and a designated member of the clergy to ascertain...'

He paused, searching for guidance. It was Carmichael who raised his head and looked me soulfully in the eyes.

'To ascertain if the accursed thing buried in the meadow is still alive down there.'

I staggered back to grasp at the door frame. 'There's someone alive underneath the meadow? How is that possible and what on earth—'

'Not alive,' corrected Jessop. 'Moving, but very much dead. The poor men and women were innocent at the moment of death in the eyes of God. It's what unholy spirit possessed them afterwards that's causing them to be restless.'

'Restless?' I said, searching for any hint of sanity in the word.

'Yes,' said Jessop. 'Ever since the sixteenth century we've been re-interring those that refuse to lie still after death. We encase them in salt and lead, which causes the spirit ultimately to leave the body and return to whatever infernal kingdom they came from. There is one boon, however.' He clicked open the latches on the bag and withdrew the stained cloth.

'The coverings they crawl from hold certain strange qualities that aid us in—'

I glanced over at the cloth in his steady hands. 'I know what the cloth does, or at least what it shows if you lay it upon the ground.'

The three men looked at each other in bemusement.

'Did you tell her about this, Mac?' said Carmichael, frowning.

He shook his head.

'No,' I replied. 'I discovered that the cloth shows things hidden beneath the floor last year while I was—'

'Eavesdropping and trespassing?' offered Carmichael.

I shuffled from one foot to the other thinking of a defence but the priest saved my blushes.

'It's a cerecloth,' he said. 'A waxed shroud used to bury the dead, but this one has unusual attributes. Our order found it in northern France five hundred and fifty years ago wrapped around one of the earliest souls to suffer this particular indignity after death. Somebody stole the cloth once its strange properties were discovered and used by grave robbers to locate the dead before the church could reclaim it.'

'How is that even possible? Magic doesn't exist; it's some sort of trick, Mackenzie?'

The solicitor shook his head. 'There are thirty-three burials dotted around the country, and the cerecloth shows their particular state of play. It's where I've been all year, meeting the guardians, checking and recording the internments. Don't panic, I do other solicitor stuff like wills and conveyancing as well—'

'It's true, Fran,' said Carmichael. 'It's the one caveat to living here in paradise with no care for money and all the time in the world to enjoy it. You'll be secure for life. I didn't dare to tell you earlier – it's what I asked you to forgive me for when I'm gone. I never got to hear it from my mother's mouth.' He glanced up at the brooch on my left shoulder. 'But I understand now – she didn't have the strength. It's why I never had children of my own; courage is not a Carmichael trait, I'm afraid.' He looked up at Mackenzie, who nodded sympathetically.

'I wouldn't say that now, Mr Carmichael,' he said.

I brushed back my hair, trying to comprehend the enormity of the secret both of them had been keeping from me.

'You are offering me everything you own and a life without a nine to five as long as I live alongside something allegedly undead not six hundred metres away—'

The men looked among themselves and nodded.

'And you call that security?'

'Yes,' said Carmichael. 'It can't get to you unless something removes it from its salt-filled, lead-lined coffin fourteen feet down. It's why there can be no development or change in circumstance for the house or the others around the country. Can you imagine if a spa or golf hotel company got hold of the place?'

'And if I refuse?' I said.

A look of sadness clouded Carmichael's face as Mackenzie withdrew an envelope.

'Then a severance award of fifty-thousand pounds, paid following the death of Mr Carmichael, will be deposited into your account, and the guardianship defers back to The Trust before a suitable external candidate can be identified.'

'The Trust?' I said. 'Is that who you all work for?'

Mackenzie nodded. 'It's important to keep these things quiet down the years and The Trust takes care of all guardianship of the burials.'

I walked over and stooped in front of the old man. He reached out his hands to my face, and I placed my own upon them.

'I would be doing this for you,' I said. 'Not for the money or the house. For you.'

He nodded and began to weep. 'Forgive an old coward for shirking the responsibility. I didn't want to lose you when you found out.'

Mackenzie knelt and joined hands with both of us.

I looked into the eyes of the one who had witnessed the thing in the meadow for the first time a year ago and then into the eyes of the one who had seen it over a lifetime.

'I'd need to see it, first. Whatever it is.'

Carmichael was heavily wrapped under a bundle of scarfs and blankets as I pushed him past the yew avenue and out onto the terrace overlooking the churchyard. The cut grass of the circle, accomplished by the perpetually bemused gardener, contained the area where the annual communion with what lay below would occur. Jessop cast out the cerecloth, and the stitched tear caught my attention once more. I wondered if the thing that lay buried deep below the spent crocus and daffodils had once occupied the shroud and whether escape or some other method had caused the re-incarceration to be in impenetrable lead.

I barely heard the priest begin his blessing because Mackenzie caught hold of my hand and squeezed it tightly.

'You can do this, Fran,' he said. 'Just pretend it's some video nasty.'

'I think all your hints and riddles can't possibly be as frightening as what I am about to witness?' I offered hopefully. He returned my expectant gaze solemnly, and I knew I was in for a similar experience to what my beloved had gone through the previous year. I turned to the house, wishing I was suddenly at the window, watching through binoculars rather than here, at the edge of fear and the unknown.

'It's necessary,' said Mackenzie. 'Each guardian must see what is at stake; otherwise, you may become blasé, and the consequences could be severe.'

I nodded, closing my eyes as the priest dragged across the cloth, searching for the coffin below.

'It can't hurt you, and it can't get out,' said Carmichael. 'It has to stay like that and your role will be to live here and make sure that thing stays down there when Jessop and I are gone.'

I exhaled deeply as Mackenzie continued.

'With any luck, it won't be moving anymore. The spirit binding the body together eventually quits, and the corpse decays naturally; something to do with the salt, we think. I've been lucky enough to see it myself. This is one of the later ones, so there may be a few years left on the clock in this case—'

I held up my hand to curb the conversation. 'Too much information. I think you need to stop talking now, Mac.'

'Sorry,' he said.

'It's time, Frances,' said Jessop.

I opened my eyes to see the others staring down at the shroud. It was Carmichael who spoke first.

'I declare the thing is still whole and unmoving. I discharge my duty this day as guardian and swear that this is my true and honest word in front of the church and the judiciary.' He spat as though bidding farewell. 'I won't be seeing you again – my place is in the holy ground over the wall.'

Father Jessop frowned in disapproval before speaking.

'I concur; the creature is still whole and unmoving. I discharge my duty this day as the appointed member of the church and swear that this is my true and honest word in front of the guardian and the judiciary.'

Mackenzie leaned over and flinched momentarily before relaxing.

'I concur; the caveat is still whole and unmoving. I discharge my duty this day as the appointed member of the judiciary and swear that this is my true and honest word in front of the guardian and the church.'

I turned my gaze downward, but Mackenzie spoke again to the others. 'I think it's gone quiet finally—'

'Hush!' said the priest, watching me as I accustomed my eyes to the bizarre projection below.

The cloth appeared to vanish to all but my peripheral vision. The centre opened up to a shimmering hole showing the movement of worms, gnarled roots from the oak tree, and pathways made by insects and small mammals.

'I can't see anything but what is going on a few feet down,' I said hopefully, returning to the priest for guidance.

'Deeper,' he said, pointing to the centre. 'Concentrate on the centre. Don't let your eyes wander.'

I held my breath and gazed without blinking as the image descended past small skeletal remains of rodents and birds until it reached the rectangular and alien casket made and buried by man.

'I see the coffin,' I said. 'Is that far enough? I believe you.'

The grip of support tightened as Mac shook his head and whispered.

'A few inches more.'

I returned to the lead casket, and the top surface melted away, revealing something indistinct and huddled inside. I drifted my eyes over the entire decaying body that lay within.

It was a woman, or had been, lying within a light covering of salt. Its lank, wispy hair still clung to some vestige of skin across its skull. Arms, like leathered poles, were bound within clasps on either side of its shoulders. Its hips appeared to have been deliberately dislocated to fit within the permanent sarcophagus. It was missing a foot, while the other was at such an angle that someone must have comprehensively broken it during or shortly after death.

'I see her,' I said, hyperventilating. 'She has a foot missing.'

I retraced my eyes to her head when I saw it twitch, and I intensified my gaze in disbelief. The thing shuddered as though aware of the light pouring through the magic of the shroud and twisted round to gaze fully back through sunken eye-sockets and sewn lips into my face.

Suddenly it was aware of me and shook like a caged wild animal desperate for release.

I fell back, scrabbling to recover and gain some distance as Mackenzie let go of my hand and grabbed hold of the cerecloth, bunching it into a roll and tossing it to the priest. 'Enough,' he said. 'She's fulfilled her duties as inheritor.'

I looked at the ground, flattened and covered with the bleeding sap and tufts of stubble of the mown ring, the image of the thing deep below attempting impotently to escape its perpetual prison permanently imprinted in my mind. I would never unsee my first time.

'It's over,' said Mackenzie, coming over to help me to my feet. I brushed him away as I regained my feet and rested my hands on my knees, gathering my composure.

'Do you need to be sick?' he asked.

I shook my head. 'Just give me a minute, I'll be alright – it's still moving. It's not dead or whatever it needs to be.'

Carmichael nodded and sighed. 'I'd hoped to see it gone within my lifetime.'

'What is it?' I said, turning to the priest tidying away the religious items and the cloth.

'It's what the unenlightened used to call a witch, lych, or ghoul,' he said. 'We know of many such creatures, all of which cannot be killed by any device known to man.

'We call them revenants.'

'You were lucky,' said Mackenzie, engaging his mouth before his brain. 'The one still moving over at Stonehouse has been hung, drawn, and quartered.'

I punched him forcefully on the shoulder. 'Jesus, Mac! Shut up.'

The priest continued, offering me a token silver crucifix from his pocket. 'It's not like in the movies,' he said. 'Even the church can't do anything about them except guard their positions, so no harm comes to anyone.'

'So, is it living or dead?' I said.

'It's dead, but inhabited by something that will ultimately leave it be. There hasn't been a case since New Orleans at the turn of the century. We don't know why or how, only that if it were to escape, it has only one desire.'

I held up my hand to interrupt the priest. 'Do I need to know what that is, or can I just assume that it is something terrible, please?'

Jessop looked across at Mackenzie for confirmation, and I was relieved when he spoke.

'It's unnecessary for her to know that part.'

I breathed a sigh of relief.

Carmichael looked up at the tree. 'I won't see your leaves fall, old oak, but you watch over this spot and my Frances.'

I approached and adjusted his scarf back to his unprotected neck. He caught my shaking hand.

'You see why I was frightened of losing you,' he said. 'I've been powerless and helpless to do anything about it all these years, and now I'm burdening you with it. I can see it's startled you and you want to run. I remember the same urge. Just promise me you won't leave without saying goodbye; it would be the end of me straight away if you did that.'

He leaned over and brushed my hair away from the brooch.

'It's a lot to take in,' I said, looking back at the beauty of the house and the idyllic surroundings. I turned to stare at the flattened grass and the memory of the revenant beneath, wondering if it still raged, unheard and unseen, to escape. 'My whole worldview has just been shattered—'

'You need to choose now,' he said, requesting the brooch. 'If you think about it, you won't be able to decide, or you will say no to be free of the decision. I respect you either way.'

I unclipped the brooch and handed it over to his shuddering open palm.

Carmichael held the circular filigree between thumb and forefinger as I turned to see Mackenzie put his hands in his pockets and purse his lips, unable to sway me either as legal counsel or lover.

The old man took a long and rattling intake of breath and blew out with tremendous force, setting the central garnet whizzing around on its tiny spindle.

'You have the time it takes for the jewel to cease spinning,' he said. 'Choose now.'

A beam of sunlight struck the corner and glittered off the silver crucifix in my hand. I turned it over, conscious of the spinning garnet beginning to slow in its revolutions within the confines of the brooch. Engraved on the reverse of the smooth cross were the words '*Thy will be done*'.

I watched, hypnotised, as the garnet came to a slow stop, and I lifted my gaze to the dearest person I had ever met.

'I've kept both my promises to you,' I said, seeing the garnet wobble to a stop.

Carmichael asked me the fateful question.

'So, what's it going to be, Fran?'

I watched you tumble and cartwheel across the lawn, my beautiful child, year after year. Full of life, catching the mayflies without care, or knowledge of what lay down in the meadow. Mac and I decided you should be free from any sense of dread surrounding the grassy corner, but I still bit my lip as you picked corncockle and camassia from the tall grass for 'Grand Uncle Carmichael's' grave. We hoped, in some way, to exorcise our own feelings of the place.

Carmichael outlived Jessop by a few months, and I grieved for the loss of his company. Mac continued his unusual legal career alongside a new priest, frequently journeying for days away from our happy home. Even though I had Mac, I wanted

Carmichael to fill the need for spirited companionship, and I welled up with the irony. There were days when Daddy returned and swept you up into his arms, giving me a wink.

'Good trip?' I would ask, readying his gin and tonic.

He would place you down, spoiling you with some brightly wrapped and expensive gift to deflect the flash of triumph thrown towards me.

'Yes. Another one's gone.'

I felt a pang of guilt for feeling jealous of the guardian who could now sleep soundly and pass on their inheritance without caveat or the fear of having to tell their children that the sanctuary they grew up in was, in fact, a bastion against an unseen horror. Ten more years of watching and waiting until The Trust would sanction the site as cleansed. Ten years of hopeful expectation that the revenant would be gone from the world and the guardian would be free to live in their particular paradise without the annual communion or constant reminder of their burden and the caveat.

'When will it be our turn?' I would whisper back, coming over to clasp my arms around you.

'In our lifetime, I'm sure of it.'

The years passed, and you grew beautiful and strong, determined to be master of your own fate; a passion we encouraged. Every second week of May became a game of subterfuge as we packed you off to Mac's relatives or spring camp, waving you off in one car before welcoming in the new arrival, dog-collared and carrying the Gladstone bag, to complete our annual communion.

Wilkins retired and his replacement dutifully carried out the cutting down of the long grass without complaint or enquiry; perhaps the old gardener had primed him concerning our eccentricities.

'You've fallen on your feet, Fran,' Wilkins said when word

had got out about my inheritance, but with no hint of condemnation or jealousy. 'I'm glad.'

I remember him offering his hand, which I shook.

'You've got no worries now, have you?' he continued.

'No,' I lied, observing the strict silence on the matter of the burial as stipulated by The Trust. 'I guess not.'

May rolled round once more, and you begged to borrow the car shortly after your eighteenth birthday for a girls' weekend in Malvern; I remember the shock on your face when we both agreed.

'You are both up to something,' you said. 'You didn't even put up a fight.'

'We trust you,' I said, digging my nails into my palms at letting you fly from us for the first time, while providing us with the privacy we needed.

'I'd like you to have this,' I said, unpinning my brooch and thinking of a spring day long ago. 'For luck, if you like; it's no use leaving it to you when I'm gone – where's the fun in that?'

Two days later we stood together in the meadow, Mac and I, while Monseigneur Humphries laid out the cerecloth and peered down. I was always the last to commit and confirm.

Mac squeezed my hand, and my heart sank. He shook me from my stare at the lower branches of the old oak and smiled.

'It's okay,' he said, urging me to look. 'It's gone, look.'

I caught sight of Humphries kneeling and muttering some blessing or thanks as I peered over into the cloth and the ground beneath.

Down my gaze went, rushing to find the coffin that held the revenant.

Could it be true, or was it just waiting to mock me?

I gasped and grabbed Mac's arm as though fearing to fall into the cloth and onto the creature below.

Something was different.

Something wonderful.

The body was barely discernible, as though age and decay, kept back in some small fashion by the spirit that once possessed it, had suddenly caught up with the mortal remains.

'Is it true?' I stammered. 'It looks—'

'It's up to you, Mrs Simmons, to begin the assurance,' said Humphries, breaking into a smile and making the sign of the cross.

I looked down once more, daring the thing to move, knowing in my heart it was finally dead. I glanced across the church wall to Carmichael's headstone, gleaming in a sunbeam, and broke into tears of joy. My days of feeling powerless and my fear of having to tell you were ending.

Mac put his arm around me and kissed my head.

'Go on, Fran. Say it loud enough for the old bugger to hear.'

I sniffed back the growing tears and held up my hands to the oak and the hopeful spring sky beyond its emerging new life.

'I declare the thing is unbound and unmoving. I discharge my duty this day as guardian and swear that this is my true and honest word in front of the church and the judiciary.'

ST MARK'S EVE

Everyone at *The Times* considered Claydon Fenchurch to be the greatest obituary writer of the 1960s, including him. Naturally, I was eager to be given my first real step up at the newspaper to shadow his final year before retirement.

'Nice piece of work on the collapse of Callaghan's banking empire,' he said, blowing sweet pipe tobacco smoke above the typewriter and pushing back his round-rimmed spectacles.

'That means a lot coming from you, Mr Fenchurch,' I said, seated with my hands buried in the pockets of the most expensive pinstripe suit I could afford on a junior reporter's salary. I watched and waited for any sign that the oldest serving stalwart in the newspaper's history had ratified my transfer and imminent promotion.

Fenchurch had been writing about the dead for close to half a century. The veteran's prosaic, illuminating and, above all, timely obituaries, which formed the third most-read page after the features and foreign affairs sections, were a master-class in the concise use of language. Understated and packed with wry sensibility, the obituaries he composed were all adapted to fit the deceased's persona and contribution (or lack of it) to humanity. It was joked, well out of earshot of the Old Etonian, that even St Peter read his section in *The Times* to determine the measure of the men and women on their way up to the pearly gates to save time and avoid any unnecessary queues.

I had rarely been in his company and had never been alone with the godfather of the broadsheets in his office overlooking Penning Street in the heart of north London. Kings, prime ministers, despots, and social icons had all been graced or disgraced by his skilful send-off. He was planning on leaving the paper in the following twelve months, once a suitable replacement had undergone sufficient probation and purgatory at the expense of his uncompromising high standards. More qualified writers than I had waltzed into the ring and suffered scathing editorial knock-outs, like inexperienced boxers in a title fight, and they licked their wounds back in the dugout of the lower floor, scarred from the experience.

There were writers, and there were obituary writers; one could not rely upon the former to be any good at the latter.

And here I was, relatively fresh-faced and burning brightly from my eighteen months as go-between and copy-writer for others until a tip-off had landed me my first real scoop on a failing bank about to go under and stripping the company of assets to off-shore private accounts.

The paper got a lot of credit for the early inside story, and here was my reward – an interview with God's own weigher of souls.

The silence in his office, only interrupted by the tapping of workers extending the scaffolding on the building, made me nervous, and I wondered if I wasn't best suited back on the noisy tip-tapping typewriters of the lower floor with the other column-writing rats.

He returned his pipe to his mouth and rose to close the

sash window from the sound of the men fixing steel clamps to heavy metal poles outside the second-floor window.

'Not very *swinging*,' he said casually, frowning at the whiskered navvy appearing at the window, thirty feet above the busy London thoroughfare.

'Pardon me, Mr Fenchurch?' I said, unclear about his meaning.

He turned and spoke from the side of his pipe-filled mouth.

'Obituaries and writing about the dead – not very *swinging sixties*, Mr Johnson. Wouldn't you prefer to be doing something more life-affirming at your age?'

I countered, fortunate in my hasty research on the old fellow. 'If I recall, you took over from the previous incumbent, Mr Fairfax, only a few months younger than I am now.'

He spun around, and I was unsure if I had overreached in my arrogance, comparing myself to the might of the man standing before me who held my future in his hands. I was relieved to see a wry smile appear from the side of his mouth as he puffed out another billow of smoke.

'Now there's a name I haven't heard in a long time,' he said. 'A real taskmaster was old Fairfax and a hard man to please, but he taught me everything I know.' He looked past me as though recalling a memory.

'*Everything I know.*'

I waited for him to return to the present. After a moment, he perched at the end of his long ebony desk.

'You've done your research, Johnson,' he said, crossing one arm and adjusting the pipe with his other hand. 'That's the first rule of journalism.'

'Thank—' I began before being interrupted without a glance.

'What do you think the others are, as they relate specifically to obituaries?'

I sat uncomfortably trying to eliminate the obvious and unrelated qualities: contacts were useless unless they were someone in the know at a hospital or a very rare undertaker needing to break a code of silence to fuel an expensive drug habit. Writing skills and the sparing use of words, as though their very cost mattered, were too generic to mention, so I thought laterally.

'Timeliness, tone, and fact-checking,' I said hopefully. 'Those would be the secrets from what I understand of the craft.' It was well-known that Fenchurch rarely worked late and he kept a mistress who he often visited. Yet, despite the serene and effortless gentleness of his working day, he still hit the right spot at the right time with an obituary written and ready to go as though he had some insight into which bright young thing or senile old lord was ready for the big sleep on the following day. It seemed ironic that one of the largest parishes in London also housed many of the illuminati of the capital and the editorial offices that housed the greatest writer of the glorious send-off.

'Secrets?' he said, neither confirming nor denying my answers to his initial question. 'Maybe so, Johnson, and always passed down from mentor to apprentice in an unbroken chain from the old world to the new.'

I nodded from habit and the desire to understand my superior while unsure what he was referring to. He emptied his pipe and opened the top drawer, then retrieved and offered me a list of handwritten names with accompanying notes.

'It's obvious you have some talent,' he said, looking through the window disdainfully at the worker readying himself for the climb down to the pavement and the end of his shift. 'If you want to help me build up a bank of ready-to-go *OBs*, then I'll expect you to work hard and keep secrets –

one in particular. I'll also expect a full copy on those to me by tomorrow morning.'

'What?' I exclaimed, hearing the nearby church tower chime for six o'clock. '*All twelve?*'

He did not look up.

'Is there a problem, Mr Johnson?'

I thought ahead to the long and sleepless night fuelled by black coffee and flirting with filing cabinets and microfiche while my colleagues headed to the sweltering basements of the swinging clubs and bars outside in the cold February air.

'No, Mr Fenchurch,' I said, correcting myself and rising to make an early start in the hope of a few hours' shut-eye in the mailroom hammock, providing it wasn't already in use. 'First thing in the morning.'

I turned to go, but Fenchurch stopped me.

'Pay particular attention to the former Lord Chief Justice on that list, Johnson,' he said. 'You were right with all the qualities needed, especially timeliness, but you missed the most important one out – luck.'

'How the hell did he know he was going to die, Sam?' I asked my former colleague as he passed me a cigarette and another cup of bitter black coffee. My eyes burned from toil and lack of sleep, and I desperately needed a shave and a change of clothes.

'He didn't,' said Sam, rubbing at the pencil behind his ear. 'Got word of him being ill, I suppose. He's got a nose for this sort of thing, and you'll pick it up eventually now that you have the pleasure of kissing his arse until he gives you the job permanently.'

'That's not down to him,' I said, 'but I agree it would go a long way. The thing is, after last night, I don't think I can do this now.'

Sam shook his head. 'That's nerves and tiredness talking – it was a test of stamina and dealing with deadline pressure, that's all. Fenchurch was just pushing your buttons to see what you are made of. You got the transfer and said yourself he was happy with the results?'

'I wouldn't define it as being happy,' I replied, yawning. 'Just a slight pursing of his lips without comment.'

'That's high praise coming from Fenchurch,' he said, slapping me on the back to wake me and compliment me in equal measure. 'He chucked a glass ashtray at Harry Seagrove for his attempt on the obituary for an obscure Dutch cleric that no one had ever heard of.'

'He's not using any of what I wrote, though,' I said. 'Fenchurch already had something prepared in that locked cabinet of his and ready to go – Bill in proofs said so.'

'You can't run before you can walk, mate,' he said. 'We are talking about the obituary for one of the greatest political players of the last thirty years, after all.'

I couldn't shake the unease and coincidence, but knew that intuition wasn't something easily defined, quantified, or gained. The typesetter had obviously been mistaken when he revealed Fenchurch had dropped off the copy on the evening before, invalidating any possibility of my own work being used.

What I could not fathom, in my exhausted delirium, was that the drop off had occurred nine hours before the great lord had passed away within the bounds of his home nearby.

My new taskmaster had me working late for several months until he was confident I would not quit. Either that or he just got bored with being an arse. During one particularly weird moment, I felt so symbiotic with the typewriter as to wonder where one of us began and the other ended.

The hard work paid off, and I soaked up his wisdom, writing style, and sense of the public mood and legacy of the dead person to build up an obituary that was a thing of succinct literary beauty.

'It's not about the deceased,' he would say over his pipe during our afternoon sessions together. 'It's about giving the reader the impression they are coming to their own conclusion, not our own.'

Throughout it all, Fenchurch remained incredibly astute and timely with the release of copy to the typesetter, and I marvelled at the potential vault of well-crafted obituaries locked away in his cabinet, hoping that I would inherit them one day and pass them off as my own.

Hour after hour, I would scan through the dry and dusty tomes of peerage lists or academic affiliations, looking to make advance writings and notes on elderly members. Near endless browsing proved a tedious affair, searching through our back catalogue on leaked medical interventions and procedures regarding the great and the glorious, just in case anything should suddenly require an urgent hour's work to polish their final fitting words on page seven.

'I can understand how I might get a heads-up on the demise of the really old candidates,' I said one day in mid-April above the annoyance of the building work outside the window. 'But what about the younger ones, especially those belonging to the parish hereabouts? You've got a knack for delivering those with clockwork timeliness.'

Fenchurch put down his copy of *Punch* and stared over the top of his glasses like a head teacher, unsure whether a detained pupil was offering a genuine question or just wasting his time.

He made me uneasy when he adopted that look, as I was always uncertain of the outcome. Usually, it was a gentle but constructive rebuke, but there were moments of brimstone if my innocent question was not framed correctly or was too base for his mood at the time.

I qualified my question to ensure the former. 'You've taught me all the qualities we agree make a great obituary writer, but you can't teach me luck. Will you tell me how you knew old Lord Coughton was going to pop his clogs that first night you had me slaving away for you?'

To my surprise, he lowered the tabloid political comic and studied me.

'I didn't,' he said. 'Though he was next in line, you might say, and my brand of luck works only with those passing away within the boundary of this parish. I mentioned him because I was interested in your reaction, or should I say lack of it.'

'You gave me the job as your assistant because I didn't make a fuss about a strange coincidence?'

He shook his head. 'No, I recommended you for my position on retirement because you saw no causal link from natural causes. I intend to shake that last remaining bias from you providing you keep the information to yourself – the future cannot be altered; I've tried.'

I was stunned at his sudden revelation of my upcoming promotion and barely registered the rest of what was about to emerge.

'Think you are ready to learn the secret, Johnson?' he said, flipping through the desk calendar for the remainder of April. He flipped over the playing-card-sized dates, turning it in my direction until the 24th was displayed. 'Luck's secret can be taught, or a distinct and unquestionable advantage, if you prefer. Meet me at the porch at St George's in the East, a week tonight. Around midnight normally does it.'

He tore off the paper and handed it to me. The large red

numbers dominated the page, but it also included other important anniversaries and noteworthy events for the day in a smaller black font:

French revolutionary Jean-Paul Marat is acquitted (1795)
88°F highest temperature ever recorded in Cleveland (1925)
St Mark's Eve

'I never understand why they put saints' days on calendars,' I said. 'What's there to celebrate about St Mark's Eve?'

Fenchurch rummaged through his drawer.

'Your future,' he said cryptically, removing an old key from a set on a ring. 'At the expense of someone else's. You are a journalist, at heart, are you not? Do your research.'

It sounded ominous, and I looked over at movement from the window. The crumbling stonework repairs blighted the exterior of the building and interrupted the office's quiet necessity. The workman outside on the platform chiselled and tapped away with a variety of hammers and chisels. Just for a moment, I glanced back at the newspaper veteran and wondered if there was no mistress at all and that his nocturnal wanderings were something altogether more nefarious.

He held out the small key, and I took it warily.

'You can go now,' he said. 'I need time to think.'

I collected my coat and briefcase, glad to be away from the teeth-jarring sounds of the workmen and Fenchurch's brooding melancholy.

I turned and opened the door to the hectic evening hubbub of the late shift as he issued one last request.

'Oh, and Johnson?' he said. 'St Mark's Eve – come alone.'

I caught Sam pretending to research cloud formations while creating his own, smoking outside the canteen.

'Don't worry,' I said. 'Your secret skiving place is safe with me. Can you do me a favour later if you get the time?'

He flicked the spent filter end into the stray dog alleyway beyond the high wall. 'Sure,' he said, listening to the raucous, indignant barks from beyond. 'What do you need?'

'Ever heard of St Mark's Eve?'

He scrunched his face and put his hands in his pockets. 'Is that the new club on Craven Road?'

'Can you stop thinking about women, booze, and the Rolling Stones for one minute?' I said, unfolding the calendar sheet. 'It's a saint's day – April 24th.'

'Never heard of it, though I'm not one for the church. Is it important?'

'I'm not sure,' I said, offering him a cigarette from my jacket pocket to seal the deal and ready him for my next request.

'If I don't turn up on the 25th, will you call the coppers and arrest Fenchurch – he's asked me to meet him late at a nearby church in the evening.'

'Everyone knows the sun shines out of your backside at the paper,' said Sam, spluttering from a cough of smoky surprise. 'He probably wants to take a closer look. I didn't know you were into *that*, let alone him. You'll get yourself arrested if you aren't careful.'

'*Hilarious*,' I said, rolling my eyes. 'No, this is something that sounds a bit heavy for my liking. I'm supposed to learn something to my advantage, something he has been keeping back – the secret of his success, so to speak.'

'Sounds shady and too pulp noir for my tastes,' he replied. 'It's London at night, after all. Just be bloody careful, alright?'

His concern momentarily humbled me before his true nature returned.

'If anything happens to you,' he said, staring up at the

brightening stars now waxing in the setting sun, 'you'll get the best possible obituary.'

'What do you mean?'

'Traditionally, any fallen newsmen get their name on top of the second column on the OBs.' He smirked and continued.

'I'll be able to read about his arrest for sodomy and murder, and your obituary in the same edition.'

I wilfully tried to erase the thought of the invitation and quite succeeded, so busy was I during the intervening days. I forgot all about the meeting until I discovered the folding calendar sheet in my coat pocket as I prepared to hit the town for a few drinks. Fenchurch had not reminded me of it or mentioned it again after the initial invitation. Sam had avoided eye contact for several days, and now I recalled my request for information being the cause. No wonder the scoundrel had avoided reminding me about my imminent demise or whatever I was supposed to see or hear, for fear of being reminded about his promised look into St Mark's Eve for me.

I caught several buses back to the office, passing by the scaffold-scarred editorial building. The streetlamps cast spidery shapes through the web of steel against the white-washed walls. The wind picked up, and I saw the structure wobble and shudder alarmingly before settling back. It did not look safe, and I was glad I had chosen an office job; until I recalled where I was going with no understanding of the context or consequences.

I looked at my watch – 10.30 pm – and hurried the half-mile along the pavement as the rain began to lash into my face, driven by the strengthening storm funnelling through the tall-building-lined thoroughfare.

I reached the ornate Victorian gate to St George in the East, behind which lay the public park of St George's Gardens; the entrance was locked fast. I frantically padded my coat pockets until I pulled out the small but heavy key and tried the gate. I had assumed that it was to unlock the recently restored church interior that had been burned out during the Blitz. Still, at that moment, I was glad to be through and running for cover towards the eighteenth-century Palladian painted facade that surrounded the restored glass and concrete structure within.

I raced for the semicircular bay of the vestibule housing the altar within and along a wall lined with propped head-stones. It provided a momentary respite from the direction of the inclement weather. I drew my coat collar tightly around my sodden neck and wiped back my dripping hair to look up at the twin pepper-pot baroque towers that once would have had a clear sight of their greater cousin, St Paul's Cathedral.

Feeling my way along the wall, eyes half-closed to avoid the blinding sleety rain, I reached the front porch of the towered entrance doorway. To my dismay, the church door remained locked and would not open to the gate key. I felt frustrated with the lack of information on where to meet – had Fenchurch said to meet him at the entrance porch or at the gate? What was the time I was supposed to meet him? Did he say 11 pm or was it after midnight?

I was alone, huddled within the few feet of protection afforded by the porch, wondering how long I could put up with the shivering and the cold.

The clock tower above me struck for 11 o'clock.

I then caught sight of Fenchurch, wearing no coat above his blazer and flannels, walking towards the porch from the dense laurels alongside the older section of the graveyard.

The rain lashed against his path, but he did not hurry, as though walking on a fine summer's day without a care in the world. He made towards me but did not return the greeting of my raised arm. I felt the rain seep into my cuff, and I lowered it immediately, waiting for his arrival. I stamped my feet and called out.

'The bloody door's locked. You only gave me a key for the gate—'

Fenchurch ignored me and turned calmly to the right, back towards the direction I had taken, disappearing beyond the grave-lined wall.

'Mr Fenchurch!' I called, racing out in annoyance to follow the old duffer. How he had missed me from the porch a mere twenty yards away I could not tell. Even the rain and the darkness of the alcove could not hide my animated attempts at signalling. I resigned myself to another soaking as I ran into the path of the gale, searching for my superior.

He was nowhere to be seen.

Light from several dim lamps above the perimeter wall washed over the trimmed lawn and isolated memorials, revealing no one within sight. I called out again and circled the church, retracing my steps to the porch to no avail, and waited for a further ten minutes before giving it all up as a bad joke. I didn't bother locking the gate and took the late bus home, watching the bending of great tree branches in the terrific wind and thinking about what I would love to say or do to the old man for ignoring me and leading me on some ridiculous errand. I could have been warm and dry in some dimly lit Soho bar, sipping snowballs with Sophia Loren lookalikes.

Perhaps Fenchurch was being an arse again and was looking forward to some satisfaction when I came in the following day to complain. I promised myself I would not allow that to happen, no matter how my temper raged through the rising steam of my drying jacket on the clothes horse in front of the five-bar electric heater. I stripped off and soaked in the bath, listening to the shipping forecast to calm me down before falling asleep on the settee just after 4 am.

———

'You're still alive, then,' said Sam, poking me awake in the quiet canteen just before noon. 'How was your little tryst with Fenchurch last night?'

'Don't ask,' I replied, rubbing my red eyes. 'I think it was some sort of wind-up, just to press my buttons and keep me on my toes and guessing. I figure the secret he's keeping back from me is that there is no secret.'

'He didn't show up and teach you how to tell when local celebrities are going to pass away, then?'

'Fenchurch showed up, or at least I thought he did. Someone just like him walked straight past me, ignoring my calls through the rain. It was horrendous out there last night.'

Sam nodded. 'The building work out front took a battering and a load of tiles came down; they wouldn't get me up there on that load of badly fixed Meccano.' He looked outside at the continuing foul weather. 'You got soaked for a load of old nonsense last night, my friend, while I pulled at that bar on—'

'Old nonsense?' I said, ignoring the mention of his victorious evening and attempts to rub salt in my wounds. He passed me several sheets of handwritten notes.

He folded his arms and pointed to the manuscript with mock pride. 'St Mark's Eve − its history, folklore, and bullshit by Sam Chambers; you've been the butt of his little joke.'

I scanned Sam's notes as he sat opposite, bringing to my

attention the varying ridiculous superstitions of the evening of April 24th.

'It's known as *porch-watching* if you believe in that sort of yokel folky crap. The details vary a little according to location, but you sit in a church porch and the spirits or wraiths of those in or around the parish who are going to die soon will be seen as ghosts. When the church clock struck 11 pm, a procession of the dead predicted that year would appear either leaving or entering the church in the relative order of their deaths, with the first ones seen being the first to pop their clogs. It's really rather a clever stitch-up.'

'What's clever about being stitched up?' I said, my ego and pride bruised.

'Think about it,' said Sam, always quicker on the uptake. 'It's an "in" joke for obituary writers. Wouldn't it be amazing to know ahead of time if someone was going to die so you could get your iron in the fire and be the first to whet the public's appetite for the definitive precis of their existence to that point?'

'You think I asked too many questions and came across too pushy?'

Sam winked in affirmation, and I thought back to the afternoon of the invitation:

You are a journalist at heart, are you not? Go do your research.

'Not a word,' I whispered, feeling humiliated.

Sam crossed his heart with his fingers, which gave me no confidence in his confidence whatsoever. 'I didn't realise Fenchurch had it in him to be a wind-up merchant of the highest class. Do you think he got stitched up like that just before old Fairfax handed over the reins?'

I watched as he shrugged and struggled to hold back a snigger.

'You don't think Fenchurch believes the nonsense, then?' I

said, trying to avoid any office-wide humiliation by insinuating that my boss was a believer in the supernatural.

'Nice try,' he said, getting up. 'Not a chance, and I don't know how long I can keep this to myself.'

I took out my pack of cigarettes and threw them into his chest. He caught them and gave me a look of feigned innocence.

'You've got till tomorrow morning to come up with a way of getting him back, which I'm happy to help with, before I break the story; I might even write it as a feature on the noticeboard...'

I barged into the office, not caring if Fenchurch minded; my days of being courteous and submissive were now at an end, and I would be my own man and no one's fool.

Fenchurch hurriedly pulled out and turned over a typed sheet of paper as I entered and stomped over to my desk with a pathetic attempt at a scowl. To my surprise, the old man was more concerned with hiding and putting into an envelope marked 'Proofs' whatever he had been composing than my undignified entry into what remained one of the innermost sanctums at *The Times*.

'You're late,' he said, getting out his pocket watch like an Etonian schoolmaster. 'Where have you been? I've been worried.'

'Drying out and trying to stay awake,' I said abruptly, readying my typewriter. 'You went too far last night.'

'Where were you?' he said, picking up my defiant tone. 'I was worried—'

'You know where,' I said, staring at the rain lashing down against the window. 'Standing outside a sodding church in the pouring rain while you and the senior editors all had a good laugh from those laurel bushes, I shouldn't wonder.'

He got up and stood to my side, trying to gain my attention.

'Why would you be worried about someone like me?' I said, turning to look into his concerned face. 'You don't care about me. It wasn't kind, Mr Fenchurch, to send me on a fairytale. St Mark's Eve and the procession of dead folk for the year to come like some obituary shopping list, indeed! You could have just told me there was no secret to your good fortune, and I would have believed you; you know how hard I've been working on getting this gig, and now the whole damn paper is going to find out you humiliated me.'

'What do you mean?' he said, suddenly agitated.

'Well, if you and whoever was in on your joke don't tell, then Sam Chambers will; I'd do the same probably if I were in his shoes.'

The colour dropped from Fenchurch's face. 'No!' he said, shaking visibly and fumbling with his pipe. 'He mustn't let on. Things like that can't be changed, nor can the future and its consequences.'

He raced around the table, opening drawers to locate a notebook. He returned and slammed it down on my desk at a randomly opened page. A long list of names, some of whom I was familiar with, having written snippets of obituaries for them, were written in Fenchurch's hand; each one crossed out like a completed shopping list.

'It's true,' he whispered, coming so close that I could smell the nicotine on his breath. 'Fairfax told me about it not long before he left that chair over there to me.'

I scanned over at the antique leather bureau chair and back at the sincere look in his eyes, willing me to believe the fantastical tale.

'It only works at that church from all accounts, and folk

have forgotten all about what happens if you go there after midnight on the 24th. That's the secret, lad, but there's no point in trying to persuade you; I can see that now. You'd have to wait another year now to see it with your own eyes, and it will shake every remaining close-minded thought and bias against the unseen that's left inside you.'

I studied his face, trying to comprehend whether I was seeing the delusional end to a great man's career or someone so desperate to cling on that he was trying every effort to push any chance of a successor from his path.

'You should stop it, right now,' I said. 'And go get some professional help.'

He grabbed me by the arm, and I flinched, eager to be rid of the man, the office, and the opportunity to be an obituary writer.

'Where are you going?' he said, sweating and protective like a worried parent.

'Away from you; I quit.'

I freed myself and pulled on my coat.

'No!' he cried, as I opened the door. 'Stay here where it's safe, at least until the old MP for Whitechapel and St George's dies; it'll be soon, I promise!'

I marched down the corridor, giving Sam a two-fingered salute through the interior glass windows, but he didn't see me and nor did those lining the adjoining offices. They all watched Fenchurch racing in pursuit like some overbearing parent. Newspaper men put down their pens and looked out over the developing story in the corridor.

'You're too good a writer to be lost!' he said, out of breath and closing on me. I turned and raced down the stairs, desperate to be free of the office and his company for the afternoon. I felt empowered, in charge of my destiny, and the red mist that was still ruling my cognitive functions told me I'd deal with the fallout tomorrow.

Perhaps *The Telegraph* or *The Daily Mirror* might need a half-decent writer, as long as it wasn't obituaries.

Fenchurch stumbled down the flight behind me as I strode across the lobby, tipping a wink at the new girl on the reception desk. This was too good an opportunity not to impress the new office sweetheart. I lit a cigarette and threw open the entrance doors to the howling wind. It all but drowned out the desperate cries of the old man begging me to come back inside.

The force nine gale checked my path, and my temperament suddenly cooled in the face of the wind.

Fenchurch was suddenly upon me, urging me to listen. I pouted back through the glass at the bemused beehive-haired beauty as he spoke in sudden bursts between breaths.

'You mustn't go out or do anything stupid until I'm sure you'll outlive the MP,' he said.

'What are you going on about, Fenchurch?' I said. 'Leave me alone.'

A gust of wind rattled the windows and set the heavy doors swinging behind us. I looked up to see the scaffold creaking and buckling under the strain of its own weight in the ferocious onslaught.

'I saw you first last night,' said Fenchurch. 'You were first, Johnson. Do you understand?'

'Of course I was first,' I said. 'I was there twenty minutes before you and saw you around 11 pm. I know it was that time because the bloody bells were going, but you could have at least acknowledged me rather than just being an old arse and walking on by.'

He stepped back against one of the steel uprights, which swayed gently like the mast of a ship in a light swell.

'I wasn't there until after midnight,' he said, shaking his head nervously. 'You are making it up to get back at me. I saw you first, just after midnight.'

'You are off your head,' I shouted, above the sound of the wind. 'I caught the late bus at 11.30, so you are talking nonsense, man.'

'You mean we each saw the other on St Mark's Eve when neither of us could have been there—'

One of the last things I thought before the scaffold buckled one final time before collapsing above us was the shocking realisation that he might have been telling the truth. From the look on his face, he realised far quicker the folly that had led us both to the same place and the same end. The upper sections of the scaffold twisted and snapped, colliding on their way down in a deafening crescendo of clanging metal like the bells of inescapable fate pealing for payment.

I looked into his eyes at the calm stillness that descended in the moments before our deaths and widened my own, thinking of the turned page on his desk upstairs. Claydon Fenchurch, the greatest writer of the craft, had written my obituary that morning, and he had been endeavouring to change an outcome he knew to be impossible.

My last thought took me to my grave.

Who would now write his?

GETHSEMANE

Lieutenant Wade peered through a slit in the sandbags at the top of the trench. His legs slipped on the wet, muddy rungs of the makeshift ladder, and he held his breath, waiting for the command to go over the top. He peered down at the captain, studying his watch, a silver whistle perched on his parched lips.

Through the fog and desolation, Wade scanned the distant ruinous wall to the remains of the church, halfway to the German line. It always appeared there, the only living thing in no man's land. No one could kill it, and no man had tamed it.

Wade's eyes widened as the shape revealed itself slowly and distantly within the fog, then hurried along the top of the wall. It always appeared during the fleeting moments of calm between the carnage and cruelty.

It jumped down, and Wade lost sight of it for a moment before the creature emerged between a stand of distant, smouldering trees. It paused periodically to look around before dropping into a shell hole to feast on something. A circling crow mocked and startled the beast and it loped back into view, heading towards the church, hind legs caked in mud. Its white-tipped tail streaked in a sudden break of weak November sunlight; the last remaining thing of colour on a field of toneless clay.

Wade fidgeted and rubbed at his khaki-covered legs, relieving the pins and needles from the interminable wait. A numbing breeze funnelled up to him from below, and the stench assaulted him. It was the smell of the Great War: months of labour and habitation, the labyrinthine warren of tunnels and trenches pockmarked with latrines, cesspits, bodies, and sweat. He pressed his nose against the tarred sandbags, and the smell of safe resinous hessian and protective sand provided relief.

He had learned to cope with the dreary monochrome of the field ahead and the reek of the front-line. What he dreaded above all was the complete absence of sound. He could deal with the barrage and bombardments, the sound of men singing, wailing, or crying. The tinnitus that followed was worst of all in the silence before the blowing of the whistle. Silence brought unimaginably consuming fear.

The mist cleared momentarily, and Wade followed the beast as it made its way to the church ruin. It circled the remains of the pitiful structure, disappearing through the tower door that hung limply ajar. Wade had made it to the sanctuary on two occasions, once on the glorious advance, and then on the dreadful retreat. He pondered on the previous eventful and ultimately fruitless enterprise and readied himself to do it all over again.

The advance, two weeks earlier, had been rapid but tiring. Exhausted and searching for cover, Wade and three of his company had stumbled into the ruin. The bombed-out church had little roof remaining or internal structure, but enough remained to show its original peaceful purpose. Long gone were the embellishments and precious items of faith, but on the side wall of the nave, there remained a faded fresco, masterfully painted.

Wade's men slumped down, backs against the blocks of a collapsed pillar, and lit cigarettes while he searched the rubble for traps. He examined the ancient fresco, mostly untouched except for a few shrapnel marks. It was of a garden at night. Christ knelt and leaned upon a large flat stone, head bowed, hands clasped in torment. Above the figure soared a bright and majestic angel holding a cup in one hand, the other pointing towards three apostles standing guard. At its base, there was a title, *The Agony in the Garden*. It raised a thin and wry smile, and Wade ordered a watch at the door and along the exposed wall.

They ate a meal early in the evening, leaving their bully beef and plum jam tins open and half-eaten, and broke cover to advance on the German position, once they had dispatched the snipers.

They had gained the enemy trench the following day, and the tug of war between the two sides seemed to have turned in their favour. Momentum had been building, and for a while, the new surroundings were an almost holiday-like experience. They enjoyed the relative comforts of the well-built German defences for the next three days.

Then mustard gas and flamethrowers drove them all out and back to their lines in a disastrous rout.

Wade and two of his comrades had returned to the ruin during the retreat, less well provisioned or armed. The hasty retreat had caught them off guard, and they slumped against the broken blocks of the altar, demoralised with the thought of their trench, a half-mile distant.

They had found the abandoned tins and supplies of their

previous sojourn, but they were empty and clean of their contents. Wade noticed the plum jam tins, pushed forwards along the dusty aisle until they could go no further at the fresco wall. Something with four paws had gained something from the effort because pungent scatt droppings lay close by.

The men had a meagre supper in the failing light, while Wade re-examined the fresco to discover something rather odd. Parts of the fresco were missing or changed from a few days earlier, though not in a physical sense, as the wall was intact. Instead, the scene presented subtle differences.

Christ now gazed skywards towards the angel. The cup was now tipped to one side, spilling the bloody contents onto the grass and staining a patch of the foreground into a faded and washed pink. The other hand remained pointed at the apostles, now soundly sleeping. Turning around, Wade mentioned the oddity, but his words failed when he found the two men slumped and dozing as if in imitation of the figures on the wall. He raised the sergeant and corporal, but they were more interested in sleep than the ill-remembered details of a mural from their commanding officer.

All three had made it safely back to the trench and enjoyed a reunion with comrades. They enjoyed cigarettes and chicory coffee, and a few days away from the front to recover. Wade sought the local priest, who could only shine a faint light on the fresco and a brief history of its origins.

'Gethsemane, monsieur, Christ is requesting that the cup of suffering and sacrifice be taken from him if God willed it.'

God had willed otherwise in both cases, and Wade had returned to active duty the following day for the next great push. The British artillery was softening up the enemy upon their arrival, and the bombardment was intense. The Germans had attempted the English line in the intervening days, catching the English off guard though ultimately proving unsuccessful. The tug of war had continued for several days before the Germans retreated to their lines, miserable and demoralised.

The sound of the present suddenly and piercingly returned to Wade, breaking the remembrances of the past few weeks. Whistles blew along the mile of the trench. It approached like a sonic wave, broke overhead, and cascaded away down the line before detonating into the distance with a starting cannon.

All sensation came jolting back, and Wade felt his arms gripping the top of the wooden rung, the coarseness of the khaki uniform, the heaviness of the pack, and the tight holster of his Webley revolver biting into his waist. He felt his legs primed to run, to launch into danger. Wade was fast, and it was a half-mile to the wall. There he would wait until the infantry caught up before assessing and advancing to the enemy line.

A great battle cry broke out in the trench below, and Wade leapt forwards from the confines of the earth, sprinting towards the nearest cover. Men rose like corpses from open graves and clambered out onto the killing field, some wary, some looking for a speedy resolution to their part in the war. They would reach the German line or they would not, and Wade saw in their eyes that many no longer cared how, why, or if.

Weaving through the cratered and barbed wire landscape, pistol in hand, he urged the men forwards; it would be some distance before the enemy opened fire with purpose. Looking ahead through breaks in the fog, he saw the rapid retorts and amber flashes of gunfire, woefully out of range, but reminding the advancing soldiers they were ready for them.

Wade covered another four hundred yards, intimately

acquainted with its diversions, mines, and piles of broken humanity. He noticed a familiar shape crawl out of the church ahead and head back along the wall; calm and serenity had passed, and the beast was making a rapid return to its den.

The dense fog became patchy and drifted haphazardly across the field. Wade slowed, disorientated, unsure now of the obstructions he saw ahead and the safest route through them. Dimly, and on either side, the blossom of England jogged forwards, some falling, some stumbling. The fierce stinging sounds of molten metal hurtling through the air replaced the echo of the whistle – ill-aimed spray from the German machine guns ahead. He was now in range and glimpsed enemy snipers taking up positions between the corridors of machine gunfire.

Leaning on his thighs, he caught a breath and peered through the fog; there was a growing shadow weaving this way and that towards him. A German? A retreating Englishman? He knelt and aimed his pistol at the formless shadow.

Out of the fog loped the silhouette of a great fox. It plodded forwards, staring mournfully into his astonished face. It circled him close enough for its musk and hot panting breath to permeate Wade's nostrils. Whining, it moved away, looking back just as it disappeared once more. Wade got up and followed the fox as it weaved around obstructions, always knowing where and what it was trying to avoid ahead. Wade followed the twisted path, snaking his way through the barren and scorched earth in the wall's direction.

He ran, faster and faster to keep up with the fox, now almost out of sight. He saw the beast vault the materialising wall and disappear. Wade followed along with it, creeping low and shielding himself, giving orders to the men arriving and taking up defensive positions along its sinuous safety. He moved towards where he knew the church to be, somewhere two hundred yards away.

The fog lifted, and the ruin came into relief; a light wind was blowing against the advance. Wade jogged forwards, picking his way through grey-skinned bodies and the remains of a sunken tank before warily making his way in through the open door with several of his men.

He made a quick scan on entry to make sure they were alone and climbed the remaining stairs of the small bell tower, pausing at the first opening in the wall to take stock of the battlefield. He took out paper and pencil and hurriedly sketched the enemy positions before making his way back down and past the fresco.

He stopped in his tracks. The image was different, subtly, but it had changed. Christ was now standing, blood weeping from his tormented face. The angel had all but vanished, the finger of its barely visible hand pointing to a line of distant soldiers appearing through the gates of the olive grove. One lonely apostle remained with his back turned – St Peter?

A fox in a lower part of the scene caught his attention. It bent to lap or sniff the faded contents of the spilt cup. On the back of his enemy markings, he rapidly sketched the scene showing the position of the figures and dated the top corner with '13th October 1916'. In a minute, he was back outside with the information to advance, searching for the wall.

Beyond the enemy line, several loud thumps of mortar fire signalled the last movement of the doomed British advance. A short whine and the high explosive landed behind Wade, launching much of the ground beneath him. He flailed forwards through the air and pounded into concussive uncon-sciousness, landing on the inside wall of a deep, steep-sided crater. He slid to rest on the bottom, into an intensely cold pool of diluted blood and filth.

Wade woke several hours later, and his first sight was that of dead men lining the shallow pool. He knew many of the men that now floated upon it, blasted from their proximity to the mortar impact. Whether it was the bottom of a deep well crater or the church's deep underground crypt, Wade could not tell. One thing was obvious: the sheer-sided hole was immensely deep.

Imprisoned in the deathly pit, Wade recovered his wits and scrabbled up the slippery clay walls without success. Glancing down, he saw blood from the pool staining his sodden trousers and rising ever slowly up to his loins. In vain he attempted to staunch it and tried again to gain purchase on any rock, body, or piece of timber that would lead him out back to the field. Wade panicked with every weary attempt, and with each slide back into the reeking pool, he became weaker and more desperate.

He fired five rounds into the air, calling out each time between the shots, knowing to keep the sixth for a final option; he was missing his ammunition belt and pack. He sat on his haunches out of the water's reach and surveyed his prison.

The pool was roughly circular and twenty yards across; the sheer walls rose like a well to the roof of fog, fifteen yards above. Bodies lay strewn around the margins of the pool, blue-black from weeks of exposure and decay, leaching their lifeblood into the stagnant water. Some had slipped in whole, dying later, others had blown in from nearby artillery, blasted apart at the surface and reunited in a shower of spray and flesh in the tomb below. There was something curious about the bodies; some were half-naked, and something disturbed them.

He was not alone – the familiar sound of scratching and hard, gritty chewing pointed to brown rats somewhere nearby.

'You cannot get out, Englishman, save your strength,' said a croaking, accented voice on the opposite side of the pool.

Wade shot up and slid backwards, coming to rest ankle

deep in the shallow water. He took out his pistol shakily, aiming in the sound's direction.

'Who goes there? Show yourself!'

A rat scurried from the opposite side of the pool, where a mass of bodies heaved and writhed. A living hand broke through and pushed away from the dead, finally revealing the face and upper body of a fair-haired and youthful man who spoke again.

'If you shoot me, you will have used your last bullet. Perhaps you want to keep it a while longer for yourself? It's impossible to kill yourself with a rifle. I've already tried it.' The man nodded his head left and right at the weapons lying haphazardly and entwined with the bodies of the fallen.

The young German officer held up both hands in submission and then rested back against the muddy wall. Wade could see additional clothing on and around the man, obviously to keep warm. The man adjusted himself and pushed away a dead arm that had fallen back onto his chest, forcing Wade to point the pistol more intently and demand his name and rank.

'Are you thinking of taking me as your prisoner?' said the man. 'Very well, I will humour you, Mr Second-Lieutenant. My name is Christian Luyken, also lieutenant.' He pointed to the single muddy yellow pip on his epaulette.

'I am at your service, and your prisoner, if you can get me out of here.' Luyken got up slowly and awkwardly raised his hands.

Wade nodded towards the young officer's pistol, still in its holster.

'Out with it, slowly, and over here.'

The German obliged and unbuttoned the leather strap under the watchful gaze of the Englishman, withdrawing the pistol and throwing it at Wade's feet. Assessing the rifles lying nearby, Wade motioned the German to the side, out of range of any sudden movements.

Luyken was passive and slowly lowered his arms. 'I have been here for two days, Englishman. I could have killed you when you landed, but I don't have the motivation or the strength to fight you, so do as you will; you will find my Luger pistol empty.'

Wade picked up the long-muzzled German weapon caked in bloodied mud and checked the magazine. It was vacant. He relaxed his grip and holstered his revolver, motioning him to sit. 'You came over with the last assault two days ago?' he asked.

Luyken nodded and sat down on a German body. 'Yes, my first and last attempt at bravery or folly. I am not sure which. I sprinted through the fog and did not see this pit until I met the bottom.'

'Just you? What about all these others?' Wade nodded at the piles of bodies nearby. 'You speak excellent English for a Fritz.'

'Thank you,' answered Luyken. 'Two others only, one before and one after.' He pointed at the man beneath him. 'This one was blinded and came yesterday from the sky; he landed badly on his neck.'

'And the other?' asked Wade, noticing the prosaic and educated nature of the man's speech.

'That one died this morning. He had been drinking from the pool for over a week, and he had — how do you call it — disintestry?'

Wade grinned at the slip. 'It's dysentery. How is it that you are still alive?'

Luyken pointed to a body floating between them. 'He was a medic. He carried antiseptic and a small cooking kit. I made a fire from the clothes and boiled the pool water, adding the medicine and some of this—'

The German's hand went quickly to his inside pocket, and Wade raised his pistol rapidly.

'Careful now, Herr Luyken,' he said sharply.

Luyken held his other hand up in submission and withdrew the other from his breast pocket, carrying a slim silver flask. 'I've nothing left now to offer you as a welcome gift. It is a shame because you get used to the taste after three days.'

The battle above seemed to lessen, and Luyken looked up at the clearing azure sky.

'I tried to make a mound of the bodies to climb up,' he said. 'But there weren't enough, unfortunately.'

Wade spat in front of him. 'Unfortunately? For Christ's sake, don't you have any feelings, man? Most of these are bloody Krauts. And what was with you underneath all of those bodies a while ago?'

Luyken rose and smoothed down his uniform. He pushed back his blond hair and formally bowed. 'Forgive me, I prefer to see them as they were, laughing and singing. I know many of their names. After three days here you will try all things to get out, and keep warm, as I have done.' The young man seemed genuinely sorry for his earlier comment and continued, voice shaking. 'The worst was this morning, covering myself with them to avoid being seen and shot by your British soldiers. They would not help me climb out, but I know that some of you have some compassion of a different kind; I'm not ready to die yet.'

Wade understood. The soldier's code, a modern form of chivalry, dictated the rapid dispatch of one's enemy where aid could never come, or where death was preferable to life.

'I have lived in England as a boy,' Luyken continued. 'I know you have some honour. We are not so very different.'

Wade encouraged him to sit once again, and he duly obliged, this time sitting on his haunches away from the dead soldier as if to re-enforce the shame of his earlier misdemeanour. Wade stooped and got out a cigarette from his top pocket and searched for matches, only to discover them sodden in his trouser pocket.

Luyken pointed to a dead man three paces away to his left. 'He has some, and they are still dry.'

'You get them and throw them to me,' said Wade, 'and then you can tell me where in England you pretended to live.'

Luyken dutifully rummaged through the top pocket of the corpse and threw the matches to Wade, who caught them one-handed. 'Nice catch. Do you play cricket, perhaps?'

Wade nodded. 'Yes, before all this bloody mess.' The German was talkative, though the conversation was in complete contrast to the surroundings.

Luyken's eyes widened, and he continued. 'Before the war, I kept wicket for my school near Worcester; that is where I lived from age four. I discovered English cricket and a love of art there.'

Wade struck the match and watched the young German as he lit the cigarette. He was younger, that was certain, well-spoken and calm, almost as though they were talking to each other at an art gallery.

'Who was Captain of Worcestershire in 1913, then?' said Wade.

Luyken beamed. 'That would be Knollys, Henry Knollys Foster. Did you see him play?'

Wade nodded. 'Yes, every time he came to beat Middlesex.'

Luyken laughed, a gentle sound, so strange but so precious and rare in this time and this place. Wade caught himself grinning, too.

Wade walked over, lit another cigarette and offered it to the German. The young officer gratefully accepted it and lay back against the muddy wall, coughing several times before getting used to the strong tobacco.

'What are you doing fighting for the Kaiser, then?' asked Wade.

'My mother is German and remarried after the death of my father. She married an English gentleman, of sorts, and we moved to a house in the country with my stepsisters. I spent the summer before the war in Rome and Paris visiting the galleries and studying art before ending up in Stuttgart with my grandmother.'

'You got stranded, then?' Wade asked.

Luyken nodded, staring at a scurrying rat skirting its way over debris at the back of the pool. 'Stranded, yes. Just like now, just like you and that creature over there.'

Something up on the rim of the crater dislodged soil and small stones. They came raining down into the pool in front of them. Both men looked up to see the fox peering down, framed by the cloudless sky beyond. Luyken put up a hand in greeting.

'He is a sly fox, always coming to see me. Perhaps he is guarding me against harm.'

'I doubt it. He led me into this mess,' said Wade. 'I was following him moments before I landed here. We often see him from our trench; I think he shelters near the church up there.'

'The church with the wall painting!' said Luyken sharply.

Wade frowned at the sudden outburst. 'Technically, it's a fresco because they apply the pigment to the wet lime plaster,' said Wade. He reached into his breast pocket and pulled out his notebook. 'You have seen the painting, you know its name or association?'

'It is a masterful copy of Christ in the garden, the day before his crucifixion,' said Luyken. 'I have seen the original in Rome, and it is by Benvenuto Tisi. But there is a problem with the figures.'

'Yes, I know,' said Wade, 'like they aren't where they are supposed to be, compared to the original?'

The German was astonished. 'You have seen it, too! The painting appears to change. I have seen it twice, and it was different three days ago.'

'Yes, it was,' said Wade. 'I have seen it three times now, most recently before I ended up here. It has changed twice from the original.'

He opened the notebook and flipped to the sketch he had made earlier in the day, extending it to the wide-eyed German. Luyken took it and shook his head.

'No, that is not right,' he said. 'The soldiers have already arrived, and Peter is denouncing the Christ. It looks like I am ahead of you, Englishman.' Luyken flipped through a few pages to see the reverse of the rough map Wade had drawn from the tower. 'These points you have drawn here are dummy positions,' he said, pointing to an area at the top of the page. Wade grabbed the sheaves back sharply and looked at the marks before putting away the book.

'So why do you think the painting changes?' Wade whispered, gazing up at the empty rim above.

Luyken shrugged in his heavily wrapped overcoat. 'Perhaps it is trying to tell us both something?'

Wade snorted. 'Yes, like one of us will die at the hand of the other,' he said. 'I'm not a God-fearing man, Mr Luyken, even after two years of hell.'

Luyken frowned and looked around him as if to press home his point. 'This is man's doing, not God's. Christ was betrayed, yes, but without Judas and Petra—' he corrected his English '—without Judas and Peter, a greater good could not be.'

Wade smiled. Here he was discussing cricket and theology at the bottom of his tomb, most likely, with a charismatic German.

He began a counterargument while his cigarette went out. 'Much good it did them both. Judas hung himself, and they crucified Peter, upside down, if I recall,' he said. 'What about the fox in all this, does he get out alive?'

Luyken stood up slowly, stretching his aching legs. 'The fox symbolises cunning and intelligence.' He paced a little further around the pool, and Wade alerted him once again to his loaded pistol. Luyken held out his hands while he thought on his premise. 'You saw the fox drink the blood from the cup, the first time that the picture changed?'

'Yes,' said Wade, 'and was the fox still there in the change that you saw, the one I am yet to see?'

Luyken nodded. 'He was climbing back to his den, high above on the sheer cliff face beyond the garden wall. There were exposed tree roots he was using—'

Wade sprung up, breaking Luyken's recollection. An idea was forming in his mind. 'How many rifles are there?'

'What do you mean?' asked Luyken.

'We can use the bayonets as pitons and rig them to our feet as crampons. We can claw our way up like the fox and the tree roots.' Wade made a comical imitation of a mountaineer.

He picked up and disassembled a rifle. 'Hurry, man. Help me get these off. We can hammer in a few of the rifles into the clay with the butt end of that floating log over there.'

'And if we get to the top, Englishman, what then?' Luyken asked. 'Who betrays who?'

Wade discarded the stripped rifle.

'We both agree not to hinder the other in getting back to our lines, but we go to that church first and see if that fresco has changed again; agreed?'

'Agreed,' said Luyken, 'but I don't know if I have the strength to do this.'

Wade put away his revolver in a display of cooperation.

'The top is barely fifteen yards, less if you can grab hold of that wire fence dangling away up there. We can pile some of your fallen to get a head start. With a few rifle ladders, you'll only need to climb eight yards.'

They removed the bayonets from eight rifles. Luyken hammered the metal blades into right angles and wedged them between the front toe caps and the leather soles of their boots. 'They only have to stay on for a short while,' he said.

Wade wrapped pieces of cloth around the other bayonets to act as handles, stripping fabric into strands to tie around their wrists in case they dropped them partway through the climb.

They dragged and lifted ten bodies, making a mound to begin their climb. Luyken held the rifles, point first, into the mud wall as Wade hammered in the butts with the slimy wooden log. Several of them slid in as far as the trigger.

'I'll go first,' said Wade. 'No need for both of us to fall to our deaths if my plan doesn't work.'

Wade pushed his way up onto the bodies and stood, puncturing the final dead German with his foot-mounted bayonet. He tested his weight on the first makeshift wooden rung. It bent slightly but held firm as he sidled up to the next rifle. Reaching the end of the third butt, Wade turned to look down just as his revolver slipped from his holster to land several feet away from the German below. Luyken picked it up and hesitated.

At eight yards up, Wade was helpless. He couldn't go back and was a sitting target if the German below proved false.

Luyken emptied the chamber and put the revolver inside his breast pocket. 'We go to the church, yes?' he said, and Wade breathed a sigh of relief inches from the wet clay. He clawed his way up like a splayed and timid spider, digging in his right foot and hammering his left hand into the wall. Wade heaved himself slowly from the safety of the last rifle.

His weight held as he clung, shaking, to the sheer face. As long as he balanced and distributed himself evenly, he would not slide.

He made another step up, carving down into the clay with his feet and hands. Adrenaline coursed through his muscles with the fear of losing his grip and the thrill of getting out. Wade yearned to get back to the comparative paradise of the English trench. He barely heard Luyken, trying to guide and reassure him until the gentle voice called out that the matted wire fence was close at hand. Wade looked sideways, caked in mud, and saw the twisted squares of stock fencing, tangled with rotten and blasted posts. If there was a flaw, it was this. He had planned to grab a hold and use it to drag himself the final few yards to the top. His body ached, and lactic acid burned his limbs, but he had not considered what would happen should the wire not be connected to anything.

He thought of abandoning the idea but was unsure whether he could manage another six or seven pulls up to the top. The decision, however, was taken for him.

Something disturbed the top of the rim, and he looked up, fearful of seeing a German face peering over the lip. What looked over was the fox, barely three yards away, and the shock caused Wade to lose his handhold. Just as his feet were about to leave the wall, he launched himself at the wire netting and grabbed at its cold and biting strands. Wade swung like a pendulum, hearing the blood pounding in his ears, and the shouts and yells from Luyken below. Whether they were shouts of congratulations or warnings of the fox, he did not know or care. He scrabbled to hammer his feet into the wall as the netting unravelled and spooled over the lip. Wade slid down, arresting his fall repeatedly as he dug his feet and hands into the wall, using the bayonets like an ice axe to control his fall. The fencing continued to drag over the edge, and he knew that he would not have the strength to do this again. Lumps of earth and falling posts dislodged him from the wall, and he fell backwards several yards into the open arms of the heavily bundled Luyken.

He was winded, bloodied, and unrecognisable; but he was alive.

Luyken got him to his feet, precariously in the mud, and they looked over at the metal rigging that had unfurled before them.

They tugged at it carefully. A few yards spooled over and then stopped. Luyken put his weight at the base, and the squares strained and stretched in protest. Somewhere above, the fence remained attached.

'Get your breath back, Mr Wade,' Luyken said, taking off the makeshift crampons. 'I go to try my luck now on your excellent ladder.'

It was a challenging climb, trying to find the safest squares as foot- and handholds, but after a laborious ten minutes, Luyken pulled himself out of the hole and rolled over onto his back, out of sight.

Wade called out from below, and Luyken appeared at the lip, giving a thumbs up. Wade navigated the climb out. He reached the top, and Luyken grabbed at his uniform to extricate him from the tangled mass of wire. They knelt, mid-way in no-man's-land, and out of range of both sides. Wade glanced sideways in both directions into the rapidly diminishing light.

They stifled laughs and gripped each other's arms in overwhelming relief. Wade took Luyken's hand and shook it furiously, pulling off the German's signet ring.

'Keep it, Englishman,' he said. 'I owe you my life.'

Wade removed his own and handed it to the grinning young man.

'You could have killed me down there – you had the chance. You could also have pushed me away from the top.'

Luyken placed the foreign ring on his third finger, rubbing at the thistle motif engraved on its face. 'You owe me, then, Mr Wade, and a third time pays for all.'

They were out, but not yet safe. The church was only a few hundred yards away, but they waited until darkness cloaked them before risking the open ground. Wade scouted the ruin before calling Luyken into the relative safety of the roofless building. They glanced around, finding nothing but a few mouthfuls of bitter-tasting water from discarded canteens. What they were here to see loomed in front of them, dark and difficult to make out.

'Do you have the matches still?' said Luyken. 'There is a small soaked rag over there that smells of paraffin.'

Wade considered the danger. Would either side send out anyone to check on a single curious light?

'We need to be quick, then,' he said, fetching the rag and wrapping it tightly around a splintered piece of carved wood.

The brand burst into flame and Wade waved it in front of the damaged and dim fresco like an Egyptian tomb-robber. Luyken gasped at the revelation from the torch.

'Look!' he said, pointing to the far left corner. 'Over here, the soldiers have taken the Christ, and Peter remains alone. It has changed again.'

Barely believing his eyes in the dim light, Wade squinted at the retreating backs of the Roman soldiers and the solitary figure of Peter in the foreground, a face full of grief and remorse for the recent denial that he was one of Jesus's apostles.

'Three times they asked Peter if he was a follower of Jesus, and three times Peter denied him,' said Luyken. 'Look over here. There is the cock greeting the dawn.'

'*Before the cock crow this day thou shalt deny me thrice...*' whispered Wade, recalling his Sunday School. 'It seems we have an end to the story, but what is its relevance if we both know of it already?'

'I do not know, but put out the light,' said Luyken. 'There is no more to see.'

Wade extinguished the diminishing rag, plunging them into darkness. He slumped against the base of a pillar and rubbed his filthy form for warmth. 'Best wait until things quieten down, then you go your way, and I mine.'

They remained silent and shivering for over an hour before Luyken stirred.

He joined Wade at the base of the column and looked across. 'When this is all over, we should meet in better surroundings, Englishman,' he said and held out his hand. Wade took it and was about to reciprocate the sentiment when they heard the slip of rocks from outside.

'The soldiers are coming for us, Mr Luyken, but whose?' said Wade, dragging the young man behind the pillar.

Wade was all but invisible, a caked golem of clay, and he risked a glance above the blasted stone. He heard the whispers of several men. One slipped in the dim light on some loose piece of masonry.

'Bollocks!' it hissed, shortly followed by a sharp remonstration from a senior man. No German swore like that, and Luyken tugged at Wade's muddied uniform.

'Here is your pistol,' he said. 'You must pretend to capture me; I am your prisoner finally.'

'What do you mean?' said Wade.

'I must be captured and taken as your prisoner. It will afford me protection if such conventions still exist between our peoples,' he said. 'You found me here on your retreat, and took me as your prisoner, yes?' He shook Wade vigorously. 'Yes, Englishman?'

Wade thought on the bitterness of the flamethrower attack and whether such conventions would apply if Luyken was captured. Perhaps better to end the poor man's life here, swiftly and honourably, than take him back to be tortured or worse. He glanced down at the new ring on his hand in shame.

'Get down,' he said. 'Let me do the talking.'

The small company sent to investigate the advance of a raiding party had now entered the ruin, and he could see their vague rifle-carrying silhouettes against the blasted walls. Wade thought of the only safe way to attract their attention, and he began the opening line of a familiar song.

'*It's a long way to Tipperary; it's a long way to go…*'

The soldiers in front took up defensive positions and called out. A flashlight blinded Wade, and he aimed the empty pistol towards the heavily clothed Luyken at his feet.

'Is that you, Lieutenant?' asked the sergeant. 'Mr Wade, sir?'

'Yes.' He nodded. 'Don't point the bloody light at me, point it at the Jerry here, and have your men watch out along the far wall. If you've seen the fire from the torch, then so have they.'

Five men took up defensive positions as the sergeant came over and bound Luyken's hands with rope. 'Is it just you, sir?' he asked. 'No one else?'

It sounded ominous to Wade, and he nodded, knowing that he may have been the only soldier to make it back from the failed advance.

'Do you know this man, sir?' he asked. 'Orders are to leave them be or finish them where we find them. Considering what happened the other day, sir.'

Wade looked down at the German, doing his best to look passive and captive.

'The man, sir,' repeated the sergeant.

A soldier from the opposite wall whistled the alarm.

'They're coming, sir, twenty of 'em, about two hundred yards away.'

'The German at your feet, Lieutenant, do you know the man?' the sergeant asked for a third time, readying his rifle.

Wade grabbed the flashlight and turned it off, but not before a rapid and cursory glance at the painted wall. Luyken saw it too.

The fresco had returned to its original form. Christ was once again praying at the stone and looking up into the sky. All was as it had been. If there was any difference, it was in the subtle placement of the angel's eyes.

They weren't looking down on the Son of God, but down on Wade, waiting for his response. Would he deny the man before him?

'Yes, I know the man,' Wade replied before the sergeant raised his weapon to shoot. Wade got out the damp drawings from his inside pocket. 'The man is a double agent. He has told me these sniper nests are unmanned, and these here—' he pointed down in the gloom '—are dummy positions. We need to let him get back to the German line.'

The sergeant called his men together and glanced at Luyken. 'What he says is the truth, sir, or at least part of it,' he said, relaxing. 'We spent the best part of yesterday blowing up nothing but sandbags in that area. A waste of bloody ammunition.'

Luyken held up his bound palms and joined in with the ruse. 'My dear fellow, it wouldn't be cricket to shoot a bound man, but as long as those plans reach headquarters, then I've done my bit for Blighty.'

'We'd better be going,' said Wade, too eager for the German's life to be amused by his dreadful attempt to sound like one of them.

'Call your men, we need to get out of here, and cut his

bonds; he won't call out till we have gone.' Wade looked into Luyken's eyes, trusting his instinct one last time. The German nodded and put his bound finger to his lips as they cut his cords.

They slipped out and were several hundred yards away when they heard Luyken sing something energetically patriotic in German. Wade glanced behind, going to ground in the light of a rising quarter moon. The small company lay down, watching and waiting as a significant number of Germans made their makeshift camp within. Seeing themselves pinned down while the enemy held the higher ground of the ruin, the British waited for several hours, hidden behind the blasted remains of the wall.

Dawn broke, and the Germans headed back to their lines with enough daylight to get them safely identified by their snipers.

Wade took a last look at the bundled silhouette of a man, last to disappear over the rise. The heavily clothed man looked back and raised a hand to the sky in farewell, then pointed over at the distant form of the fox, a hundred yards away. Wade saw them both and then heard something else.

Far away, behind the English line, a distant cockerel crowed to meet the rising sun. When Wade turned back to the church, Luyken and the fox were gone.

1926

Wade drained his bitter coffee and threw some change onto the outdoor café table. The September sun shone down on the piazza, and he looked forward to the welcome relief in the cool of the nearby gallery. The holiday was in its infancy, but Wade was determined to see as many sites in Rome as possible. He made his way through the hawkers to an afternoon's cool and contemplative study of the sixteenth-century masters.

After paying the attendant, Wade headed through the brick-lined and labyrinthine gallery. Interesting, but unrecognised, works held his attention briefly as he wandered through the empty halls. The lateness of the season afforded a much deeper experience with the artworks, despite the interruptions of several workers applying restorative render to flaking sections of the wall. Wade saw repetition in many of the works, typically those on a religious theme. Wealthy patrons of the time had commissioned works, and countless artists reimagined the various biblical scenes.

He was not prepared for what greeted him in the quiet antechamber ahead.

The painting of *The Agony in the Garden* loomed large and solitary on the far wall. It was the original, and Wade looked upon Gethsemane for the first time in all its intricate glory. He stood transfixed but respectful for the figure kneeling at its base. The darkly veiled woman got up, made the sign of the cross, and pushed a fragment of paper into a joint of the brickwork below. She turned and made her way out, acknowledging the Englishman as she passed.

Wade glanced down to discover he was rubbing at the signet ring on his right hand. The token had become so familiar that he had almost forgotten its origin and the fresco in the distant country church. The nightmares from the war were less frequent than they had been, and he wondered, not for the first time, whether the owner of his ring had survived the war.

The painting covered most of the wall, pockmarked with tightly rolled prayers scribbled on paper stuffed into the joints – offerings to the self-sacrifice of the figure within the frame, kneeling at a time of great anguish. Wade recalled the prayers and offerings at the Wailing Wall, from an earlier visit to Jerusalem.

Christ looked up in anguish at the angel on the eve of his interrogation and crucifixion. All the elements were here, in masterful detail. Wade scanned the right edge to the outcrop of stone cliffs to see the form of the fox. A wave of recognition and thankfulness welled up within him, tinged with the sadness and uncertainty in the fate of Christian Luyken.

Recent plasterworks immediately surrounding the frame showed signs of graffiti, mostly benign or religiously motivated, and he glanced along the edge to see something he instantly recognised was meant for him.

In line with the fox, the plaster showed the impression of his former signet ring. A thistle, surrounded by the oval of the raised frame, had been pressed into obviously still wet plaster. The initials C. L. were scratched nearby, followed by a small line to the brickwork. Wade caught his breath with the discovery and message meant for him, made in hope in the not too distant past; a confirmation that Christian Luyken had survived, a signal made in hope to another who might not have survived, or ever visit this exact spot. That the young fair-haired chatterbox had survived moved Wade deeply as he pondered the faint line leading to the plaster's edge and the tightly rolled paper, barely visible and stuffed between two closely set bricks. Wade looked around at the empty chamber and made several attempts at removing the fragile object at arm's length.

The tiny paper partially unrolled as it fell into Wade's trembling hand, revealing an address.

An address in southern Germany followed by the single word 'Wade'.

'Can I help you, sir?' asked the attendant behind him.

Wade tightened his fist, hiding the revelatory fragment, and turned.

'How long ago was the plaster added?' said Wade, pointing to the surroundings of the painting.

'A strange question, even from an Englishman,' said the man, scratching his head in thought. 'It would have been early in the spring, March perhaps. We have to be sensitive to the many prayers and messages secreted in the wall, so we do the repairs to the wall every year before the tourists arrive. We believe that giving our Lord a year to answer the prayers should be sufficient for the Almighty.'

Wade nodded and quickly left the gallery, knowing that he was fortunate to have discovered the note before it was lost to the plaster of the Italian workers. Perhaps he could reach the address by telegram and cut short his holiday in Italy if there was a favourable reply? There was no doubt in his mind that he would make for the address gripped tightly in his palm and already committed to memory.

The rail journey was scenic and pleasant, but Wade could not enjoy the mountain views, desperate as he was to see, first-hand, the man who had replied several days later to his initial telegram from the hotel. Luyken lived, and expected Wade in the coming days at his family's vineyard, deep in the Bavarian countryside.

Wade alighted from the carriage and scanned the emptying platform, unsure whether he should wait or call for a car to cover the remaining ten miles. He felt the tap of something against the side of his shoe and glanced down at the cherry red cricket ball coming to rest on the stone paving. At the far edge of the platform waved a young child with a mop of bright blond hair. Wade stooped and rolled back the ball, much to the delight of the youngster.

'Vater!' The child pointed over to the man emerging from the waiting room.

'Father,' corrected the similarly blond man in his late twenties. The child attempted the unfamiliar word, staring warmly into the face of his father. 'This is an Englishman, Karl. He's here to teach you how to play cricket.'

Wade dropped his case and met the man halfway. They embraced and shook each other from shoulder to hand, fearing to lose touch once again.

'I doubt if I would have recognised you, Wade,' said Luyken. 'You were very dirty as hell—'

'I would know you anywhere,' said Wade, messing the hair of the young boy at his side. 'And my name is Christopher.'

Luyken beamed. 'Christian and Christopher saved and reunited by a painting of Christ. What do your sceptical sensibilities have to say about that?'

'I'd say it was a remarkable coincidence, though I often wondered if I had dreamt the whole affair,' said Wade. 'It all seems so implausible. Perhaps we would have got out of the situation with or without it, but I'm just glad to know you have survived and prospered.' He smiled at the boy below.

'I too believed I was living a fantasy,' said Luyken, ushering him towards the waiting motorcar. 'Even as I made the mark in the plaster with your ring, I asked myself how could it not have happened when I had proof sitting on my right hand? I never thought you would find my message.'

'Perhaps all you needed was a little cunning and intelligence, like your fox,' said Wade, looking into the clear blue sky and picking up his case. 'And perhaps a little faith.'

COCK CROW AT CANDLEMAS

'He's quite a looker, Jen,' said Kane, pointing his pen in the figure's direction. 'Right up your street.'

Jen put down the antique book and glanced up at the oil painting of the handsome Victorian gentleman mounted on the library wall. The man sat on a window seat looking out of the window of a grand library. A large wall-mounted floor-to-ceiling mirror with mounted candles reflected the contents of the room, skilfully rendered in minute detail by the artist. A shaggy-haired wolfhound lay at the man's feet, with a matching melancholic look to that of his master's face. Below was an epitaph:

Edward Melson Esquire, 1857.

'Right up your street, too,' said Jen, winking at her supervisor as he resumed the cataloguing of books on the dusty country house shelf. 'How could someone who once owned all this look so sad?'

'Maybe he's sick,' said Kane, pushing back the half-moon glasses to the bridge of his crooked nose. 'What's sad is *Mr Darcy*, here, died the year after that was painted; he's in the local graveyard about a half-mile away.'

'It's unusual to see a room virtually unchanged in a hundred and sixty years, don't you think?' said Jen, looking around the cluttered library. 'It's as though Mrs Fellows, and those that came before her, wanted to keep the room just as it was in the painting.'

'She was probably just sentimental, like the rest of them,' said Kane, inspecting the next book on the shelf. 'Another diary, by the look of things. Not much value in them, sadly, if you've no kin to make sense of them; still, they might interest a museum of social history?'

'Is it full of questions, like the others?' she asked. Many of the volumes were written in a strong, male hand, consisting mostly of questions with unrelated answers. Reading them made little sense; it was as though the author was holding a correspondence but not recording the other party's replies.

'Yes,' said Kane, flicking through the pages. 'It seems our Victorian gentleman continues to be obtuse.'

Jen studied the pages. She recognised the same flowing hand and the date – '1857', just like the other diaries piled up to the side. They were the strange work of Edward Melson, and several entries contained women's names, including the recently deceased Katherine Fellows.

'It's like he's writing or talking to someone who can't hear,' said Jen.

'He's probably been at the laudanum, or he's mad,' said Kane, retrieving the book and starting a new pile. 'It would explain the look on his face.'

Jen shook her head. 'The diaries written in that pile with the women's hand are similar – almost as if they are talking to each other without copying what the other is saying?' She twitched her nose. 'Perhaps they match up somehow?'

Kane shrugged and typed the latest entry and estimation into his laptop.

'Possibly, but it's not our job to go poking about in centuries-old love letters or whatever they are. We are here to catalogue the curious, not explain it.'

Jen glanced above the piles of books being catalogued for sale, comparing the room to that shown in the painting. The candlestick on the dresser was there, though bent and misshaped by damage and the ravages of time. The limestone-carved fireplace lay bare, in contrast to the bright but cheerless blaze of 1857. The bookshelves were now fuller than those above, and they still had many to value before the auction of the contents took place after Christmas.

They discovered one or two interesting volumes, several first editions of Tennyson and well-worn second-print-run copies of Austen and Hardy. Apart from the collections of literary magazines stretching back a century, the rest were mostly unremarkable books and diaries, filled with bizarre questions and unrelated answers. The only constant appeared to be the greater numbers of volumes written in the steady hand of Edward Melson, all dating from 1856.

Kane lowered a book and glanced at his apprentice, frowning at the great oil painting.

'You are a proper fantasist and a hapless romantic,' said Kane, nodding to the painting. 'You need to find yourself a guy like that, not moping about in old libraries and closing-down sales with a dusty old queen like me – you should be at Christmas parties meeting Mr Right.'

'Please,' said Jen, rolling her eyes. 'I'm happiest here, doing triple-paid overtime with you.' She nudged mischievously into the fatherly figure of the archivist. 'Besides, you always get Moliere mixed up with Maupassant.' Jen returned an unprofitable book to the shelf. 'Don't worry about me, Kane. I'll get my man, one day; I promise. I was born in the wrong century, that's all.'

Her superior nudged back in the pretence of reaching for the next book. There was a bond between them – an odd couple bound by a passion for books, dusty old houses, and the past. He didn't want her to end up living alone, outside of a library, where true loneliness could not exist among leather-bound companions.

'You might try a less unorthodox sense of dress if you want to attract the right sort,' he said. 'Look at those boots of yours – just a suggestion?'

He pointed to the calf-length purple Dr. Martens and tutted at her penchant for dark and sombre clothing.

'What's wrong with them?' said Jen. 'There's no one around to be offended, except the ghosts, and you.' She pointed back to the painting and continued. 'Anyway, I'd be happy in something from 1856 – the women had style in that era.'

'You, in a dress?' snorted Kane. 'I'd pay to see that!'

Jen stared at the mirror within the painting. Lit candles surrounded it, and a delicate rosewood lectern lay to the side. She turned to scour the chilly library and discovered the book-stand tucked away in the far corner. A thick, plush drape covered a large rectangular section of the wall nearby.

'Why have they covered the mirror?' asked Jen, glancing up at the ceiling to see recent soot marks directly above the hidden object.

'Superstition would be my guess,' said Kane. 'The solicitor said Katherine Fellows died after taking an overdose in front of it, sitting in one of those big armchairs back there.' He gestured to a haphazard collection of furniture and continued.

'It was lucky the Macmillan nurse turned up last week; otherwise, she'd still be watching her reflection. Country folk hold that the spirits of the dead can get trapped by certain things – quicksilver in mirrors, for example.'

'Where'd you learn that?' asked Jen, picking up another of the diaries.

'I read books,' said Kane, 'as well as cataloguing them. Now back to work, Miss Morticia Addams, there's plenty to get through before midday; I don't want to be working *all* Christmas Eve, and the weather is getting worse. It's five miles to the nearest village, and I prefer a white Christmas from the comfort of my London flat, if you don't mind.'

Jen turned to the window. The snow was falling in fluffy shreds and laying inches thick on their cars outside.

They worked meticulously and quickly through the remaining shelf. Several rare ghost-story authors, contemporaries of the master, M. R. James, came to light, much to Jen's delight.

'It's against our policy,' said Kane, noting her interest, 'but as long as they reappear precisely on the same shelf in January along with your Gothic backside, then consider it a loan as a Christmas gift – I didn't get you anything, by the way.'

Jen pretended not to mind, but smiled at the prospect of reading *The Stoneground Ghost Tales*, by E. G. Swain, over the festive period.

Kane glanced at the window rapidly covering in snow and called it a day.

'The books will still be here in January, Jen. Time to make a move.'

'I can return the key to the agent if you like?' said Jen, bunching her wayward hair back into her ponytail. 'It's on my way home.'

Kane nodded and hugged her awkwardly. 'You drive safe, okay? I'll see you at the office in the New Year, complete with a picture of you in a dress and news of the new beau you met at a New Year's Eve disco – or whatever you call them these days.'

She nodded and pecked her old mentor on the cheek with

genuine affection, glancing up at the painting. 'You belong back there more than I do, talking like that. You be careful of those Christmas parties yourself, okay?'

Kane grinned and grabbed his coat and laptop bag. 'Don't leave it too long. Just turn the lights off and make sure the—'

'I know how to lock a house down, Kane. Now take your advice and get out of here.'

Kane fought his way to the driveway and his estate car, clearing the snow from his windscreen, and that of her small city car. He turned, covered in snow, and blew her a farewell kiss. She attempted to catch it and closed the door behind her, hearing the car rev its choke-hearted engine until it met with the lane in the distance. Jen was alone in the isolated country house, in the middle of a developing Christmas Eve blizzard. Still, she wanted to soak in the library's atmosphere and sit, as Edward Melson had done over a century before, before collecting her things and the books to be borrowed.

The window seat was chilly, and the leaded glass was steaming up with the closeness of her breath. The snow blanketed the garden and sundial. All was still.

She closed her eyes, grateful for the moment alone, before the bustle and stress of the traffic congestion to come. The sigh of the swirling wind filled her ears, along with the faint sound of a barking dog. She smiled at her imagination and looked within the room, from where the distant sound seemed to emerge. Dust motes swirled in the chilly air, disturbed from the partly emptied shelves, and Jen rose, taking a picture with her phone of the sad and beautiful painting.

There was a weak signal, and several texts arrived from companies informing her of their seasonal opening hours. There was a final message from her mother's carer at the rest home, letting her know all was well. It would be her mother's final Christmas, and she thought of her lying there, morphine clouded and unaware, just as she had been when Jen last visited at the weekend. There was no text from her absent father, there never was, and Jen shrugged. She glanced down at her purple boots and clicked the heels together, hoping for a quick return to Kansas, or failing that, Hemel Hempstead.

'Merry Christmas, Mr Melson,' she said to the figure in the painting. She put on her coat and wandered the ground floor, switching off lamps and the light to the downstairs cloakroom. As she tried to set the alarm near the door, there was a clunk of a distant circuit breaker, and the panel flashed with the power outage. She briefly thought of locking the door and leaving the house, calling into the land agent's office to inform them, but she put down her things and picked up a nearby torch with its fading battery and went in search of the fuse box in the pantry.

No one had yet cleared the kitchen stores, and several tins, jams and household essentials, boxes and jars remained and hindered her from reaching the antiquated fuse board. Jen reached out, stretching to reset the fuse to the main supply, only to discover it tripped immediately with every attempt. She meandered her way back into the passage and back to the front door – there was no more she could do for the sad old house, alone itself for perhaps the first Christmas in its existence. She turned to see the snow, much thicker and falling faster than it had done just twenty minutes before. The small blue car was barely visible, and the steps down to the drive were now covered and indistinct.

She cleared the windscreen, kicked away the snow preventing her from gaining access to the driver's door, and turned over the engine. The car sputtered and shuddered as it attempted to fire into being. The sparks within the engine ignited the fuel momentarily, before flooding from the purple boot eagerly depressing the accelerator pedal. The instrument display lit up with many blinking fairy light warnings as Jen tried again.

And again.

The battery light flickered, and the combination of worn battery and the piercing cold resulted in no other sound or action. Jen got out her depleted phone and dialled Kane; perhaps he wasn't far away and could call out a mechanic or return himself. The phone hunted for a signal before joining the vehicle in an unplanned and inconvenient Christmas Eve shutdown.

Jen slammed her hand onto the dashboard and looked out at the covering windscreen; she was rapidly becoming cocooned within the frigid city car.

Peering out, she gauged whether the five-mile slog to the village was possible. She was a competent walker, and her travels in the Chilean Andes earlier that year had left her with a rucksack full of cold-weather and high-altitude items. Jen was glad she had packed the down-filled sleeping bag and gaiter-covered hiking boots, along with a solar-panelled phone charger and a camping stove. It would be dangerous, and the landscape looked so different in several feet of snow. Jen decided against it, at least for now. *Better to hole up, at least until the snow stops*, she thought.

She fought to open the door and slithered her way to the rear of the car, head down, to open the boot. She grabbed at the rucksack within and brushed against a wicker box; it was a hamper with a note.

I lied. Merry Christmas, Jennifer. The Boss xx.

Jen shouldered the rucksack and hooked the hamper into the crook of her armpit. She navigated the slow route back through her footprints to the steps of the house. Withdrawing the key, she pushed open the door and slipped over into a bundled heap on the threshold.

Tonight, at least, would be spent in the house. The Georgian building would not spend Christmas alone after all.

It was three o'clock before Jen got everything in order. She found dry wood and kindling in the back storehouse, along with an oil lamp and a propane-fuelled heater. The fuse box did not endear itself to her exposed fingers, as they were shocked for the fourth and final time. She resigned herself, with little opposition, to spending the evening, and at least some of tomorrow, without power. The phone lay on the library bay window seat, connected to its solar strip, and soaked up the last pitiful white-out light filtering through the snow-drifted leaded panels. Jen prised open a key cupboard and unlocked a guest bedroom that would serve for the evening; there was no need to use the master bedroom – there was such a thing as respect, after all.

She opened the hamper in front of the crackling fire and blessed the contents, one by one, as they emerged from the basket: Dundee cake, exotic cheeses (eaten only at this time of year), jars of cognac-infused spreads and pickles, Belgian chocolates and mince-pies, and to crown it all – a large bottle of modestly expensive champagne. There were enough calories in the house, it seemed, to last most of the winter. She dragged the deceased lady's leather armchair closer to the blaze and relaxed into a packet of cheese straws. The room was accommodating, now that the fire and lamps were lit. Jen forgave the blizzard and the car and soaked in the solitude and the silence.

With an hour of daylight remaining, she worked through the rest of the piled diaries. The earlier ones were written in the confident hand of Edward Melson, stretching back over a hundred and seventy years in four volumes. Each entry began with the year, closely followed by the month and day. Jen arranged them from February 1856 until they ceased in late November of the same year. The list of questions, mixed with several unconnected answers, followed a similar pattern:

Edward Melson
What is your name?
What year is this?
I am cursed, but know that I mean you no harm.
Is my beloved dead?
Only when another has passed. The candles allow it.

Jen turned the pages. After every few months, around the time of the changing of the seasons, the list of similarly asked questions would repeat, as though addressing a new correspondent. The last page of the fourth volume ended with a list of four women's names. A thrill of recognition and coincidence greeted her as she recognised the last two – the lady recently deceased, and her own. The former names were crossed through with a single stroke of fine red ink:

Marie-Ann Harper
Constance Genevieve Munro
Katherine Margaret Fellows
Jennifer Callow 'Jen'

She grabbed the diary written in the hand of Katherine Fellows and opened the first page, dated 1975. A series of unrelated sentences and questions began with a similar one-sided correspondence.

Who are you?
Where, why. How?
What must I do?
What happens at Candlemas?
I cannot, even for you.

Jen flipped to the final entry. It was made close to Katherine Fellows' death and dated several weeks prior.

I am dying. I am sorry, please forgive me for what I am about to do.

Jen knelt on the floor in front of the fire and opened the last volume from Edward Melson alongside, dated September 1856.

Today, I learned that my beloved Constance, the blessed summer of my remaining year, is no more. A young woman has inherited and has fallen upon the secret, revealing to me the sad news. It begins again; the year beyond is 1975, and it is very curious. The questions, the same answers, the falling in love? I pray to God that I do not have to grieve again; the pain is too great. I hope only for a solution to the riddle, or a swift end at Candlemas to my suffering and heart-ache.

Jen checked the other diaries, each written by one of the earlier women. She sat back and glanced up at the painting. Edward Melson stared out of the painted window, sad with news of grief. But how could he be in mourning for the passing of women decades and over a century after his death?

There were glimpses in the women's diaries that corresponded with answers or questions from Melson's pages. They were not, however, complete and they were mostly out of order, but snippets of conversations, cross-matched, could be read and understood.

The light failed, and the torch battery died. Jen got up to check on her phone. There was barely any power and no signal. She glanced back at the painting and the bright candles burning merrily, at odds with the figures within – she needed more light. Jen hunted for candles in the pantry and returned to the library with an assortment of sizes and shapes. She began fitting them into the bent pewter candle-stick and pressed several more into green foamy bricks, removing the dried flower arrangements and casting the brittle stems into the fire.

The light in the room held its own against the

encroaching darkness outside, but it would prove difficult to read and study the diaries further without more. Jen moved over to the covered wall and tugged at the dark velvet drape, revealing the carved floor-to-ceiling mirror in the painting.

It was a thing of strange and pagan beauty. The frame was carved with writhing blossom and vines. Several branched from the sides to terminate in four cup-shaped candle sconces. The mirror reflected the image of the candlelit room behind, and Jen tested and tried the remaining candles to fit the four holders. All but one holder contained some relic of burned wax, and Jen cleared out the sockets, ready to accept the new sources of light. She lit the candles, and they crackled into life, illuminating and reflecting into the mirror and out to the warm room.

She stared at her reflection, pondering on Kane's words to get out and socialise. Jen stared down at her purple boots and bobbled black leggings.

I'll find my soul-mate one day, she mused to herself, *but for now, I'm content to read ghost stories and weird country house diaries, and eat chocolate-covered cherries with champagne.*

She turned and lit a remaining candle before leaving the room in search of a glass. The kitchen revealed a few pint glasses and a chipped mug, which she rinsed under the tap. The water spat from the tap as it struggled against the formation of ice in the pipes.

Back near the hearth, Jen resumed her study and order of the diaries. She got out a pad of paper and noted down promising cross-references between the scripts of Edward Melson, and those of the three women. A shadow crossed the far wall, and she looked over, suddenly fearful there was someone in the room.

'Hello?' she said, reaching for the iron poker.

The shadow appeared again as though something was writhing or turning, cast from light coming from the other side of the room. Jen spun around and saw the mirror and its candles bobbing merrily on the frame; it was the only source of light coming from the direction of the opposite wall. The candlestick on the dresser was reflected, but it took time for the shock to register.

The candlestick reflecting was unbent and burned with new candles. Jen pivoted and saw the lop-sided candlestick in the room, complete with its mismatched lumps of burning wax. The shadow appeared again, and she returned to the mirror. Then she saw it − or didn't see it...

Jen no longer saw her reflection.

She raised a hand to touch the glass and saw nothing but the room beyond, subtly different, but the same room. The firelight coming from within the mirror was briefly blotted out as a large wolfhound got up and stretched, casting a shadow into the room beyond. The dog circled and lay down again, nestling into a comfortable pose and basking in the warm glow of the fire.

Jen looked behind the mirror for signs of trickery. The slit between the mirror and wall showed nothing but dust and cobwebs. She put her hand on the glass and tapped to convince herself there was no illusion. The dog rose with pricked ears and wandered over to her hand. It cocked a head at her as though looking through clear glass on the other side. Jen moved her fingers, and the dog followed her hand as she traced a pattern on the lower silvered surface. She stooped and held out her palm on the glass. The wet nose pressed against the inside of the mirror, leaving a greasy mark. Jen put her hands to her mouth in astonishment.

The dog wagged its tail and opened its mouth, as if to let out an inaudible whine. Jen tapped on the glass once more, and the dog let out a silent series of barks, bringing in a well-dressed young man Jen recognised instantly. She shot up and instinctively grabbed one of the fireplace tools.

On the other side of the mirror, Edward Melson hurriedly made his way to the mirror with a look of happiness and eagerness. His lips moved without sound as he called the hound away and looked upon the young, strangely dressed woman looking back, armed with an iron poker.

Jen stared back, shaking with the sudden appearance of someone familiar, however far removed. Edward's face turned from one of curiosity to sudden understanding – the woman before him was not the one he had expected to see. Edward bowed his head in greeting and dragged the lectern to meet the mirror from his side. He disappeared from view, and Jen stepped back, fearing some sudden appearance from a secret door in the panelling. Edward returned with a blank book and wrote with his back to her. Jen looked at the claret frock coat and the tall, muscular outline of the young man; he was more impressive in the flesh than the painting suggested.

Edward moved away with a look of profound sadness to reveal the page upon which was a single line of the familiar flowing script.

'*Where is my beloved Katherine, is she gone?*'

Jen nodded.

Edward placed the open book on the stand and covered his face with his hands. The hound rubbed against his master's muscular leg and let out a silent whine of comfort and shared sadness. He took out a handkerchief and wiped his eyes before returning to write in the book once more. His hand wavered with grief as the words appeared to Jen through the portrait mirror beyond.

'*It begins for the final time; there is so little of it left – What is your name? And what is the year?*'

'Jen Callow, it's short for Jennifer, but only my mother calls me that. It's December 24th, 2018. Can you hear me?' Jen winced at the embarrassing and stumbling waffle, wishing the purple boots were in her mouth to prevent her from talking.

Jen watched as the young man struggled to understand her silent speech and shook his head. He pointed to the book on the stand within the room where Jen stood. Edward raised the quill and pretended to write on the glass. He came closer, and Jen saw his blue eyes plead for understanding as his breath steamed a halo around his striking face.

Jen put down the poker and retrieved a notepad from her bag. She wrote her name and the date on a blank page, holding it up to Edward's astonishment.

Jen dragged the stand from the corner of the room to copy the image from beyond the mirror. She removed the book from it and placed her note pad face-up.

Edward turned and scratched out the words from his side of the mirror.

'*I have little time*,' he wrote. '*What is it that one woman can give but no other?*'

'What woman?' replied Jen, via the notepad.

Edward turned and pointed directly at her, mouthing the word '*You*'.

Jen shook her head at the riddle and lowered her pen to the paper. 'I do not know. I'm sorry. Are you dead or alive? My boss saw your stone—' She scribbled out the last line, but it was too late. She glanced up to see Edward understand his impending mortality.

'*February 1858?*' he scribbled, after dipping his quill into a small jar of ink.

Jen nodded and blushed from the faux pas.

'*Why are you here and are you alone?*' wrote Edward.

Jen nodded, breathed on the mirror, and drew the word 'snow' backwards on the condensation. She pointed at the windows and Edward followed her finger to the snow-blasted panels.

The nobleman copied her and did likewise with the word 'Safe?'

Jen nodded and scribbled on the pad. *'Are you alright?'* she wrote, seeing the struggle in his face to hold back the tears.

Edward silently scratched at his parchment. *'For the present, but the curse will come true, and I am lost. Death by the feast of Candlemas for following the wishes of my family, and not my heart.'*

'What should I do?' wrote Jen.

He scribbled a final line before getting up, despondently, and snuffing out a candle on his side of the frame. The image began to darken, and Jen could just make out the outline of her reflection. Edward pinched out another of the four candles and pointed to his book.

Jen read the last line before the remaining two candles from beyond the mirror were extinguished and the tear-stricken face of the most beautiful man Jen had ever set eyes upon faded, to be replaced by her sorrowful reflection.

'Follow your heart, Mistress Jen, wherever it leads.'

The night was cold and dark. The snow did not relent until the early hours, and Jen woke from her sleeping bag upon the musty old mattress to look out on the serene landscape as far as the distant hills. The child-like joy of being snowed in for Christmas Day gave way to her adult common sense, and she wondered whether the depth of snow would allow her to make it to a nearby farmhouse, or even to the village to get help.

Downstairs in the library, she poked at the embers in the grate, coaxing them back into life. She sniffed at the open bottle of champagne and took a swig before tucking into the cheese and oatcakes from the hamper.

Not a bad Christmas breakfast, she thought, looking over at the mirror and the depleted candles. The smear from the hound's nose could be explained as simply a tarnishing of the glass-bound silver and her writing on the pad simply an act of silliness brought on by anxiety and whimsy. She looked across at the oil painting and the seated figure of Edward Melson.

'Let's see if you're truly there or just in my dreams,' she whispered to the mirror, breathing a patch of condensation and forming a heart shape with her finger. She fumbled with a box of matches in her nervousness to light the four candles and discover the truth.

The mirror remained constant and reflected the bright, snow-lit windows and fire from the library. Jen looked at her dishevelled appearance and tapped on the glass before catching herself blushing at her stupidity and fertile imagination. *Cold air will cure such nonsense*, she thought as she looked out of the frosted bay window with apprehension.

After collecting her coat, she left the house and fought her way through the drift of snow to the submerged car. She followed the line of the long drive to the distant crow-cawing lane. The ruts were filled with fresh snow, and despite there being only a gentle sprinkling now falling, there was no chance to make it to civilisation on four wheels, in or out. Jen plodded through a hundred yards of deep snow, lifting her sodden leggings and boots high with each awkward stride until she turned around, exhausted. The distant sound of a church bell signalled the end of a Christmas Day service, and she retreated in the face of freshly blown snow back to the house via her compacted footprints.

Back in the cosy library, the phone on the windowsill buzzed into life from its trickle of solar charge. Jen rubbed at her frost-nipped fingers and waited for the phone to show her the message, miraculously arriving during a momentary chance encounter with a fleeting and wayward signal. It was a text from the land agent, sent the day before:

Post key in door, we are closing the office because of bad weather. Will be in touch after Xmas to conclude the evaluation of the contents. Merry Christmas from all at Hampton's Estates Office.

Jen tried, without success, to send texts to Kane and her contact list. The battery was fully charged, and she smiled, knowing that she could play her favourite mobile game, *Candy Burst*, when the books and diaries became tiresome. After a warm meal of tinned ratatouille, courtesy of the pantry and gas-cooker, Jen wandered the house with a cup of black coffee. On the upstairs landing, she paused at the painting of an Irish wolfhound, proudly standing guard in front of the country house. The similarity to the animal in the library painting was too much to be a coincidence, as was the resemblance to the hound from beyond the mirror. She stroked the rough, oil-painted fur, recalling the bizarre experience of the previous evening.

'You look after him, and the house, okay?' she whispered to the hound, and descended the main staircase to return to the library.

The sky outside darkened with the threat of further snow, and Jen lit the candles of the bent candlestick on the far dresser. It was bent as though the pewter had been dropped or flung against a wall in the past. Munching through a layer of macaroons, Jen cross-referenced the questions and answers from the various diaries to understand a story being retold to three women over the past one hundred and sixty years.

The three women, struck out in red ink, appeared to have been corresponding from 1874, 1933, and finally 1975 respectively. They had all believed they were communicating with Edward Melson over the past one hundred and fifty years. Considering Jen's vivid experience, the thought that she had been corresponding similarly with the year 1856 was over-whelming.

The diary entries revealed the initial shock and confusion and a coming to terms with the bizarre reality that allowed such conversation across the centuries. The mirror was closely tied to repeated mentions of a curse and was acting as a conduit to those who had inherited Edward's estate following his untimely demise.

Jen pieced together the entries, from several volumes, detailing how Edward had fallen in love with a Romani girl, in defiance of societal norms and family who were firmly against the union. The couple had planned to elope and be married the following day, but a maidservant revealed the secret, and Edward's father decreed that the young man would give up any right of inheritance if he pursued the matter. Edward did not meet his beloved at the stag-headed oak, as planned, and did not marry at the woodland chapel the following day. He locked himself away in grief at his predicament, comforted only by his hound, as he tried to come to terms with the breaking of his promise. Several days later, the spurned lover and her family stood outside, beyond the sinuous ha-ha wall. They stopped a great caravan and brought out a grand mirror, setting it against a great elm tree. Edward had watched as the Romani girl kissed the mirror and called out to him:

'I curse you, Edward Melson, and your faint heart. May you watch as others you love grow old and die, while you remain young. May you take their love and your cowardice to your grave. Our wedding gift I leave to you, along with my broken heart, the names of four women you will encounter over the following seasons, and these words:

'*Mark well this mirror and protect its glass, for by cock crow at Candlemas, you too shall pass. You took from me what only one other can give; learn this truth and you will live.*'

Jen read on, late into the afternoon, of the gentle, lonely

man struggling to understand and come to terms with the women that appeared in the mirror. Their corresponding diary entries revealed a passionate but unactionable love on both sides, until one by one, except for Katherine Fellows, they married, grew old, and died while the man in the painting and the mirror remained hale and youthful. How they kept such things a secret, Jen could only guess, but the entries in Edward's pages continued – reaching out until they ended, desperate, with a poem of such intense passion that Jen thought her heart would burst.

Time was no longer linear between each side of the mirror, though the seasons changed with each passing of the woman beyond. Spring, summer, and autumn had now passed. The house and its mirror image now entered snowbound winter, and Jen glanced at her name – the final entry in the series.

Jen discovered the date of Candlemas on her mobile app – by February 2nd, no matter the year, it would be all over and Edward would die unless he could answer the gipsy's riddle and break the curse.

He had placed an advertisement in *The Times* and received several macabre and disturbing suggestions, none of which a gentleman or human being in their right mind would contemplate.

From the initial confusion and surprise of discovering the mirror's properties, the women had suggested many ideas: a woman's heart and love, her fortune, her children, and finally her life – but another could give all these. Jen opened the last entry from Katherine Fellows, the page that had lain open to the mirror at the moment of her death.

Here at the end of my life, I give it to you, in the hope it allows you yours and answers the riddle, know that I have loved you and always will. Let there be an end to your suffering and mine.

Life was not the answer. The self-sacrifice and suicide,

despite her great pain, of Katherine Fellows had not broken the curse. Edward Melson was out of options.

Darkness dawned as the sun sank on Christmas Day. Jen replaced several of the candles and stared into the mirror. It was unchanged, except that on closer inspection, she noticed a tarnished mark as though confirming the Romani girl's kiss. Jen flushed and brushed her lips against the spot in the glass.

'Let the answer be a kiss,' she said, knowing in her heart that another could easily give such a boon. Jen was no prude and had given plenty of them away, all for little gain over the years. Books were more faithful than boys and could be put back onto a shelf and exchanged without remorse or guilt. She stood back as the breath and outline of her naked lips disappeared, leaving only her reflection and that of the room.

A glint of light from the fire reflected from the antique plate of a gramophone funnel, and she turned, seeking the musical device. After a few moments of winding and searching for the thick, grooved record plates, hidden in a drawer beneath the turntable, the first crackles and treble-rich sounds of a Charleston filled the room. Jen clapped with delight and took off her boots to frolic and romp on the polished wooden floor, as though no one was watching.

She whirled faster and faster, banging into the outstretched corner of the central marble table.

'*Bugger!*' she exclaimed, grabbing at her toe to deaden the dull ache. She grimaced and hopped to the armchair to rub at the sore foot. The gramophone wound down after a few minutes and stopped. A large shadow moved across the wall, and she spun to the mirror to see Edward Melson standing amused at the antics in the room beyond his own. It was obvious he had been there for some time. He bowed and pointed to his book.

'*Is this how a lady should dance and cuss in 2018?*'

Jen blushed and slapped her hands to her face to hide the

embarrassment. She peeped through to see a smile so warm and kind that she nodded and laughed until the ache in her foot receded.

She wrote in the book on the stand. Edward glanced down at her bare shin and feet before looking away in modesty.

'*I thought I was dreaming. Does the mirror only work at night?*'

'*No,*' replied Edward, '*but the candles on both sides must be lit. Even then, there must be a strong emotional necessity.*'

Jen pointed to her foot with a questioning look.

Edward shook his head and wrote with his swan-feather quill. '*No, not that. It must have been me – I wanted to see if you were safe.*'

'*Thank you,*' mouthed Jen, wondering how long the noble-man's son had been there and if he had witnessed the earlier kiss. The irony struck her as she watched him fidget with his signet ring, as though unsure what to say next. Here she was, conversing with a man from two centuries ago, while her phone couldn't even send a text half a mile.

Her phone...

'Wait, I have an idea!' she said out loud, unplugging the charger and starting up the speech-to-text app. The remark-able piece of software translated all manner of written media, speech and snippets of conversations into a multitude of media forms. Given time, the clever app could even lip read providing the camera function was not deactivated. She rested the phone on the lectern.

'Can you read this?' she said.

Edward turned and squinted into the mirror, nodding excitedly. He opened a nearby drawer, removed the ink-bottle from its well and plugged in the handle of an ivory magni-fying glass. He returned to scribble wildly on the parchment below. Jen's camera on the phone picked up the script from beyond, translating back into speech:

Katherine oozed sand at the vice sushi the larger and some primer.

Jen held out her hands and lowered them to the ground in the universal symbol to slow down. 'You must write individual letters,' she said into the phone. The magic box cannot read your elegant joined-up writing, not yet. It needs to learn.'

Edward understood and wrote individual letters to make up the words.

'Katherine used a hand telegraph device such as this, but it was much larger and more primitive.'

Jen nodded. 'Yes,' she said, as the phone perfectly translated to text. 'It's the latest model. It's a pity you don't have one also; we could save so much time.'

'I wanted to see if you were safe, Miss Callow, and to wish you a happy Christmas,' said Edward via the phone. The American voice did not seem quite right, and Jen held up her hand for patience as she scrolled through the British alternatives. She reached the voice of Colin Firth and restarted the app.

Perfect! she thought.

With each line of writing, he turned, ready to receive the reply, but Jen noticed they were both looking far more at each other than the pages.

'Have you spent the day alone, too?' asked Jen, kick-starting the conversation following a long and pleasant examination of many of his best features.

Edward nodded but then qualified the answer by pointing to the wolfhound, sound asleep by the fire. He returned to the book.

'Why are you in the house? Are you a relative or servant of Katherine's?'

'No,' said Jen, forgiving the notion of servitude. 'I'm trapped by the snow. I am here to collate and inventory the library – your library. It's being sold now that Katherine—'

The pained look on his face returned.

'I've read some of the diaries,' she continued. 'Not all, but enough to understand your loss and your predicament.'

Edward swallowed hard and placed a hand on his side of the mirror. Instinctively, Jen raised hers and came so close as to breathe a fine mist on the glass, revealing the image of the heart. Edward's eyes widened with surprise, and Jen bit her lip with embarrassment. She wasn't entirely sure if she said 'sorry' out loud; she certainly didn't mean it.

'*Did she die peacefully?*'

'Yes,' said Jen, lowering her hand and retrieving the open book containing Katherine Fellows' last entry. 'She left this for you.'

Edward lowered his hand and turned to read the final lines of her long and happy life, and the sacrifice she hoped would free him from his fate.

'*She committed an act of suicide? Will she not be damned?*' wrote Edward.

Jen shook her head. 'We don't believe this anymore, well most of us anyway.' She held up her hand to the glass and continued. 'She peacefully ended her life on her terms, knowing she had little time left. I believe she was trying to help you.'

'*But the headstone shows my death next year still?*'

'Yes. I've tried to understand what happened and what the answer to the riddle could be. My name is in the book – did you write it?'

Edward nodded and held up his hand with a look of thankfulness for the compassion on show. Jen knew he had wanted to see she was safe, but also to reach out to another human being, however distant in time, in his moment of grief.

'*Yesterday,*' he wrote. '*How many more names are there?*'

'I'm the last,' said Jen, desperately wanting to comfort the man inches away, but over a hundred and sixty years in the past. They were not so very different for all that; empathy was timeless, and she wanted him to know it had survived the industrial age.

'*Then, I accept my fate. I have tried to find her and the gipsies, but they are gone.*'

'What about your family?' said Jen, returning to the fire to add more wood.

'*I disinherited myself. I have only the house and Cairn.*' Jen watched as Edward put his fingers to his lips and gave a silent whistle. The dog rolled over, cocked an ear, and returned to his slumber. '*I cannot afford servants, but if I were to live, I would write. I have a publisher that believes I could make a living as an author.*'

'What kind of literature?' said Jen, intrigued.

Edward paused, as though revealing something deeply personal. He turned and looked bashful before dipping his quill into the ink and resuming the script.

'*I have written a work of romance, but under a pseudonym. Please do not think me unmanly. I adore the works of the romantic poets and hoped that one day I could write something that would long outlast me. Alas.*'

Jen returned to face the mirror.

'Men and women in the modern age change their gender and write under pseudonyms, but we call them "pen names"; George Eliot, for example.'

Edward brought the quill to his nose and frowned. '*I do not know this author – is he famous?*'

'He is actually a *she*,' said Jen. 'Her real name is Mary Ann Evans, and you will know her—' She held up a hand to pause the conversation and consulted the bibliography database on her phone. '*Adam Bede* was her earliest novel in 1859, and it's remained in print to this day. You must wait until then.'

Edward shook his head and put pen to paper. '*I think not, Jen.*'

There was an awkward silence, and Jen and Edward stared at one another once more, not knowing what to say, but happy in the quiet of each other's company. Edward rose and removed his coat and cravat, revealing a billowing shirt and flawless frame. Jen watched as he drew a small and plain book from the shelf. Edward stepped over the hound in his hurry to show her the newly bound novel. He wrapped it in the silk cravat and placed it next to the stand, then dipped the quill into the nearby ink; his inclination became clear.

'*I have a single volume, the last from a small run. If it is not presumptuous, I will make a gift of it in thanks for your company on Christmas Day, but also to ensure something of me remains – I have an idea.*'

'I accept,' she began, watching as he left the room, returning some moments later with a bar and lever. After lifting the rug and prising a floorboard, he placed the wrapped book into the void and hammered back the polished plank.

Jen understood the possibility and worked her way back from the mirror to find the exact spot in the library of 2018. She took a final step backwards and collided with the marble table for a second time. One leg lay secured above the floorboard.

Jen left the room with the phone acting as a torch and returned from the cloakroom toolbox with a hammer and crowbar. She returned the phone to the stand and tried to push the table away but could not budge it a single inch. She prised open an adjacent board and hacked out a large chunk of its corner to lever it open wide enough to jam a large and unremarkable encyclopaedia within to prevent it from springing back.

'*Be careful!*' said Edward, in translation as he wrote in the book. '*I only just purchased that.*'

Jen rolled up her long-sleeved top and reached into the void beneath, in the table leg's direction.

'Don't panic,' she said, getting down on to the floor and wriggling her arm further into the confined space. 'It's not worth much, maybe a hundred pounds, tops.'

'That's extortionate – I only paid six shillings for it.'

Jen stretched out her fingers, pinching her shoulder against the sharp edge of the board. There was something there, just out of reach. She dug her long nails into something soft and dragged out the silk-wrapped book that had lain in Edward's timeline for only a few minutes; one hundred and sixty-two years in Jen's. The rough underside of the board lightly scratched her arm as she withdrew the gift.

She unwrapped the book and held it aloft for Edward to see. He clapped in celebration and bowed with a flourish of his muscular arms. He returned to the open page on the stand and picked up the quill.

'A Merry Christmas, Jen Callow.'

Jen got up and kicked away the encyclopaedia, snapping shut the floorboard once more. She rolled down her sleeve and opened the book. The pages were mottled with age and historic damp, but the typeface was clear and legible. She held it to her breast and blew a kiss in reply.

'Perhaps I can offer you something that no man or woman has ever seen in 1856?' she said, picking up the phone.

Edward looked confused and watched as she set down the device.

Jen had considered several worthy authors: Nora Roberts, Virginia Woolf, and even Jackie Collins in a moment of mischief. She settled on George Eliot and spread both her hands on the glass as Edward read the opening words to *Adam Bede*, the scrolling text of something that had yet to be written in 1856. He glanced up in amazement and placed both hands against her own, leaning his brow against the glass to gain an even closer bond. He closed his eyes, and Jen brushed her temple against the glass.

'It's okay,' she said, knowing the phone would not translate while it scrolled through the modern foreword about the author's life. 'I know.' She looked into his opening eyes as a tear streaked down his face. A mix of emotions welled in his eyes, but the most poignant of all, perhaps, was the knowledge that this Christmas would be his last. He wiped away the tear and smiled, sitting to read the opening chapter.

Jen retreated to the fireplace and poured the remaining champagne into a chipped teacup; now that she was in the company of a gentleman, swigging from the bottle seemed very unladylike.

Jen wrapped herself in the velvet drape and snuggled down to read the small book, occasionally looking up to see Edward returning her glance.

The work was beautiful and profound, and Jen had read nothing so personal and moving. That anyone, let alone a man from the mid-nineteenth century, could provoke such a response was astounding. She wiped away her tears, knowing that if the curse proved true, no more beautiful words would make it into print.

She fell into a doze and slept by the fire. The book slid quietly from her hand as Edward Melson stood and watched over her until the candles burned low and went out.

Jen awoke to a cold morning in the library. The fire had gone out, and she unravelled herself from the velvet drape and squinted across at the mirror. Her slovenly appearance was reflected, and she smoothed down her unkempt hair.

Outside, the snow had stopped and a thin Boxing Day sun beamed through the high windows. Thoughts of leaving and returning to the outside world came flooding back, conflicting with the emotional turmoil of leaving the mirror and the man within. She imagined him lighting the candles tonight, but over one hundred and sixty years ago in his world, to find her gone. Perhaps when the work continued in January, she could show Kane the portal to another time. Kane was smart and well-read; if anyone could find an answer to the riddle, he could.

What is it that one woman can give but no other?

She boiled a teakettle on the gas hob, and the cyclical reasoning to determine an answer began once more. How could she give anything to a man dead for so long, regardless of what it was? Katherine Fellows had given her life, and that had not worked. Doubt and reality intruded into her thoughts as she slapped her cold feet on the hallway tiles and back to the library to dress.

She looked into the mirror at her appearance. Perhaps Kane was right – a new year, a new you...

The sockets in the frame contained melted stubs, and she looked at the four remaining mismatched candles on the sideboard, desperate to see Edward again, but fearing that she was captivated by someone and something she could never have. She ran through the events of the previous night, squirming and delighting with the remembrance of the virtual embrace through the glass. Just fantasy, she told herself, to assume such a man would find her at all attractive. She had come on too strong and needed to grow up – it was time to get back to the outside world.

She decided she would end the encounter, painfully, but on her terms and with a deeply personal message. Jen wrote in the book for the final time.

My dear Edward, I must return to my life, despite the snow and my desire to remain here with you. I will return with others in January to solve the riddle. Know that I have strong feelings for you, despite the short time I have known you. Your work touched me deeply, and I feel I would be happy to spend a lifetime, or whatever remains for either of us, with you.

She sighed and replaced the candles, ready to light them when she left the house for the final time. With any luck, she would be the first back inside within a few weeks and could snap shut the book before others noticed things were amiss. She turned and began the clean-up operation, rearranging the room as Kane had last seen it, except for the drape. She bundled it close to the edge of the mirror in a mock pretence of it falling over the festive period.

An hour later, she was ready to leave. She drew herself away from the oil painting, after a long last look at Edward Melson, and lit the candles. She promised herself only a brief look but set down the phone with the speech to text running just in case.

... both sides need to be lit, and even then, there must be a strong emotional necessity...

The mirror remained stationary, reflecting the present.

From a distant ground-floor room, there came the sound of breaking glass. Jen swung around, startled, unsure if it was just a bird strike or a slipped roof tile.

She tiptoed into the hallway and heard the dragging sound of a sash window opening in an adjoining room. Her anxiety rose as she creaked her way across the floorboards as stealthily as she could, back to the library to collect the iron poker. A heavy thud gave no doubt that someone was in the house and moving similarly, listening for any other signs of life. Jen made it back to the library and lifted the makeshift weapon at arm's length, setting off the clang of the tongs and shovel. The sound of footsteps stopped, now aware that they were not alone. A door creaked open across the hallway. Jen shook with fear and looked over to the exit, trying to gauge the distance to the front door. Should she call out and try to frighten whoever it was? Maybe it was someone from the village coming to check?

Don't be stupid, Jen, she thought. *Good people come in through the front door, not the back window.*

Suddenly she heard her phone dictating the messages from beyond the mirror. The machine learning was now able to lip read and translate directly from the silent movements of his mouth.

Edward had lit the candles in 1856 and was even now calling out, having read the message before him. She needed to turn it off, to make it stop, and to get out through the back window and across the buried lawn to the thicket of trees, a few hundred yards away at the edge of the fence-line. She abandoned all attempts at stealth and ran back into the library. Edward stood there, confused, and pointing to the opened page. He silently shouted, '*No!*' and she shook her head.

'There's someone in the house, Edward! I have to get out.'

The phone translated the speech to text, and Edward banged on the glass in futility. He screamed and pointed over to the doorway; Jen did not wait for the app to translate; she saw his words clearly:

'*Run! Get Out!*'

Jen forgot all notion of saving her things and raced to the window, trying to raise the swollen, damp wood of the sash window. It rocked ajar, and she levered the base with the poker, raising it a few inches. A blast of frigid air raced in and took her breath, closely followed by the gloved hand of the intruder, gripping her throat and dragging her back into the room.

'No, you don't,' said the hoarse voice of the intruder. 'Not until I'm done here. You behave yourself, missy, I'm not a nice man, and I know you're alone.'

The grip was tightening, and he shook the poker from her

hand. She struggled to pull the wrist from her throat and then remembered a trick from a scene in a film.

Jen grabbed the assailant's little finger and twisted it, dislocating it. The man released her with a yelp of pain. She turned to see the burly man in a balaclava gripping his hand.

'Take what you want and let me get out of here! The valuables have gone, you are wasting your time.'

The burglar recovered his wits and roared in anger and pain. He grabbed at the silk cravat wrapping on the edge of the marble table and advanced, tightening both ends. His little finger stuck out to avoid further injury, and Jen feared it was no longer a question of whether she would be gagged, bound, or strangled.

Jen backed to the window and glanced over at Edward silently but furiously banging on the inside of the mirror.

The intruder glanced over, fearing some misdirection, to see the strangely clothed man throwing himself against the glass. A large and vicious hound snarled silently beside him.

'What the devil?' he said, searching around the room for a hidden camera. 'Where is it? Where's the damn thing? There's no power, so why is the screen working?'

'You are on tape,' said Jen, lifting the poker and waving it in front of herself. 'Edward, help!'

The phone translated to text, and Edward turned, grabbing something out of view. It was a rifle. The intruder turned his attention back to the shaking young woman in black, someone he had not expected to find in the old house, known to be empty. He saw the man behind the glass load the weapon and point it in his direction. Seizing an opportunity, he lunged at Jen, ready to take a hostage.

The iron poker flailed and struck the arm of the burglar to little effect. He grabbed her wrist and attempted to grasp hold of her little finger to return the painful favour. Jen scrunched her hand into a fist and lashed out with the other.

It was not enough, and a deft and practised manoeuvre swung her around. She screamed, and he dragged her before the mirror, in front of the man with the loaded rifle.

Edward stood resolutely, muzzle raised as the hound below scratched ferociously at the glass. The burglar paused, unsure, then laughed.

'It's just a screen!' he said, spitting upon the glass. 'You nearly had me there, missy.' He spun Jen around and struck her with the back of his fist, sending her sprawling into the base of the mirror. The frame wobbled, and the candles quivered in their sockets but did not go out.

The ringing in Jen's ears gave way to the sound of tapping from behind. A tremor from the glass thudded with the rifle butt as Edward hammered on the glass from beyond. Jen wiped the blood from her cut lip and glanced up. A crack appeared in the silvered surface, though only from Edward's side. The burglar paused in his advance as further cracks appeared, but not quickly enough. The robber dragged Jen to her feet and forced her against the mirror, his lips inches from her face.

'One last time, where's the bloody camera?' With one hand pressed against her throat at arm's length, he drew a wicked-looking knife.

'There isn't one, you animal!' croaked Jen, struggling to breathe. 'He's coming, and he'll be no gentleman when he gets here.'

Jen heard the distant echo of the hound barking as the crack developed. She saw the confused look on her attacker's face. The phone also picked up the sound and translated it into speech.

'*Possible match – Bark, Bark...*'

Edward threw down the rifle and raced to retrieve the candlestick from the back of the nineteenth-century library. He hurled it at the glass and retrieved the gun as a hairline fracture spread across the inside of the twenty-first-century mirror. His deep voice became clearer as the crack ran to the mirror's edge.

'*I will kill you if you lay hands on her again!*'

The phone repeated the phrase, distracting the burglar.

Jen drew in a rasping breath and forced her knees into the man's groin, sending him sprawling to the floor.

'Grab the candlestick!' came the muffled cry of Edward. 'It's the only thing that connects us that can break the mirror.'

The phone repeated the words as Jen stumbled to the far dresser and lifted the heavy object. The lit candles flailed and toppled over as she made her way to the mirror and threw the solid pewter against its surface. The metal rebounded from the glass and wobbled precariously.

'Again!' cried Edward, seeing the burglar rise from the floor brandishing the knife. Jen did not see the reflection of his approach, but from the expression on Edward's face, she knew that the final swing of the candlestick would be her last.

She hurled the object into the mirror like an Olympian hammer thrower and watched as a small crack developed into a web of fine lines. She kicked at the glass with her purple boots and saw Edward raise the rifle, taking aim and shouting at her to get down. The intruder plunged the knife forwards as the distant sound of an Enfield rifle-musket followed by the showering of glass stopped him dead in his tracks.

In an instant, Edward and the hound were in the room, grappling with the wounded man. The intruder grabbed at his shoulder in disbelief as a trickle of blood issued from the wound on his shoulder. The hound grabbed at his leg, biting deeply as the man slashed with his knife, cutting deeply into Edward's thigh. Jen screamed and got up from the shards of glass, cutting her hands. Edward stumbled back, expecting a renewed assault, but the burglar turned and staggered from the room and out of the house, pursued by the wolfhound.

'Get the cravat,' said Edward, looking at her hands. 'Bind them until we can—'

Jen turned and fetched the silken cloth. She knelt to bind his leg.

'It's not deep, but there's a lot of blood. We need to get you to the hospital.'

She got to her feet, panting, and looked into his eyes.

'Is it you? Are you really here?' She grabbed his forearm, squeezing into the toned muscle to make certain.

He nodded.

'I didn't know you were Scottish?' she said, noting his accent.

'The lands I will or will not inherit are on my father's estate in Dumfriesshire. I came south with what I had. Is that a problem?' he asked, checking the cuts on her hands.

The phone repeated the last phrase in the voice of Colin Firth.

'Who's that talking?' said Edward.

'It's my ex-boyfriend speaking from the hand telegraph,' said Jen with a wink.

'What happens now?' said Edward, looking around at the familiar but changed room.

'This,' said Jen, throwing her arms around him and kissing him on the lips.

Edward blushed as she removed herself from the kiss, longer than he had expected.

'I meant about the mirror?' He pointed to the opening. A candle wavered from the room beyond and went out. The open space between the worlds misted as though the boundary was closing. The mirror was returning. He put his arm through the opening and whistled for the hound.

'It will close soon, and I think for the final time,' he said.

'If I stay here, I may bleed to death long before your flying machines can procure the services of a surgeon. You are also in need of a nurse.'

'Is there a doctor in the village in 1856?' she said.

The hound came bounding in, breathless, and licked at his master's bloodied bandage.

'Yes,' said Edward, 'I can ride, but not without help in saddling and mounting my horse.'

Jen nodded. 'We can relight the candles later when you are well?'

'I think not,' he said. His face became pale, and he turned to face the mirror's opening. 'This is our final moment, and the mirror will not reveal its secrets again now that it is broken. I do not begrudge what I have done, despite my heart, knowing you are safe for the present. I do not think the vagrant will return, but you must call for the beadle.'

'This is 2018, Edward; there is no beadle.'

He drew her to the mirror frame and pointed through the haze to his library beyond. 'I must go, the candles are going out.' A gust of wind from the narrow slit of the sash window blew out another candle before she rushed to the open sash and slammed it shut.

'What have you done to yourself?' she said. 'The curse said to look after the mirror?'

'I do not know,' he said, stepping through to his time. 'I no longer fear any retribution. I have been punished enough. Is it not enough to repent until all feeling and love are driven away? Perhaps this wound here causes my death ultimately, but I do not regret it.'

He pointed to the candles.

'When they go out, we will never again have such comfort. Remember me as I was, in the painting over there.'

'What if I came with you?' said Jen, thinking of the curse and the unanswered riddle.

I was born in the wrong century...

'The mirror would trap you in the past, with me,' he said. 'I only have a few weeks to live, Jen, and you would be alone in a strange time without your televisual sets and gramophone machines.'

'You will die either way if I don't.' She took a long look around the room and gazed upon the painting of the man with whom she had fallen in love.

There was a moment of clarity, and Jen answered the riddle.

'I offer you what no other woman can do on my behalf, or any woman has done – I offer you my *future*. I renounce my future in 2018, to save yours before Candlemas.'

Edward shook his head. 'You would give up everything you know to save my life, a man you barely know except through words?'

'And deeds,' she said. 'I do not know what is within me to save your life, but what I read in that book and feel right now should not be snuffed out from one missed chance. I will be with you on Candlemas Eve, whatever happens, curse or no curse.'

She threw herself into his arms. The wolfhound howled in glee and jumped up, desperate to be part of the binding.

'I promise to honour and protect you—' he began.

'On this side of the mirror, it's the 21st century,' she interrupted, with a twinkle in her eye. 'I'll settle for love and respect.'

'That is such a small price?' he said.

'Don't worry,' she said, releasing him and gathering her things. 'I'll make sure I get my money's worth.'

'You need to be quick! The candles are going out.'

'Wait for a second,' said Jen.

She grabbed the phone and the charger, along with her

bag. She threw several books from the shelves through the portal.

I can't wait fifty years for these to be written, she said to herself.

Leaving her car keys on the rosewood lectern with a note, Jen held up the phone.

'Come on, come on,' she said, searching for a signal. 'Just this once.'

The mobile buzzed into the last of its useful life in the twenty-first century and sent the uploaded translations and transcripts, along with a farewell text to Kane.

'Hurry!' shouted Edward. The hound whined, joining the urgency.

Jen rushed across the room and through the boundary in time. 'I'll hold you to your promise, Mr Darcy,' she said, burying her head into his chest as he caught her.

'My name's Melson,' he said, watching as the candles burned low and the portal began to close. 'Are you referring to that despicable rogue in Austen's work?'

'Yes,' she said, holding up her phone. 'Remind me to show you the BBC adaptation I have downloaded; it's a classic.'

Jen hesitated and looked at the cloudy vision of the library through the closing portal. 'Will I be okay on this side?'

'Yes, though the boots and clothing will attract attention and I would recommend a more conservative fashion in company.'

'And in private?'

'I will love you, just as you are.'

The dog pawed at the boundary between the worlds as the candles blew out. Jen did not turn as the vision of a country house library in 2018 was replaced by the wall of the splintered mirror. It was 1856, she had her man, and had given away her future.

One of them at any rate.

The frame remained ever after, mounted on the wall and outlining a bare patch of flocked burgundy wallpaper, a happy reminder of an altogether different time, left behind in pursuit of a better future.

Kane entered the library with some trepidation. It was a month since he and Jen should have been back at work. Only six weeks since he or anyone else had set eyes upon her, and now he would resume the cataloguing alone.

He set up his laptop on the marble table, noticing some recent damage to the floorboard below. He glanced at the mirror frame and the dirty, faded flock of the wallpaper behind. What the hell had gone on here? The police would not say, only that a missing person investigation was underway following the discovery of a badly wounded and wanted man in the district. His strange confession had, fortunately, absolved Kane of any suspicion, as he no longer was the last person to see the young woman alive.

Here and there, patches of melting snow slid from the roof, thawing in the bright February morning. He picked up a series of books and tapped into the database server for the first time since Christmas Eve.

He opened the cloud-based file with the laptop, boosted by the signal enhancer brought along to photograph and speed up the cataloguing of the library now that he was down by a man.

A notification of an email and attachments, sent December 26th, flagged up on the screen:

Kane, it might be hard to swallow, but I'm okay. The files attached and the diaries will explain if you can believe it. Sorry, I took a few books with me back to 1856 – look under the floorboard next to the marble table – it should pay you back. Thank you for everything, now and forever. Jen xx

Kane scanned through the attachment, desperate to understand the nonsense and babble. Through it all, a thread of conversation that began on Christmas Day and ended with the final transcripted words of Edward Melson:

'You need to be quick! The candles are going out.'

He picked up his phone, deciding whether to call the police. He hesitated and stood over the broken floorboard. Lifting the damaged corner with his large finger, he shone the phone's flashlight into the recess; something lay wrapped within. He put down the phone and forced his hand into the void, retrieving several books wrapped in black time-moulded cotton.

He opened the cloth to discover it was a black T-shirt, the same that Jen had worn at their parting. Decades of dust and the faded label in the collar showed a size 12. The books were first editions of J. E. Melson, the pseudonym of Edward Melson, the famous romance writer of the mid-nineteenth century and in whose house Kane now stood. It was worth a fortune and inside the first was an inscription, written in Jen's hand:

I got my man – Jen x
Ps, I look great in a dress, wouldn't you agree?

He glanced up at the painting to see the debonair figure of Edward now looking across at a woman, richly dressed with a baby on her knee. The child's illuminated face was holding a curious black rectangular object and looked absorbed by its cover. It could have been a phone except that the painting was dated to 1858. The woman's face was instantly recognisable, and he gasped in recognition. The hair was longer, but it was unmistakeably the face of his former assistant. He wept with joy as he looked down at her hand, lifting the hem of her exquisite dress, provocatively, to reveal a purple boot.

'You definitely did, my beautiful Jen. And you certainly do.'

The End

GET EXCLUSIVE CONTENT

Thank you for reading *Midnight's Treasury*.

Building a relationship with my readers is the very best thing about writing. I send monthly newsletters with details on new releases, special offers and other news relating to my books.

Sign up to my readers' group at www.jtcroft.com or by scanning the QR code below, and I'll send you further stories in my collection, *Free Spirits,* exclusive to my reader's group– you can't get this anywhere else.

ABOUT THE TALES

QUEEN OF HEARTS

I was triggered to write a story that gave a hefty and whimsical nod towards the craft of writing and independent publishing. It is a story winked firmly towards my fellow authors and those responsible for me picking up the proverbial pen at all. What better than a ghostwriter that takes dictation from a ghost? A common theme in ghost stories is something unresolved in the spirit's former life, preventing them from leaving the influence of the physical world. Usually, it is to impart some information or retribution on a mortal so they can 'move on', but what if the ties that bind us to this world long after our days are done are our passion in life?

I wonder if there are ghost anglers, ghost knitters, or ghost jigsaw-puzzlers pursuing their pastimes peacefully all around us?

TREVELYAN'S EYE

At the most south-westerly tip of England, Cornwall can arguably claim to be the country's capital county for smugglers, shipwrecks, and ghosts. It is a dramatic location for a spooky tale, dominated by its Atlantic sea-battered cliffs and granite-toothed moorland. The region is a haunt (if you will pardon the expression) of many a seasoned holidaymaker. This is my Cornish ghost story.

It began with the vessel foundering against the rocks on a whitewashed wall, projected through a stationary ship in a bottle, and spread out from there. I have always enjoyed the 'sins of the father' motif where unresolved crimes or misdemeanours return to plague future generations. It certainly takes some inspiration from James Herbert's masterpiece, *The Fog*, but with an altogether more adventurous tone. I love the idea of two descendants of smugglers working together to put right the faults in their family history, something that humanity could do more often to make the world a better place.

THIN AIR

I was once alone and high in the mist-crowned Cumbrian fells. Below the summit of Bowfell, the domain of ravens and towering stacks of frost-shattered boulders, there is an unusual geological feature known as the 'Great Slab'. Surrounded by great moraines of tumbled rock, the modestly smooth surface rises steeply to the ridge several hundred metres above. The more experienced climber can traverse the slippery plateau, but the more modestly kitted, timid, or cautious scrambler reaches the summit via a rocky route known as the 'River of Boulders', running parallel to the Great Slab.

It was at a large boulder that I turned to look behind through the mist, catching my breath as I strained for any view of the surrounding Langdale Pikes. The sun filtered through the haze, and a curious atmospheric phenomenon akin to a sun dog ringed my shadow at the edge of the precipice. I waved, and the silhouette, visible against the dense water droplets in the air, waved back. I turned to look ahead, preparing myself for the final lung-bursting exertion to reach one of the finest peaks in the Lake District of northern England, to see someone else.

For a moment, I thought it was another walker looking back, and I raised my hand. The figure copied my movements, and I realised it was a rare double refraction. Between the two shadows, I looked back to the past and then ahead at the figure standing in my future before continuing my ascent.

The figure beyond remained until the mist cleared, vanishing as though completing his task of picking out a safe route to the cairn.

I fed the ravens in that lonely place on morsels of remaining Kendal mint cake and dried fruit until they departed for the more popular pickings on the summit of Scafell, and I was left alone. I searched in the silence for my shadows, but they had long departed, and I never encountered them again.

It is comforting to have companions in the thin air, even if they are of your own making.

NEIGHBOURHOOD WATCH

I once heard tell of a graveyard blighted by vandalism and graffiti, and the agency of vigilantes unknown had rid the site of the scourge. In the absence of any obvious living contenders, I wondered if the 'residents' of the churchyard had taken matters into their own hands.

It is the only story written 'on location' in a pretty country churchyard that forms part of a collection of my special places. It is protected by Neighbourhood Watch and, perhaps, by other agencies.

Just for the record, I always pick up my litter.

THE CAVEAT

There is always a catch, no matter how good an offer or opportunity seems to be at first glance.

Caveat emptor – buyer beware.

I like tough choices and creating scenarios that force the reader (and the writer!) to postulate on the dilemma for themselves:

Would you choose to live a life of ease with a caveat that you were powerless to forget or affect?

The story was originally conceived to end with the question but without an answer, leaving the reader to fill in the response from an emotionally charged cliff-hanger. My advance readers, *The Muses*, revolted and insisted on an epilogue – it was simply too great a decision to be left unresolved. While the answer the protagonist gives and the decision she makes ultimately leads to a satisfactory conclusion, I ask you to consider your own response as the spinning central garnet within the brooch slows and stops.

For my part, I have yet to come down on one side or the other.

ST MARK'S EVE

This story was long in the tossing and turning of many midnights. As is often the case, the ending came first – an unmoving keystone that I hoped would throw the reader off and, for just this once, provide a sudden and unexpected 'curve ball'. Britain is brim-full of bizarre customs, and I doubt the well of inspiration for contemporary tales based on pagan or medieval folklore will ever run dry.

GETHSEMANE

I have a recurring dream. A fox leads me across a blasted wasteland; to what end, I know not because the imagery ends before I catch up with the beautiful creature. In folklore, the fox represents cunning and intelligence and I wanted to bring together two people, who shared more in common than their differences, from both sides of a conflict, not of their making. Thrown together, quite literally, they had to work together to escape to the chance of a better life and solve a mystery that would unlock the path towards a brighter future.

The story ultimately hearkens back to one of the earliest 'changing picture' stories, *The Mezzotint* by M. R. James. Rather than being mere passive observers, my characters strove for a hopeful resolution based on the principles of shared human experience, resilience, and values in the face of the terrible circumstances of the Great War.

No monster, fiend, or horror story holds more terror than what man can inflict upon the land and his fellow man. There is no greater counter to this than the peace-makers – those who refuse to be pawns in a game where no one can win.

COCK CROW AT CANDLEMAS

I'm a sucker for a ghost story set at Christmas. I'm also deeply and unashamedly romantic. I needed a tonic during a torrid year of isolation, so I combined the two. Cue a story of sacrifice and big decisions neatly Christmas wrapped and mirroring (no pun intended) my occasional conclusion that I was born into the wrong century.

I once spent several days alone caretaking a Jacobean mansion at Christmas, daring something like this to happen. It never did, but the memory of falling snow and candlelit ambience, together with a sense of being out of time among the library's books and mirrored drawing room, still pleasantly haunts me from time to time.

If you catch me staring into a mirror, I assure you it's unlikely to be down to vanity.

I'm just checking.

ALSO BY J. T. CROFT

Bric-a-Brac

Firelight and Frost

Maiden Point

A House of Bells

Midnight's Treasury

High Spirits

"Dead Brilliant"

⭐⭐⭐⭐⭐

"An author whose storytelling really hits the mark"

⭐⭐⭐⭐⭐

"Beautifully dark and bittersweet"

⭐⭐⭐⭐⭐

ABOUT THE AUTHOR

J. T. Croft is the author of Gothic fiction, supernatural
mystery and ghostly short stories.
For more information:
www.jtcroft.com

I hope you enjoyed reading this book as much as I loved
writing it. If you did, I'd really appreciate you leaving me a
quick review on whichever platform you prefer. Reviews are
extremely helpful for any author, and even just a line or two
can make a big difference. I'm independently published, so I
rely on good folks like you spreading the word!

facebook.com/jtcroftauthor
x.com/jtcroftauthor
instagram.com/jtcroftauthor